DOVER

TWO

DOVER
TWO

Joyce Porter

A Foul Play Press Book

The Countryman Press, Inc.
Woodstock, Vermont

Second printing

Copyright © 1965 by Joyce Porter

This edition first published in 1989 by Foul Play Press,
an imprint of The Countryman Press, Inc.,
Woodstock, Vermont 05091

ISBN 0-88150-135-2

Printed in the United States of America

CHAPTER ONE

T HE PHONE rang.
  'Hello? Chief Constable here.'

'Colonel Muckle? Doctor Austin here, from the Memorial Hospital. I'm afraid I've got some bad news for you, sir. You remember our local 'Sleeping Beauty'? Well, she's dead. One of the nurses found her about twenty minutes ago.'

'Blast!'

'That makes it a murder case now, doesn't it, sir?'

'It does indeed, Doctor, it does indeed.'

The Chief Constable dropped his phone slowly back in its cradle. He stared blankly at it for a full minute and then, with a shrug, picked it up again.

'Get me Scotland Yard,' he said. 'The Assistant Commissioner – Crime.'

At six o'clock the next morning British Railways disgorged Chief Inspector Wilfred Dover and Detective Sergeant Charles Edward MacGregor, both of New Scotland Yard, at Curdley Central Station. Their journey from London had been a distressing one. The vital connexion which they should have caught at Crewe had been axed a mere twenty-four hours before by Dr Beeching, and the two detectives had spent the small hours – five of them as it happens – huddled and sulky on a hard railway bench. Eventually their train had arrived, unheated and no later than usual, and they had sat, staring bleakly through the grimy windows, as it slowly ambled its way north. One

5

dreary industrial town had followed another with no noticeable break between them, and even a crisp October dawn couldn't glamourize the gasometers, pit shafts and belching steel mills which moved slowly across their line of vision.

When they finally arrived at Curdley both men were cold, hungry and bad-tempered, but, the police hierarchy being what it is, only the Chief Inspector was allowed to give full rein to his feelings. No one could ever accuse Chief Inspector Dover of being tolerant and easygoing and now that he really had something to blow up about he went off in megatons. He cursed the Assistant Commissioner (Crime) at Scotland Yard, he cursed the Chief Constable of Curdley, he cursed British Railways in general and the author of their economy cuts in particular, he cursed the Sleeping Beauty whose inconsiderate death was the root cause of all his troubles and, naturally, he cursed Sergeant MacGregor just because he was nice and handy. By no means exhausted, but feeling much warmer, he roared into the Station Hotel and had a blazing row with the night porter, who at first was for refusing to let them go up to their rooms to get washed and shaved.

By eight o'clock Dover had calmed down a bit. Fortified by an enormous breakfast and with his eighth cup of tea steaming gently in front of him, he accepted a cigarette from Sergeant MacGregor with the graciousness which had made his name a byword in Scotland Yard.

"Strewth!' he growled in disgust. 'Filter tips!'

Sergeant MacGregor gritted his teeth manfully and gave him a light.

The Sleeping Beauty Case, as the Press had been calling it for some months now, was not the sort of investigation which made any appeal to Dover. To be perfectly frank, nothing which entailed any work made any appeal to Dover, but he reacted to murder cases like an outraged bull to a fluttering red flag. The idea that detectives spend their

6

time actually detecting is held only by the most naïve and credulous readers of *romans policiers*. As Dover never tired of pointing out to the stream of fresh and enthusiastic young sergeants who were assigned to him for general character training and baptisms by fire, all a real detective ever did (or should ever be expected to do) was to poke around the scene of the crime (so that the Press photographers could get their pictures) and then go and sit quietly in his office. Sooner or later some professional informer, spurned girl friend or disgruntled rival would ring up and tell him who the real villain was. Provided the suggested culprit was a reasonable possibility, the detective reviewed and adjusted what evidence he had so that it pointed in the right direction, and, usually, that was that. Another professional criminal was tucked up safely behind bars.

Professional – ah yes, that was the crux of the matter! Dover loathed murder because most murderers are amateurs and just don't play the game according to the established rules. Why, even when the neighbours know perfectly well who croaked that Mrs Jones at Number 7, do they ever think of telling the police? Not likely they don't! Not on your Nelly! They start remembering how often they themselves had wanted to croak Mrs Jones and what good and lurid reasons they had for doing so. They fear, not without some justification, that the police are likely to take the thought for the deed and they begin hedging and lying and generally messing things up until the poor wretched creature in charge of the case actually has to start looking for clues and making deductions.

No, Chief Inspector Dover definitely didn't like murder cases. There was too much hard work and trouble attached to them. And this Sleeping Beauty business, from what little he knew about it, looked like being a real stinker.

In the first place the actual crime had been committed way back in February, nearly eight months ago. The victim, a girl called Isobel Slatcher, had been shot in one of the quieter streets of Curdley at about eight o'clock on a Saturday night. The gun used, an untraceable German Luger, had been dropped beside the body. Needless to say, it had been wiped clean of any fingerprints. The girl had not been killed outright, although she had been shot in the head at close quarters. She had been rushed to the local hospital and there had been an emergency operation which, no doubt, had saved her life, but she had never regained consciousness. While the local police had tried, unsuccessfully, to find her attacker, the girl had lingered on in a coma until she had died, the day before Dover's arrival in Curdley. Now it was a murder case, and the Chief Constable had called in the Yard.

It had been some not very original journalist who had first thought of calling Isobel Slatcher the Sleeping Beauty. It was the kind of romantic label that the Press likes although, strictly speaking, Miss Slatcher was not asleep, nor was she a beauty.

Chief Inspector Dover wasn't very optimistic about his chances of solving the case after all this time. Most of his cases he never solved anyhow, but he belligerently attributed this to the fact that the sticky ones were always, unfairly, shoved on to him. There may have been a faint whiff of truth in this because the Assistant Commissioner (Crime) couldn't stand the sight of him (this feeling was mutual) and ruthlessly pushed him out on cases which were located in the remote provinces, whenever he got the chance.

Dover finished his cigarette and dropped the end with a sizzle into his teacup. He sighed heavily and thought longingly of bed.

Sergeant MacGregor broke the silence, otherwise Dover might have gone on sitting there all day.

'I'd better go and phone the Chief Constable, hadn't I, sir?' he said. 'Just to let him know we've arrived.'

Dover regarded his sergeant sourly. 'All right,' he grumbled. 'You do that.'

As MacGregor strode out of the dining-room Dover indolently surveyed his surroundings. At a near-by table somebody had left a newspaper. With a quite remarkable turn of speed for so weighty a man, Dover got to his feet to fetch it. Out of the corner of his eye he spotted that a rather elderly, bent woman had got designs on it too. He unsportingly increased his pace and grabbed the paper just before the old lady could lay a hand on it. He treated her to a small smirk of triumph and returned to his table happy in the knowledge that, once again, he'd got something for nothing.

He opened the newspaper and the smile faded quickly from his fat, pasty face. The nostrils of his tiny snub nose flared and his piggy little eyes narrowed with sheer fury as he read the headlines. BIGAMOUS BERTIE HANGED! they screamed. LAST TRIBUTE TO SUPER PERCY! Green with envy he plodded sulkily on through the story. Cuthbert Boys, whose exploits had kept the British public in raptures for months, had now finally got his just deserts at the end of a rope, secure in the knowledge that under his soubriquet of Bigamous Bertie he had passed into history as surely as Crippen or Joseph Smith. There was no need for the paper to give a detailed obituary for Bertie. Dover, in common with every other literate person in the country, knew the whole story bv heart. Briefly, Bigamous Bertie had, over a period of ten years, gone through a form of marriage with, at a conservative estimate, some twenty ladies of independent means. Posing as a pilot in the employ of a foreign airline he at one and the same time gave himself a touch of the necessary glamour and provided an excuse for his frequent absences. It also explained his chronic lack of money – all his salary being tied up by those confounded currency regulations which were the

9

speciality of whatever country he was supposed to be working in. There is no doubt that Bigamous Bertie was a crook, but he was also a gentleman and it was this, perhaps, which endeared him to the readers of the popular Press. All his surviving 'wives' spoke of him as kind and considerate and as a great giver of expensive presents. These presents were a consistent feature of Bertie's technique, purporting as they did to come from abroad. In actual fact he was quite an accomplished shop-lifter, but he stole nothing but the best and, as one 'wife' remarked, 'It's the thought that counts, isn't it?'

Bertie was so successful that there seemed no particular reason why he shouldn't have gone on marrying more and more wives to the end of his days. Unlike most of his kind, he wasn't excessively greedy and, although he relieved his wives pretty heavily of their income, he never made any attempt to touch their capital. This moderation helped to allay the suspicions of relations, as did his habit of posing as a devout (but broadminded) Roman Catholic. He made all his contacts through the Church and was 'married' on every single occasion with the full nuptial mass. This rather bizarre trade-mark was eventually, of course, his downfall. Somebody became mildly suspicious and, before you knew where you were the Yard had been called in in the person of Detective Superintendent Percival Roderick. Some people, as Dover remarked frequently and bitterly, had all the luck, and Superintendent Roderick rocketed to fame on the coat-tails of Bigamous Bertie.

For some inexplicable reason Bertie panicked when he heard that the police were on his tracks. He rushed around and in the space of less than a week he murdered no fewer than four of his wives by the simple, but messy, method of chopping them to bits with an axe. In doing so he naturally left a trail so obvious that, as Dover remarked frequently and bitterly, a backward child of two could have followed it, never mind a senior detective from New Scotland Yard.

10

As a story, Bigamous Bertie was a God-sent gift to the Press. While the hunt was on, they clarioned the latest developments to a waiting world. When Superintendent Roderick made his arrest, they printed special editions. Then there were the magistrates' hearings and the trial itself. Sensation! The jury couldn't agree, thanks to one woman who, in the face of all the evidence, held out for an acquittal. Some people claimed that she was a fanatical opponent of capital punishment and others that she had been bribed by a famous Sunday newspaper. But, whatever the reason, there had to be another trial and much to Dover's mounting disgust Superintendent Roderick, now called 'Super Percy', had his name plastered all over the front pages once again.

When Bigamous Bertie was eventually found guilty, Dover hoped to see a speedy end to the whole sordid affair, including the glare of publicity in which Super Percy was most unjustifiably basking. Dover's hopes were in vain. There was an appeal to the Court of Criminal Appeal. Once more the newspapers went to town. Then there was an appeal to the House of Lords. The newspapers went wild! All else having failed, Bertie made a plea for clemency to the Home Secretary. Britain waited with bated breath for the outcome. The plea was rejected and, much to Dover's relief, the Bigamous Bertie episode had come now to a final end, though not without one last gratuitous bouquet flung in the direction of Super Percy.

'Cuthbert Boys,' Dover read with his blood pressure dangerously high, 'paid a last, generous, gallant tribute to Superintendent Roderick just before he went to his death. "Super Percy," he said of the man whose determination and brilliance had brought him to the gallows, "is a real gentleman and a credit to the fine traditions of the British police."'

Dover nearly spat. With a curse he crumpled the newspaper up into a ball and flung it petulantly to the floor.

'Damn and blast Superintendent Percival Bloody Roderick!' he snarled.

Sergeant MacGregor, who had just returned from the telephone, got the full force of this in the face. He sighed. Dear lord, the old fool wasn't still on the rampage about Roderick, was he?

'There's been a slight change of plans, sir,' he began, in an attempt to divert Dover's mind to his own investigation.

Dover looked at him suspiciously. He didn't like changes.

'Well?' he demanded.

'The Chief Constable left a message for us. He wants us to go to the hospital first and then go and see him afterwards.'

'Wafor?'

'Well, I don't know, sir.'

'For God's sake, didn't you think of *asking*?'

'I only got the message from the station sergeant, sir. Colonel Muckle isn't in yet.'

'Lazy devil!' commented Dover. 'Oh well, what time's the car coming round?'

'Well, apparently the hospital's only a few minutes' walk from here and the police headquarters is just round the corner from the hospital so it didn't seem worth while bothering about a car. Parking's so difficult and, well, I thought we could walk,' said MacGregor lamely.

Dover just looked at him.

When at last the forbidding bulk of the Emily Gorner Memorial Hospital loomed into view, Dover's feet were hurting him but at least they took his mind off Superintendent Roderick.

The detectives were shown into a small waiting-room and Dover sat slumped in his chair with his enormous overcoat wrapped round him and his bowler hat plonked squarely on the top of his head. He didn't like hospitals.

'Pongs, doesn't it?' he remarked, wrinkling his nose in disgust.

12

The door opened and a little man in a white coat bustled in importantly.

'Good morning,' he said brightly. 'I'm Doctor Austin.'

'So what?' said Dover.

The doctor looked at him uncertainly. 'You *are* the detectives from Scotland Yard, aren't you?'

'We are,' said Dover unhelpfully.

'Oh.' The doctor took off his spectacles and wiped them. 'Well, I'm the doctor who was in charge of Miss Slatcher – you know, the Sleeping Beauty girl. Colonel Muckle said he'd get you to come round here first thing because he thought it would be best for me to put you in the picture straight away. The whole thing's really got rather complicated and I think the simplest thing would be if I gave you an outline of the case right from the beginning.'

'All right,' said Dover. 'Get on with it, but just see you keep it simple. We're detectives, not blooming Harley Street specialists!' And with this he settled down deeper in his chair, closed his eyes and prepared, one hoped, to listen.

'Er, yes,' said Dr Austin, who had quite a different mental picture of a Scotland Yard chief inspector. 'Well, as you probably know, Miss Isobel Slatcher . . .'

Dover opened one eye. 'Age?' he demanded.

'Er, twenty-eight.'

Dover closed his eye.

The doctor began again. 'Miss Isobel Slatcher . . .'

Dover opened one eye again. 'Virgin?'

'I beg your pardon?'

'Was she a virgin?'

'Well, yes, as a matter of fact, she was.'

Dover opened both eyes. ''Strewth!' he said.

Dr Austin looked in something like despair at Sergeant MacGregor, who gave him a faint smile of encouragement and waited with pencil patiently poised over his notebook.

'Well,' he tried again, 'on Saturday the seventeenth of

13

February, at about eight PM, Miss Isobel Slatcher was shot twice in the, er, back of the head at point-blank range. She was brought here almost immediately and we operated right away. We managed to get the bullets out but there was, er, considerable damage to certain areas of the brain. Miss Slatcher came through the operation quite well and, at first, we had some hope that she would at least make a partial recovery. However, as again you probably know, she never came out of the coma. Apart from the brain injury she was physically in quite good shape – heart strong, blood pressure normal, no sign of post-operative complications – you know the kind of thing.'

'So she died in the best of health?' asked Dover with heavy sarcasm.

'Well, yes, if you want to put it like that,' retorted Dr Austin, growing a little truculent in his turn, 'she did.'

'You didn't expect her to die at this stage, then?'

Dr Austin frowned. 'No, not really. As I told her sister only a couple of days ago, with reasonable medical care and attention she might have gone on like that for years. On the other hand, with these brain cases you never really know. She might have died at any time.'

'Was there any chance of her regaining consciousness?'

'Oh no!' Dr Austin shook his head firmly. 'There was no hope of that at all. In the beginning, perhaps. But after all these months, no – no chance at all.'

'I see,' said Dover, and eased his bowler hat slightly. 'Well, is that all you want to tell us?'

'Good heavens, no!' Dr Austin almost squeaked in protest. 'I'm just coming to the main thing! As I was saying, we were, well, surprised at her dying when she did as there'd been no marked degeneration in her condition at all. Naturally we were going to do a post-mortem, just to find out what had happened.'

'Naturally,' said Dover.

14

'Well, just before we opened her up, the nurse who was stripping the bed reported that one of the pillow-cases was stained with lipstick. We thought this was a bit odd, but we found the answer all right when we did the P.M.' Dr Austin paused dramatically in the hope that Dover would show some interest. He didn't.

'She'd been suffocated' – Dr Austin dropped his bombshell sulkily – 'presumably with the pillow.'

'Really?' said Dover. 'Well, that makes a difference, doesn't it? You're quite certain as to the cause of death?'

'Quite certain,' said Dr Austin.

'What time was she killed?'

'Well, she was found dead at about eleven-thirty AM I had an early lunch and began the P.M. at, say, about half past one. It's difficult to tell in these cases, body temperature and things like that are a bit tricky, but I'd guess somewhere between nine and eleven that morning.'

'H'm,' said Dover. 'Well, I'll want that pillow-slip and I'd better see the nurse who found it. Where was Miss Slatcher, by the way, in a private ward?'

'Yes, she was in a side room off Ward Seven.'

'Well, I'd better see the nurse in charge there as well, then.'

'They're both waiting for you in Matron's office. I'm afraid she insists on being present while you interview them, as a kind of chaperone, you know. She's a bit old-fashioned about these things, you know.'

'So,' said Dover, dragging himself to his feet, 'am I.'

The matron of the Emily Gorner Memorial Hospital was a kindly looking woman, very plump and with soft curly grey hair peeping out from underneath her starched white cap. She smiled sweetly as Dover was introduced to her.

'I expect you'll want to see the girl who stripped the bed first, Chief Inspector,' she said, and without waiting for an answer pressed one of the numerous buttons on her desk.

A side door opened and a very young and very pretty girl came nervously into the room. She smiled shyly at no one in particular.

'This,' said Matron in a voice of doom, 'is Probationer Nurse Pearson. Stand up straight, Pearson, answer the Chief Inspector's questions clearly and quickly, and wipe that stupid grin off your face!'

'Yes, Matron,' said Pearson meekly.

Dover opened his mouth but Matron was too quick for him.

'Who told you to strip Miss Slatcher's bed?'

'Sister told me, Matron. She told me that Miss Slatcher had died and that when they'd taken the body away I was to take all the bed linen off and send it to the laundry.'

'What time did you enter Miss Slatcher's room?'

'About a quarter past twelve, Matron.'

'And what did you do?'

'I folded the counterpane and the blankets up and then I pulled the top sheet off and folded that up too. Then I started taking the pillow-cases off. I took the top one off, folded it and put the pillow on one side. Then I took the second pillow-case off, and that was when I saw the lipstick stain.'

'And then what did you do?' asked Matron grimly.

Poor Pearson gulped. 'I went to find Doctor Austin and showed him what I'd found.'

'And what *should* you have done, Pearson?'

'I should have told Sister, Matron.'

'Precisely. And Sister would have told *me* and *I* would have told Doctor Austin.'

'Yes, Matron,' said Pearson with downcast mien.

'Well, Chief Inspector' – Matron turned briskly to Dover – 'have you any more questions?'

'Er, yes, I have got a couple,' said Dover, rather disconcerted. 'Can you tell me, Miss Pearson, where exactly the lipstick stain was? I know it was on the pillow, but was it next to the sheet or where?'

Matron now obliged with the answers. 'The lipstick stain was in the centre of the bottom of the two pillows,' she announced. 'The side with the lipstick on it was next to the bottom sheet. It is perfectly obvious what happened. Whoever killed Miss Slatcher, came in and removed one of the pillows from under her head. He then suffocated her with it – quite an easy job, the poor girl would offer no resistance. When she was dead, he merely lifted up the top pillow, supporting the girl's head on it, and slipped the stained pillow underneath. Anything else, Chief Inspector?'

Dover glared helplessly at her. 'Are you sure the lipstick on the pillow is the same as the stuff Miss Slatcher was wearing?'

'I have here,' said Matron, tapping a neat brown paper parcel which lay on her desk, 'both the stained pillow-slip and Miss Slatcher's lipstick, and a smear taken from her lips after she was dead. No doubt you have laboratories which can do scientific tests to prove that they are identical. I, personally, am perfectly sure that they are.'

'Hm,' said Dover. 'But can you be perfectly sure that Miss Slatcher didn't move about in the bed, turn her head, for example, and get her lipstick on to the pillow that way?'

'Completely out of the question,' snorted Matron. 'In the first place the girl was in a very deep coma and, apart from breathing, completely motionless. In the eight months we have been nursing her she hasn't, so to speak, moved a muscle. Besides, a turning of the head, such as you have mentioned, would leave a smudge on the top pillow. We have a completely clear and full imprint on the *bottom* pillow. If you are suggesting that she suddenly, against all her medical history, recovered consciousness, turned her head completely round, pressed her lips on the pillow and

17

then put that pillow underneath the other, I shall have to inform you that your suggestion is pure poppycock! Besides' (Matron held up a hand to stop an interruption from Dover) '— kindly let me finish, Chief Inspector — besides, the post-mortem showed definitely that she had been suffocated. The very faint bruising on the face clearly indicated that something soft had been used, like a pillow.'

'Oh, all right!' snapped Dover crossly. 'But whàt I don't understand is why she was wearing lipstick at all. Is this some new-fangled idea or something? I thought the girl had been completely unconscious for eight months?'

'So she had,' said Matron calmly, 'and normally, of course, we wouldn't have permitted her any make-up at all. But on this occasion I allowed one of my nurses to put lipstick and powder on Miss Slatcher's face. I did so in answer to a specific request from her sister.'

'It was for the newspaper pictures, sir,' explained Pearson helpfully.

'That will do, Pearson!' Matron squashed her subordinate quietly and efficiently. 'You see, what happened was this, Chief Inspector. On Thursday our local paper, the *Curdley and District Custodian*, published a completely irresponsible and sensational article about Miss Slatcher. As you doubtless know, she had been labelled the Sleeping Beauty and from time to time the *Custodian* has put in a bit about her — generally when they were short of news, as far as I can see. So, in Thursday's issue, it was reported that Miss Slatcher was on the verge of recovery and that her doctors were confident that she would regain consciousness within the next few days and would, no doubt, be able to give the police full information about the man who shot her. On Thursday afternoon Miss Slatcher's elder sister (and her only relation, to the best of my knowledge) came round to see me. She's a rather unbalanced woman, though devoted to her younger sister. She said that now this story

18

had appeared in our local paper, reporters from the London Press would be sure to arrive the following day and want to take pictures, and would I allow the unconscious girl to have some make-up on. Not only that, but the unconscious girl's fiancé, a young man who is in one of the Armed Forces, was coming in to see her, also on the Friday morning. It would be less painful for him if her, I must admit, quite deathly pallor were brightened up a little by the use of lipstick. Well, to cut a long story short, I eventually gave my consent, for the elder sister's sake. Nurse Horncastle – it was she, wasn't it, Pearson? – yes, Nurse Horncastle made her up at half past nine on the Friday morning, an hour or so, if we can believe Doctor Austin's findings, before she died.'

"Strewth!' said Dover, rather overwhelmed by all this. 'And the newspaper story – about her imminent recovery – that was quite untrue?'

'Quite untrue!' said Matron. 'We have known for a long time that she would never recover. Miracles do happen, of course, even under the National Health, but not to people with brain injuries like that. It was only last week that Doctor Austin, at my request, had a talk with the girl's sister and finally convinced her, or so he said, that there was no hope. He explained, for the umpteenth time, that the girl might live on for years, but there wasn't a chance in a million that she would ever come out of the coma, and if she did she would be a gibbering idiot. Very serious deterioration of the brain tissues had already taken place, to say nothing of the initial damage caused by the shots.'

'I see,' said Dover slowly. 'Who was supposed to be looking after Miss Slatcher on the Friday morning? I'd like to have a word with them.'

'It was Staff Nurse Horncastle,' said Matron. 'You can go now, Pearson, and ask Nurse Horncastle to come in.'

CHAPTER TWO

NURSE HORNCASTLE, as befitted her seniority, was allowed to tell her own story, and Matron contented herself with frequent interruptions and explanations.

Nurse Horncastle hadn't much to add. She was supposed to look in on Miss Slatcher in her private room every hour or so, just to see that she was all right. On the morning of the girl's death she had made her up, in accordance with the matron's instructions, at half past nine. At ten o'clock Miss Slatcher's fiancé had arrived, in his uniform, and carrying a large bunch of flowers. Nurse Horncastle had shown him into Miss Slatcher's room and had left him alone there. An emergency case had been brought into the main ward and Nurse Horncastle didn't get a chance to return to Miss Slatcher until half past eleven. The boy friend had already gone, and Isobel Slatcher was dead.

'I see,' said Dover, and glanced meaningfully at Sergeant MacGregor. 'Now, just let me get this straight. If you hadn't been busy elsewhere you would normally have popped in to see Miss Slatcher at about eleven o'clock, right? At which time she might or might not still have been alive?'

'Yes, sir,' said Nurse Horncastle, rather hesitantly.

'But, as it is, the last time *you* saw her alive and well was at ten o'clock when you showed this boy friend fellow into her room?'

Nurse Horncastle blushed, painfully. 'Well, not really,' she muttered, gazing resolutely at her feet. 'I only opened the door for Mr Purseglove. I didn't actually go inside the room and I didn't actually see Miss Slatcher. I was in a hurry, you see.'

'Oh?' said Dover, very significantly.

Matron chose to take this monosyllabic comment as an implied slur on the entire nursing profession. She launched herself with fury and enthusiasm into the attack.

'Well,' she thundered, her kindly blue eyes flashing, 'that's one idea you can get out of your head right away! Oh, you needn't look surprised! I know exactly what you were thinking. Well, neither you nor anybody else is going to imply for one second that Isobel Slatcher's death was due in the slightest degree to any hint of negligence by the nurses in my hospital! My nurses have looked after Miss Slatcher with unparalleled devotion for the last eight months. It's due solely to their care and attention that she lived as long as she did. Can you even begin to imagine what has to be done for a patient who is *completely* helpless? The washing, intravenous feeding, the injections, the drips and heaven only knows what? And can you imagine what it is like, doing all these things with meticulous care for someone who is *never* going to recover, never going to get one iota better? My nurses have many demands on their time, demands from people they *can* help, who *will* respond to their treatment. But, in spite of this, they continued to nurse Isobel Slatcher to the very utmost of their skill!!'

While Matron proceeded at full spate with her tirade she half unconsciously picked up a pen from her desk. Without a break in the flow of words she made a neat note in her appointments book. "2. PM', it read. 'See Horncastle. Negligence re Slatcher. Severe reprimand!'

At last Dover managed to get a word in. 'I didn't,' he observed testily, 'think for one minute that Miss Slatcher's death was caused in any way by negligence on the part of your staff. I was merely trying to ascertain at what time the girl was last seen alive. Well, according to Nurse Horncastle here she was still alive at nine-thirty that morning.'

'Ah yes,' Matron pointed out, somewhat mollified by Dover's remarks, 'but this boy friend of hers saw her after that.'

'Would he have known if she was already dead?' asked Dover doubtfully. 'I mean, if she didn't move or anything?'

'Oh, good heavens, man, you could see her breathing!' retorted Matron. 'And in any case' – she spoke as an expert – 'you can always tell.'

'Oh well,' Dover sighed, and got reluctantly to his feet, 'I suppose we'd better go and see the room, and the corpse. By the way, Matron, how many people know Isobel Slatcher was murdered? I suppose it's all round the blinking hospital by now?'

'Indeed it is not!' Matron got ready to flare up again. 'The only people who know are Doctor Austin, Pearson, Nurse Horncastle here and myself. I gave strict instructions that the matter was not to be mentioned to anyone else.'

'Well, at least that's something,' said Dover grudgingly. 'Perhaps you could tell your nurses to keep quiet about it for a bit longer. I'd better have a word with Doctor Austin and warn him to keep his trap shut.'

'There's no need to bother,' said Matron. 'I will give my instructions to the nurses, and to Doctor Austin. Nothing will be said by the staff of this hospital, you can take my word for that.'

Dover grunted.

'By the way, Chief Inspector,' she smiled sweetly, 'I suppose you must be one of Superintendent Roderick's colleagues? What a marvellous man he must be!'

Dover scowled blackly and stumped out without a word. MacGregor apologetically collected the brown paper parcel containing the lipstick-stained pillow-case, said thank you and goodbye politely and rushed off after his infuriated lord and master.

'Bossy old bitch!' muttered Dover, and lumbered off to

inspect the room in which Isobel Slatcher had been killed. He was reasonably pleased to see that the only way of entering the room was through the door. It made things simpler. Then they went down to the mortuary and had a rather hasty look at the body.

'All right,' growled Dover when they got outside, 'let's go and see the Chief Constable. Which way is it?'

'Down here, I think, sir,' said MacGregor, trying to orientate himself.

'Think?' snorted Dover. 'You walk me all round this blasted town, mate, and I'll give you something to think about!'

On their way to police headquarters they passed the premises of the *Curdley and District Custodian*. Dover stopped and gazed moodily at the selection of Press photographs which were displayed in the windows. He examined, without much interest, the pictures of newly-married couples, smirking inanely and triumphantly at the camera, and at the action shots of the town's Rugby football team, in their last match.

'I think we might as well pop in here now,' he said to MacGregor, 'and get hold of a copy of this paper that had the report of the girl's recovery in it. Might be significant, that.'

'You mean it might have been a motive for the murder, sir?'

'Looks damned like it,' grunted Dover. 'If the chap who took a pot-shot at her in the first place thought she was on the point of regaining consciousness and spilling the beans, he might well have had another go at shutting her mouth permanently.'

'The fiancé looks very well placed for the final attack, doesn't he, sir?' observed MacGregor thoughtfully. 'Seems as though he was alone with the girl in that hospital room at just about the right time.'

'Yes,' agreed Dover somewhat sarcastically, 'that point had

occurred to me, too, Sergeant. 'Course, we'll have to find out where he was at the time of the first attempt last February.'

'If he's a Serviceman, sir, he probably knows how to use a revolver.'

'That's another point which, as it happens, had not escaped me.'

MacGregor, seeing which way the wind was blowing, very sensibly shut up and let his chief inspector do the talking.

'Mind you,' Dover went on, addressing his sergeant's reflection in the plate-glass window, 'I should have had a good look at this fiancé fellow in any case. Money or sex – that's what people commit murder for.'

MacGregor thought idly of half a dozen cases in his own narrow experience in which this generalization was not true, but knew better than to draw Dover's attention to them.

'Yes,' Dover sighed, 'boy friend, fiancé, husband – you want to have a closer look at them when a woman's murdered. Well, come on, Sergeant, we can't stand here all day!'

Inside, Dover demanded a copy of last Thursday's issue of the *Custodian* and was informed by a very superior young lady that one could be purchased at any newsagent's in the town.

'I don't want to buy one!' snapped Dover. 'I'm a police officer and I want a copy of that paper for my investigations. And I want it now – so get moving!'

The superior young lady gave a supercilious toss of her head and disappeared through a swing door at the back of the counter. She reappeared a few seconds later without the newspaper but with a chubby-faced young man.

'Now then,' said the young man, 'what's all this about?'

'And who are you?' snarled Dover, who was rapidly losing what little patience he possessed.

'I'm the editor here,' said the young man.

24

'Right! Well, I'm Chief Inspector Dover of New Scotland Yard and I want to have a few words with you in connexion with the murder of Miss Isobel Slatcher!'

The jaw of the young man dropped in a most satisfying manner and the superior young lady gave a faint squeak of fright.

'Oh, well, perhaps you'd better come into my office, Chief Inspector.' The editor's voice was a little hoarse as he lifted up a hinged board in the counter and ushered the two detectives through to the back.

Once he was comfortably esconced in an armchair in the editor's inner sanctum (as he himself called it), Dover deliberately took his time. There was an ominous silence in the room as he ponderously read through the *Custodian*'s account of Isobel Slatcher's purportedly imminent recovery. The article appeared on the front page and was accompanied by a rather smudgy photograph of Curdley's Sleeping Beauty lying motionless in her hospital bed. It was a rather amateurish attempt at journalistic sensationalism and both Isobel Slatcher's name and that of the Emily Gorner Memorial Hospital were misspelt, but it made its point none the less. Anybody who read it would be quite justified in believing that the injured girl would soon be restored to full health and consciousness.

When he had finished reading about Isobel Slatcher, Dover gloomily perused the other seven pages of the paper. They were mostly filled with small advertisements and accounts of church bazaars. With a disparaging sniff, Dover handed the paper over to Sergeant MacGregor and amused himself by glaring balefully at the *Custodian*'s editor.

The young man wriggled uneasily under this prolonged and somewhat unnerving examination. He was an odd-looking creature, with a fat red face and a mass of wiry fair hair. He was wearing a bow tie and a fine-checked shirt. He had no jacket on and a pair of tight, pale-blue

25

trousers were slung low over his hips. He sat behind a large flat-topped desk which was impressively littered with all the paraphernalia of the newspaper world.

Dover, as he occasionally did, let the pregnant silence go on a bit too long. Ralph Gostage – that was the editor's name – had time enough to realize that, as he had never so much as laid eyes on Isobel Slatcher in his entire life, he had no reason to quail like a guilty felon just because a couple of blooming dicks came to see him.

'Well now, Chief Inspector,' he began brightly and confidently, 'what can the *Custodian* do for you?'

'Who wrote this article on Isobel Slatcher?' demanded Dover sulkily.

'Well, as a matter of fact, I did. We've run several front-page stories on her since her accident – after all, it's been the most exciting thing that's happened in Curdley since a gas main burst under the town hall five years ago! Yes, sir, Miss Isobel Slatcher was news, and that's what the *Custodian*'s here for – to get the news to the people. Without fear or favour,' he added in a pious afterthought.

'Is that so?' said Dover.

'And,' Ralph Gostage continued, his Curdley accent becoming more and more overlaid with American as he went on, 'we here on the *Custodian* are not unmindful of our duty, as an organ of the Press, to wage a vigorous campaign against any abuses or short-comings we may find in the running of this town. We have kept the case of Isobel Slatcher before our readers not only because she is news, but because she is a shining witness to the scandalous inefficiency and prejudice of the police force of this town.'

'Oh?' said Dover. 'So you're running a campaign against the police, are you?'

'Not only against the police,' proclaimed Mr Gostage, raising his right forefinger to stress his point, 'but against all religious prejudice wherever it may be found and from whichever side it may come.'

'Religious prejudice?' yelped Dover, feeling that the interview was rapidly slipping out of his grasp. 'What in God's name has religious prejudice got to do with the Curdley police?'

'You may well ask!' beamed Mr Gostage as he climbed with evident relish into the saddle of his hobby-horse. 'Oh, it's easy to see you boys are strangers in this town. Well, you've come to the right guy to give you the low-down on the set-up here. Say, how about having a cigar?'

Dover accepted with alacrity, as he always did. With his cigar well alight, he settled back happily in his chair. His original feelings of hostility to Mr Gostage had now been dissipated and he regarded that young man benignly as he proceeded to give the detectives the *Custodian*'s eye view of Curdley.

'Well, it's this way, you see.' His American accent, fortified no doubt by the cigar, had almost completely ousted that of his native town. 'Curdley is an unusual sort of burg if you don't know it. Several towns up here have got the same sort of problem but Curdley's got it worst. This town is split, you see, almost dead in half, between the Catholics and the Protestants. It all goes back to Henry the Eighth – or most of it does. You remember, he was the one that had six wives and started the Church of England? Well, Curdley was pretty remote from London in those days and the people up here didn't take much notice of the King's decrees and what have you. They just went on being Catholics in the same old way. Well, things got a bit tougher for 'em under Elizabeth and by the time Cromwell was in power the persecution was quite lively. The Catholics in Curdley have got twenty-nine genuine martyrs who were burnt here at the stake because they wouldn't renounce their religion. As time went by, of course, lots of people

27

switched over because life was so much simpler that way – apart from anything else – but quite a number of them never did. When things got really tough the Catholic religion in Curdley just went underground, but it was never completely extinguished. They do say that even when the persecution was at its height there was never a day that Mass wasn't celebrated properly, with a properly ordained priest, somewhere within the boundaries of the town.

'Well, you can imagine there must have been some bitter old scenes in Curdley in those days. One part of a family renouncing the old faith – and not always for the highest motives, let's be frank about it – and the other lot clinging to it and both sides denouncing each other as traitors. And when at last the Catholics *were* allowed to practise their religion openly, things got worse if anything. Both communities went mad in the effort to outdo the other. If the Catholics built a new church, then the Protestants had to shell out and build two, even bigger. If a C. of E. parish gives its vicar a motor-bike, the Catholics down the road have a whip round and give their priest a motor-car.

'Mind you, it's not as bad nowadays as it was – the war shook things up a bit and broadened a few minds – but it's bad enough. You ought to see what happens now if a Catholic boy wants to marry a Protestant girl, and vice versa! As far as the families are concerned, you'd think the end of the world had come. And naturally it doesn't stop at purely religious matters. Take the town council! Every single man jack on it has been elected because he's either a Catholic or a Protestant. Nobody gives a tuppenny damn what his political views are apart from his religious affiliations. Take education! Half the schools are Catholic ones and any Protestant kid who set foot in one'd be torn to pieces. Or take the public library! The Library Committee's got a majority of Protestant councillors and has had for donkey's years. If you're a Catholic and you want to be a librarian, you haven't a hope in hell of getting a job in Curdley. But the Parks and Gardens department – that's practically reserved for Catholics.'

'Like the police?' observed Dover slyly.

'You've got it, Chief! Just like the police! Before the war not a single policeman in Curdley was a Protestant – you'd hardly believe it, would you? Of course, they've got a fair number now – with recruiting being so bad they had to take what they could get – but they're all out pounding the beat and likely to stay there for the rest of their naturals. Every single man who's a sergeant or above is a faithful son of Rome.'

'I see,' said Dover, 'and where does the *Custodian* stand in all this?'

'Well, I'm a Protestant myself,' admitted Mr Gostage, 'but naturally I stand apart from all these petty squabbles. Intelligent people of my generation don't take these things very seriously. We've got a broader outlook than our parents had, naturally. The *Custodian* is quite impartial. We attack inefficiency and corruption wherever we find it.'

'And at the present moment you reckon you've found it in the Curdley police, is that it?'

'Definitely,' agreed Mr Gostage. 'We've been running a "Purge the Police" campaign for some time now, on and off, you know. Mind you, it's only one what-you-might-call crusade of many, but this attack on Isobel Slatcher was real grist to our mill.'

'Isobel Slatcher was a Protestant, of course?'

'Staunch C. of E. and a leading fighter in the battle against the Scarlet Woman!'

'I presume,' said Dover, looking dubiously at the cigar ash he had dropped down the front of his overcoat, 'that you are accusing the police of lack of enthusiasm, at any rate, in their investigations into last February's attack on the girl?'

'If not something worse,' said Mr Gostage darkly. 'What

do you think, Chief? This town's got – what? – a population of, say, sixty thousand. A girl's shot, not three minutes' walk from a main shopping centre with a gun which is left beside the body. And eight months later the police haven't – or say they haven't – got a clue as to who did it. After all, you're an expert – does that strike *you* as a likely story?'

'Hm,' said Dover, thoughtfully and non-committally. From what he knew of small local police forces they were more likely to be guilty of sheer inefficiency than deliberate corruption, but he loyally refrained from expressing this point of view to Mr Gostage. 'Let's just get back to the latest story of yours about Isobel Slatcher,' he said, seeing from the clock on the editor's desk that the morning was slipping away rather rapidly and they still hadn't seen the Chief Constable. 'You say you wrote it. Where did you get your information from?'

'Sorry, old chap,' Ralph Gostage leaned back in his chair and grinned complacently. 'I can't reveal my sources of information to you, you know.'

Dover forgot about the free cigar. 'Don't talk such bloody rubbish!' he snapped. 'This is a murder investigation, not a flaming television serial! There are serious consequences for anybody who tries to hinder the police in their investigations, and, by God, if you don't tell me where you got your facts from, I'll throw the whole bloody book at you! Who do you think you are, mate? Lord Beaverbrook?'

'Oh, all right,' muttered Ralph Gostage, his stand for the rights of the Press collapsing sulkily. 'It was the girl's elder sister – Violet Slatcher, her name is. She's been coming along to see me, oh every month or so since this thing happened, trying to get me to feature it in the paper. You know what some people are like – go half barmy trying to get their names in print At first it was a damned good story but, well, when it started dragging on, well,

30

people forget, don't they? I mean, what was there to say? That she was still unconscious and still in hospital – that's all.'

'But you printed *this* story,' Dover pointed out, nodding his head at the newspaper which now lay on the edge of the desk.

'Ah, yes, but that was different! Isobel Slatcher, Curdley's own Sleeping Beauty, on the verge of waking up and naming her attacker – boy, that was news! Of course we printed it!'

'When did Miss Violet Slatcher come to see you with this story?' asked Dover.

'Er, Tuesday morning she called in, I think. Yes, that's right, just in time because we go to press on Wednesday.'

'Did it ever strike you that it wasn't true?'

Poor Mr Gostage gave an embarrassed laugh. 'Well,' he said, 'you know what the newspaper business is like, don't you? I must confess that the thought did cross my mind that this "miracle recovery" business sounded a bit fishy, but, after all, my informant was the girl's own sister, wasn't she? She ought to know if anyone did.'

'You didn't think of checking with the hospital?'

'No. They wouldn't have told me anything, anyhow. You know what the medical profession's like. I phoned up the London papers, though. Thought they might have taken it up, but they didn't. Here,' he said suddenly, 'you and I might get together on this, Chief. If you keep me in the picture with your investigations, I'll try and get you into the London papers. They won't bother sending their own chaps up here – not exciting enough – but they might take the odd bit if I phone it in to 'em. How about it? 'Course, I'll want it exclusive, but you might get a bit of free publicity out of it, and even the odd quid or two if I get it accepted.'

Dover scowled. He disliked the implication that neither he nor his case was important enough to interest the

31

national Press and, although the mutually beneficial arrangements suggested by Mr Gostage were attractive, they were not the sort which could be accepted in the presence of Sergeant 'Big-Ears' MacGregor.

Regretfully he declined.

'Oh, well,' said Gostage, 'it was an idea. Now, wait a minute, I've just thought of something else! You must know Superintendent Roderick – Super Percy? Now, if you could give me a few inside details about him, we could do an article – or even a whole series. Fleet Street'd pay a fortune for it! We don't want the official stuff about his career but the intimate bits – does he take sugar in his tea, what does he think of the modern teenager, is he fond of animals? Gosh, a piece like that on Super Percy – it'd sell like hot cakes!'

This was too much for Dover. With a face as black as thunder he left the newspaper offices at top speed and in a blazing temper.

'God help,' he snarled to Sergeant MacGregor, 'the next person who mentions Percy Roderick's name to me! What's so special about him I'd like to know? Any fool could have caught Bigamous Bertie. From the way they go on about him you'd think he was the only blooming detective in Scotland Yard!'

MacGregor muttered a few soothing grunts and fell into a pleasant daydream where a kindly assistant commissioner at last listened to his implicit and explicit requests and, breaking the long and unhappy association he had not enjoyed with Chief Inspector Dover, attached him instead to the soaring Superintendent Roderick. The mere prospect of such a transfer was enough to make a young and ambitious detective sergeant swoon.

CHAPTER THREE

I<small>T WAS</small> half past twelve when Dover and MacGregor at last found themselves shown into the Chief Constable's office. Colonel Muckle was not pleased. It was, after all, Saturday, and he liked to get away early on Saturdays. At this rate he'd never make the golf course in time to get a round in before it grew dark. He frowned crossly.

'I'd almost given you two up,' he observed caustically. 'Well, we're obviously not going to have time for lunch so I've asked them to send some sandwiches and coffee up. You'll have to make do with that. Where on earth have you been all morning? I rang the hospital and they said you left at a quarter to eleven.'

'We called in to see the editor of the *Custodian* about this article,' said Dover, handing his copy of the newspaper over. 'You realize, of course, that this story of the girl being on the point of recovering consciousness may well have been the reason for this second, and fatal, attack?'

'Humph,' said Colonel Muckle. 'So the hospital people were right, were they? There's no doubt she was murdered?'

'None at all, as far as I can see,' said Dover. 'I'll get your lab to run a check on the lipstick, just to make sure it is hers on the pillow-case. But I think we can take it as murder all right.'

'Same chap trying again, d'you reckon?' asked Colonel Muckle.

'Looks like it,' said Dover. 'After all, you're hardly likely to have two people wanting to murder a girl like that, are you?'

'No,' agreed the Chief Constable, 'but, mind you, people

33

do funny things, even in a town like Curdley. We've got our problems same as anywhere else.'

'So we've been hearing,' said Dover blandly. 'We had quite a little lecture from Mr Gostage on the religious antagonism in this town.'

'Oh? Oh, well it's not as bad as all that, you know.'

'Mr Gostage seemed to think that the police dragged their feet a bit over the first attack on Isobel Slatcher – because she was a Protestant.'

'What absolute nonsense!' exploded Colonel Muckle, glancing dubiously at a brightly coloured Sacred Heart which hung on the wall opposite his desk. 'As if it would make any difference what dratted religion the girl was! Of course, it's just the kind of comment you'd expect from a fellow like Gostage – he comes from one of the most bigoted C. of E. families in the town. Father Clement was only saying the other day that there are more lies in one issue of the *Custodian* than in ten of Khrushchev's speeches. Mind you, I wouldn't go as far as that myself. I'm a Catholic' – he nodded at a small crucifix which adorned his desk – 'but I can assure you I wouldn't dream of letting my religious views influence my official actions in the slightest degree. Of course, I wasn't born and bred in Curdley so I can take a bit more broadminded and tolerant view of the whole problem. Why, when I was in the Army, some of my best friends were heretics.'

At this timely moment the coffee and sandwiches arrived. As Dover munched away, he gave the Chief Constable a brief account of what they had found out at the hospital.

'Oh?' said Colonel Muckle with great interest. 'So this boy friend was on the scene again, was he?'

'Why?' asked Dover. 'Was he around when the first attack took place?'

'Yes, he was.' The Chief Constable looked at his watch and frowned again. Drat it! By the time he'd gone home

34

and got his clubs . . . 'Look here,' he said, 'I'll just give you a short outline of this first attack last February and then I'll have to rush off. I've got rather an important engagement on this afternoon – don't want to miss it. I've got the file here all ready for you so you can go through the reports at your leisure.

'Well, briefly, the story's this. Isobel Slatcher went round on the seventeenth of February – it was a Saturday, by the way – to St Benedict's vicarage. Apparently she went every week. Well, she left the vicarage a few minutes after eight o'clock. Somebody must have been waiting for her, because as she walked round the side of the vicarage garden somebody grabbed her – well, we think they did – and shot her twice in the back of the head. Then the attacker dropped the gun beside the body and beat it. There were no fingerprints on the gun – it was a German Luger – and we haven't been able to trace the owner. It wasn't registered, of course.

'Now the Vicar – what's-his-name? – Bonnington, heard the shots in his study. He rushed outside, found the girl and thought she was dead. Not surprising, really, there was blood and brains all over the pavement. He ran back inside to phone the police and then returned to the girl. By this time the girl's fiancé, this RAF chap called Purseglove, had arrived on the scene and was kneeling beside her body. He heard the shots, too, and rushed up to see what had happened.

'Well, that's all there is to it. My CID chaps took the case on, and we got nowhere. I may tell you that as all the people concerned were Protestants they didn't exactly break their necks to co-operate with my inspector! However, we'd really nothing to go on. The gun was a dead end and it was the only blooming clue we'd got. We couldn't find any motive which looked half-way strong enough, but most of the people we questioned were only too pleased to suggest that it was all part of some fiendish Popish plot.

35

However' – Colonel Muckle spoke drily – 'I think you can discount that theory.'

He rose to his feet and started to put his raincoat on. 'So, you see, the fiancé, Purseglove, was, to put it mildly, in the area at the time of the first attack. No doubt you'll be following that line up?'

'No doubt,' said Dover glumly.

'By the way' – the Chief Constable already had his hand on the door-knob – 'I suppose you're not by any chance a Catholic?'

'Methodist,' said Dover shortly.

'Oh, yes. Wesley didn't have much success in this town. Everybody'd already taken up their sides here long before he arrived on the scene. Well, now, anything else you want?' He opened the door.

'Can you let us have a car, sir?' asked Dover, suddenly mindful of his aching feet.

'A car?' repeated Colonel Muckle as though he'd been asked for a gallon of his life's blood. 'Well, I'm afraid that's going to be very difficult. We're having a big inspection week after next and I've got all the cars off the road. Want to get 'em on the top line, y'know. If I let you have one, you'll probably get it all dirty and messed up. Tell you what,' he suggested insinuatingly, 'it's only a small town, no distance at all really. You can walk to most of the places in a couple of minutes or so, and if you've got to go a long way you can always take a taxi, eh?'

Dover accepted defeat ungraciously. 'Oh, all right,' he said in a grudging voice, 'but you'll have to give me a chit to say that there weren't any police cars available – otherwise Sergeant MacGregor here'll never get his money back.'

'Well, we can cross that bridge when we come to it.' Colonel Muckle opened the door and then turned back once again. 'By the way, how's the famous Superintendent Roderick keeping these days? On top of the world, eh?'

'Yes,' grunted Dover sourly.

'My word, I should think he's on the way up all right! Lucky devil! Still, that Bigamous Bertie do was a smart piece of work – you've got to hand it to him!'

'Yes,' said Dover.

'I did wonder,' the Chief Constable went happily on, unmindful of Dover's finer feelings, 'I did wonder if they'd send him up here. Would have been very interesting to see how he tackled a case. Oh well, no good crying over spilt milk, eh? I'll be seeing you chaps later. Must rush off now.'

''Strewth!' said Dover in deep disgust when the door was safely closed. 'He's going to be a joy to work with, he is!'

He got up with a sigh from his chair and went over to sit in the one behind the desk. He chewed away thoughtfully at the two sandwiches which the Chief Constable had left, and examined the contents of such drawers in the desk as Colonel Muckle had been foolish enough to leave unlocked. Sergeant MacGregor watched him with a pained expression. Really, this was going a bit too far, even for Dover!

Dover found one or two private letters, which were hardly worth reading, and helped himself to one of the colonel's cigars.

'He'll never miss it,' he observed to MacGregor. 'And if he does, he'll never think that *I* took it.'

'No, sir,' said MacGregor coldly, 'but he might think that *I* did!'

Dover snorted unpleasantly down his nose. Stuck-up young pup! 'Here,' he said, grabbing the Slatcher file from the desk, 'read through this lot and see if there's anything that matters!'

MacGregor took the file, quite a bulky one, and Dover with a groan of relief, removed his boots, propped his feet up on the radiator and went to sleep almost immediately.

Half an hour later MacGregor had finished reading the file and Dover had woken up.

'All right,' said the chief inspector, yawning widely and rubbing the back of his fat, policeman's neck, 'where do we go from here?'

'I think ...' began MacGregor.

'We'll go and see the sister,' said Dover flatly.

'I was just going to suggest that, sir.' MacGregor began to gather up his things with a smug smile.

'Oh,' said Dover, 'well, in that case, we'll go and see this fiancé fellow.'

The Pursegloves' house had all the blinds in the front windows respectfully lowered.

Dover dug Sergeant MacGregor sharply in the ribs as they walked up to the front door. 'Don't forget we're going to pretend this Slatcher girl died a natural death,' he hissed. 'If he did croak her, he might let something slip, see?'

'Yes, sir,' said MacGregor, and hoped that Dover would remember to keep up the pretence himself.

The Pursegloves had apparently decided to confront Scotland Yard *en famille*. Mr Purseglove Senior opened the door. He was a wispy little man, uncomfortably dressed in his best suit and with his hair pasted in stripes across his bald patch. He smiled nervously at the sight of the two policemen.

'Oh, yes,' he said. 'We were expecting you. Miss Slatcher said they'd called Scotland Yard in and that you'd be sure to want to have a word with our Rex. Will you come in here?'

He ushered Dover and MacGregor into the front room.

'Mother' – he treated a tight-lipped woman to another nervous smile – 'these are the detectives. Er, this is Mrs Purseglove, my, er, wife.'

Mrs Purseglove was sitting bolt upright in a chair by the

fireplace. She acknowledged the introductions with a watch-ful nod. Dover recognized, with a sigh, that here was the boss of the household. She looked, unfortunately, the kind of woman who prided herself on not being 'put upon' by anybody.

'And this,' said Mr Purseglove proudly, 'is my son, Pilot Officer Purseglove.'

Dover looked with interest at his Number One suspect. He was a young man in his early twenties, very carefully dressed in an RAF tie and blazer, well-cut cavalry twill trousers and elegant fawn suede shoes – all brand new and all, no doubt, purchased on tick from some expensive mili-tary tailor. At first glance he didn't look very much like either of his parents but, on closer examination, one could see sure signs of his inheritance. His rather weak mouth came from his father but it was his mother who had given him his sharp pointed nose and his eyes, which like hers were shrewd rather than intelligent.

He would, Dover judged, always have more resolution and backbone than his father, but on the other hand he would never be half the man his mother was. Dover won-dered how much she had pushed and sacrificed to see her precious son wearing an officer's uniform.

The chief inspector sighed again and he and MacGregor sat down side by side on the sofa.

'Well, sir,' said Dover, addressing Purseglove Junior, 'no doubt you understand that the death of Isobel Slatcher has turned this into a murder case? I should be very glad if you'd answer a few questions which might help us in our investigations.'

'Our Rex had nothing to do with it,' announced Mrs Purseglove.

'I never said he had, madam,' was Dover's bored re-joinder. 'And if he hasn't – well, then – there can't be any harm in answering a few simple questions, can there?'

Mrs Purseglove closed her mouth like a trap, silent but unconvinced.

'Now, sir,' Dover went on blandly, 'I understand that you and the late Miss Isobel Slatcher were engaged to be married?'

Rex Purseglove frowned. 'Well, not really, Inspector.' He spoke very carefully and precisely. 'There wasn't actually any formal engagement.'

'They was just good friends, as you might say,' continued Mr Purseglove helpfully.

'Harold!' Mrs Purseglove gave her husband a warning look. She turned to Dover. 'There was a sort of understanding between them, that's all,' she said. 'Our Rex isn't in any position to start thinking about marriage yet. He's got his way to make in the world, you know.'

Rex took up the cudgels on his own behalf. 'You see, it was like this, Inspector. Just before Isobel was shot I'd heard that my CO was going to put me up for a commission. Well, obviously I couldn't start thinking about getting married at that stage. Everything was too uncertain, you see.'

'He's had a rotten time with all this business himself, poor lad,' said Mrs Purseglove aggressively. 'What with the shooting and all the questions and Isobel never getting right and him having all these interviews and tests to do – it's a miracle he ever got through them as well as he did, with all that hanging over him. And now, just when he's got through his OCTU and everything, that girl's got to go and die and start the whole thing up again. Why, the poor lad only got home late on Wednesday night. There he was, all set for a few days' leave – and heaven only knows he needs it, three months he's been at that OCTU, you know, and you've got to work hard if you don't want to fail. Quite a lot of them did, they don't let them all get through, you know. Only come home on Wednesday night, he did, and

Friday she has to go and die. Oh, I'm sorry for her, naturally, but you've got to think of them that's left behind, haven't you?'

'Oh?' said Dover. 'So you only arrived here in Curdley on Wednesday, did you. Did you read Thursday's edition of the *Custodian*, by any chance?'

'That story about Isobel? Yes, Mum showed it to me.'

'Did you believe it?'

'Well, yes, I suppose so. I was a bit surprised because I thought, you know, she was never going to get better, but I just supposed they'd found some new treatment or something. Of course,' he added quickly, 'I was very pleased as well.'

'Hm,' said Dover thoughtfully. 'I understand that you went round to the hospital to see Miss Slatcher on Friday morning?'

Mrs Purseglove rose to this one, too. 'Well?' she demanded. 'And what of it? Nothing wrong with that, is there? Anyhow, it was her sister what asked him to go, didn't she, Rex? It was her idea that he should go round there in his uniform and everything. She said the photographers'd be there and p'raps he'd get his picture in the papers – what with him being an officer and in his uniform and everything. Oh, she'd got the whole thing organized, she had.'

'What time did you arrive at the hospital?' asked Dover after both he and Rex had shot annoyed glances at Mrs Purseglove.

'He got there like she asked him to at . . .' Mrs Purseglove was at it again.

'For goodness' sake, Mum!' said her son irritably. 'It's me the inspector's asking. I got round there just on ten o'clock, Inspector.'

'And what time did you leave?'

'About a quarter to eleven, I think.'

Dover stared pensively at Rex Purseglove and unconsciously licked his lips.

'And what did you do while you were at the hospital?'

'Do? What do you mean?'

'Well, dammit, man!' snapped Dover. 'Isobel Slatcher was unconscious. You could hardly have had a hand of gin rummy with her, could you?'

'Well, I just sat there. What else was there to do?'

'You just sat there for three-quarters of an hour?'

'I hadn't much choice, had I?' retorted Rex Purseglove crossly. 'I knew if I only stopped a few minutes Violet'd find out and get all worked up about it and there'd be more rows. So I thought I'd give her a run for her money.'

Dover paused for a moment, his eyes never leaving Rex Purseglove's face. The tension in the room was building up nicely. Dover felt very pleased with the way things were going. He put his next question in a quiet, chatty voice.

'What time was it when you noticed she was dead?'

Rex Purseglove's jaw dropped, almost audibly. Both his mother and father started to say something. Dover cut off their protests.

'Shut up!' he snarled viciously. He turned back to Rex. 'Well?'

'I don't know what you mean,' he stammered. 'I never noticed she was dead.'

'Did you notice she was alive?'

Rex gulped unhappily. 'No,' he admitted.

'Did you touch her or kiss her, or anything?'

Rex shook his head miserably. 'No, I just sat down on a chair by the door. I . . . I never went near the bed.'

'He wouldn't.' Mrs Purseglove broke in confidently. 'Never could stand illness and things like that. Even when he was a child he wouldn't go near his old grannie when she was sick. He's just like his father, isn't he, Harold?'

'That's right,' agreed Mr Purseglove with an inappropriate chuckle. 'Fair turns me up, anything like that does.'

'All right!' thundered Dover before the interruptions got out of hand. 'All right! So, as far as you know, Isobel Slatcher could have been dead when you arrived at ten o'clock, or she could have died before you left at a quarter to eleven – is that what you're saying?'

'I suppose so.' Rex Purseglove was looking very worried now. 'I never thought of her dying, specially not after all that stuff in the paper about her getting better. I just never thought to go and look. I mean, why should I?'

Dover glanced significantly at Sergeant MacGregor, who had carefully been recording all this in his notebook. The sergeant glanced significantly back again. The Purseglove family looked anxiously on.

'Well now' – Dover resumed his interrogation – 'let's go back to last February, the Saturday night that Isobel Slatcher was shot. Would you mind telling me what your movements were at that time?'

'Here!' protested Mrs Purseglove, rushing to the defence of her chick. 'What the hell are you getting at? Our Rex had nothing to do with that, had you, love? Harold! Are you just going to sit there and let them insinerate things about your own son?'

'Madam!' bellowed Dover furiously, 'if you don't keep your trap shut and allow me to get on with my investigations, I shall take your precious son down to the police station and question him there! Now, I'm warning you, one more squeak out of you and that'll be the end of it!'

'Do keep quiet, Mum!' pleaded Rex. 'They've got to ask these questions. They don't mean anything.'

'Well, that remains to be seen, sir, doesn't it?' said Dover affably. 'Now then – the evening Miss Slatcher was attacked?'

'Well, this was before I was commissioned, you see, and I

was stationed quite near here and I used to come home most week-ends. Well, on this Saturday night I wanted to have a word with Isobel and I went round to her place about, oh, a quarter past seven, I suppose. Well, of course, she wasn't in. I'd forgotten she always went round to see the Vicar for about an hour every Saturday night. I stopped and talked to Violet – that's her sister – for a bit, and then I decided I'd go and have a cup of coffee and go and meet Isobel when she came out of the vicarage. Violet said she always left about eight. Well, I went and had a cup of coffee . . .'

'Where?' asked Dover.

'Los Toros – it's a snack-bar place in Corporation Road, just round the corner from St Benedict's. Well, when I'd had the coffee I went outside and I waited around a bit on the corner of Corporation Road and Church Lane because I knew that'd be the way Isobel would be coming and I wouldn't miss her. Well, it was dark and cold and I was just hanging about, waiting, see, when I heard these shots. Two of 'em, there were. For a bit I couldn't think what they were, really, or where they'd come from. Anyhow, after a minute or two I thought I'd better go and look and I set off down Church Lane towards the vicarage. Well, just on the corner, where the road sort of bends round, I saw somebody lying on the floor and, when I looked, it was Isobel. All the back of her head was covered in blood and there was blood everywhere. It was awful – made me feel right queasy. I was just going to go and get some help when Mr Bonnington – he's the Vicar – arrived and he said he'd already phoned for the police. And we just waited there until they came. We didn't touch her or anything. Well, we thought she was dead.'

'Hm,' said Dover. 'Can you remember how long it was between hearing the shots and actually reaching Miss Slatcher?'

Rex shook his head. 'No, not really. They asked me

44

that at the time – the police, I mean. Two or three minutes, I think. It's quite a long walk down Church Lane from the corner where I was waiting to where Isobel was.'

'And you weren't hurrying?' The sarcasm passed unnoticed.

'No, not specially.'

Dover wrinkled his nose. 'Round about the time you heard the shots, either before or especially after, did you see anybody in this place, er, Church Street?'

'Church Lane, you mean. No.'

'You didn't see anybody running away, for example, after the shots were fired?'

'No. There were one or two people quite a way off in Corporation Road, but I didn't see anybody at all in Church Lane – not until the Vicar came out again, that is.'

Dover indulged in another dramatic pause while he thought this lot out. This was the boyo all right, no doubt about it! He shot the girl, dodged out of sight when the Vicar ran out, came back to see if she was dead, and was interrupted by the Vicar again. He comes back on leave eight months later, reads in the paper that the girl is going to recover consciousness, whips round to the hospital and croaks her. Simple as pie!

Dover beamed happily at poor Rex Purseglove. This was one case that Chief Inspector Wilfred (Wonder Wilf) Dover was going to get all nicely solved in no time at all. He'd show 'em that Percy Roderick wasn't the only one who could get results!

'Just one last question, sir,' he said as he reached for his bowler hat. 'I suppose in the Air Force you've been taught how to use fire-arms?'

'Yes,' admitted Rex in a thin voice, with a horrified look at his mother, 'but only a rifle! I've never fired a pistol in my life.'

Dover smiled. 'Oh, quite, sir! I was just asking, you

know. Well, I think that's all. I won't be troubling you any more – for the moment, that is.'

'Well,' remarked Dover smugly when he and MacGregor were outside again, 'not often you find a chap helpfully putting the noose round his own neck *and* tying the knot for you, is it?'

'Do you really think he's our man, sir?' asked Mac-Gregor doubtfully.

'Think?' snapped Dover. 'There's no *thinking* about it. I know damned well he did it! Stands out a mile. He knows how to use fire-arms, he's hanging round the scene of the first attack and he's no blooming alibi for the time the shots were fired. He comes back on leave, reads the paper, rushes round and smothers her with a pillow. My God, he's admitted he was alone in the room with her for three-quarters of an hour just about the time she was killed.'

'But we've no proof, have we, sir?'

'Oh, proof!' snorted Dover contemptuously.

'Well, we won't get a conviction without it, will we, sir?' asked MacGregor, reasonably enough.

'I know we won't get a conviction without it!' howled Dover. 'I don't need you to teach me my job, Sergeant! God damn it, I've only been on the case five minutes. I'll get the proof all fixed, don't you bother!'

'But,' persisted MacGregor, who occasionally couldn't leave ill alone, 'oh, I dunno, sir, he doesn't look like a murderer, does he?'

Dover raised his eyes appealingly to heaven. 'My God,' he exclaimed, 'I don't know how some of you young coppers ever get on the force, straight I don't! He doesn't look like a murderer. What bloody murderer does, eh? You tell me that!'

'But what about motive, sir? Why should he kill her?'

'I don't have to prove motive,' snapped Dover.

'No, I know, but it helps to have one, doesn't it, sir?'

Dover breathed heavily through his nose. 'All right,' he said with mock patience, 'we'll go along and see Miss Violet Slatcher. Maybe she can fill in a bit of the background for us. Maybe we'll find a motive for Mr Rex Purseglove. You play Doubting Thomas if you want to, my lad, but I'm telling you here and now that Pilot Officer Purseglove of the Royal Air Force, God help 'em, murdered Isobel Slatcher.'

MacGregor imperceptibly shrugged his shoulders. 'Yes, sir,' he said.

CHAPTER FOUR

VIOLET SLATCHER, the dead girl's sister, was not taking this latest tragedy, as they say, lying down.

'I've tried to get her to put her feet up,' whispered Mr Bonnington as he let Dover and Sergeant MacGregor into the house, 'or just rest a bit on the sofa, but there's no doing any good with her.' His dog collar gleamed whitely in the darkness of the hall. 'I'm so glad you've come. I think it'll do her good to have a chat with you. Once she's got it all off her chest she may be able to calm herself down a bit.'

He smiled unctuously, and Dover sighed. He'd had a hard day and no sleep last night and he didn't look forward to trying to drag some sense out of a hysterical woman. But Miss Slatcher wasn't hysterical. She was militant, eloquent and thirsting for revenge.

'This, dear lady,' said the Vicar in suitably hushed tones, 'is Chief Inspector Dover from Scotland Yard. He just wants to ask you a few . . .'

'Thank God!' said Miss Slatcher, loudly and fervently. 'Thank God! Now, at last, we shall get something done.'

Dover began uncomfortably to mutter some trite expressions of condolence and sympathy, but Violet Slatcher impatiently swept them aside.

'There's no need to try and spare my feelings,' she exclaimed irritably. 'I shed my tears eight months ago, when all this started. Isobel died then for me, not yesterday. What's been lying up there in the hospital all this time, that wasn't my sister – that was just a medical experiment. I've been telling the Vicar here – not that it seems to have sunk in yet – I've got past wanting sympathy. I want justice! I want the brute who murdered my poor Isobel caught and punished. And if you can't do it for me' – she glared fiercely at Dover – 'I'll take the law into my own hands and do it for myself!'

Mr Bonnington smiled uneasily. 'Come, come, dear lady,' he remonstrated without much hope of success, 'this is not a very Christian attitude. We are told to have charity, you know, and to forgive our enemies . . .'

Miss Slatcher brushed the Christian ethic to one side. 'I hope,' she said, still directing her attention to Dover, 'I hope that you don't share that milk-sop attitude. I've been waiting for a long time to have them find my sister's murderer and I warn you, I don't intend to wait much longer. You're not another snivelling Papist, I hope?'

'No,' said Dover, 'I'm . . .'

'Thank God for that! The Lord is being merciful, at last. It's taken Him a long time to answer my prayers, but I never as much as wavered in my faith that He would do what I asked. Praise be to the Lord!'

'Er, yes,' said Dover.

Mr Bonnington looked a trifle embarrassed and Sergeant MacGregor stared blankly at the virgin page of his notebook.

'Well, now, madam,' Dover started firmly, feeling it was about time he took control of the interview, 'there are just one or two questions I should be very glad if you'd answer. Do you know if your sister had any enemies, anybody who would be likely to do her serious harm, or even kill her?'

'I do!' declared Violet Slatcher in ringing tones. 'She had a hundred, a thousand – nay, ten thousand enemies in this town. She was a great fighter in the Lord, you know. Every Pope worshipper in Curdley was her deadly foe. They knew she was constantly on the watch, ready to stamp out any attempts they made to spread their idol-worship even further afield than they have managed to do already. Isobel . . .'

Dover cut this tirade short. 'Are you suggesting that she was the victim of some Catholic plot?' he asked sourly.

Violet Slatcher hesitated for a moment. 'It wouldn't be the first time,' she observed sourly, 'but, as a matter of fact, on this occasion the murderer is one whom we have nursed in our bosom! Mind you,' she added quickly, 'it's because of the Catholics that he's not yet been brought to justice. Obviously that son of Satan, the Chief Constable . . .'

'Now, just a minute,' said Dover, 'are you telling me that you *know* who the murderer is?'

'Oh, I know all right,' said Miss Slatcher with a bitter laugh.

'All right then, who is it?'

Mr Bonnington leaned forward, a worried frown creasing his urbane face. 'My dear Miss Slatcher, I do beg you once again to be careful. You must not go around making these wild accusations – for which you have not one iota of proof or justification. I've warned you before, there is a law about slander, you know.'

'I know that everybody is against me!' snapped Violet Slatcher. 'Even you, Vicar! I am a poor weak woman but in the end justice will prevail and the Lord will cast down all mine enemies.'

'Miss Slatcher!' roared Dover with a venomous glance at Mr Bonnington for his interference. 'Who is it that you think murdered your sister?'

'My lips are sealed. As Mr Bonnington says, I have no proof. I can only put my trust in the Lord, and you,' she added generously.

'All right!' snarled Dover. 'Well, I'd like to ask you a few questions about your sister. What exactly was her relationship with Rex Purseglove?'

'They were engaged to be married.'

'Mr Purseglove claims that there was only some vague understanding between them.'

'Mr Purseglove is a liar. He is also a debauched libertine, a shameless womanizer and a man who gives his promise only to break it.'

'Oh,' said Dover.

'I can imagine what sort of lying story you have had from Rex Purseglove and his precious mother and father. Well, I'll tell you the truth! For some time before Isobel was shot Rex Purseglove had been paying court to her. He was only a corporal then and he used to come over to Curdley most week-ends. Isobel saw quite a lot of him and we both thought that although he hadn't much to offer at that time he was, nevertheless, a decent, clean-living young man with good prospects. We were wrong, of course, tragically wrong, but at the time his true nature was not revealed to us. Isobel, with my encouragement, returned his affection. You have not been privileged to know my sister, Chief Inspector, but she was a girl of the very highest moral standards. Ask the Vicar here and he will tell you the same thing. Isobel loved Rex Purseglove, but she would never have permitted anything underhand or, well, nasty, in their relationship. She was not one to give her heart lightly, as

50

Rex Purseglove well knew. Naturally, she assumed that his intentions were as honourable as her own.

'You can imagine what a shock it was when this Purseglove man suddenly announced that he wished to break off their association. Isobel was heartbroken when she discovered that what for her had been something noble and sublime was, for him, merely a sordid interlude, a cruel trifling with her affections. I was not prepared to stand idly by and see him slide out of his obligations in this disgusting manner. I told him quite roundly that I was not going to see my sister callously jilted and made the laughing-stock of the whole district. I gave him a straight choice. Either he stood by his sacred obligations or we would see what redress the law of the land would give to an innocent girl. And I pointed out to him that it was unlikely that the Air Force would require the services of an officer who had been the subject of a breach of promise case.'

'I see,' said Dover. 'And what did he decide to do?'

'There wasn't time for him to decide anything. The Saturday evening that poor Isobel was shot, he and his mother came round to see me in an effort to get me to change my mind. They were unsuccessful.' Miss Slatcher smiled grimly. 'When they left I understood that Rex was going to meet my sister when she came away from the vicarage and see if he could get her to change her attitude. According to *him*, this meeting never took place, but even if it had Isobel would not have weakened in her resolve.'

'I see,' said Dover again. 'So Rex Purseglove would have got out of a very difficult situation if your sister had died, eh? As, come to think of it, he's got out of it now.'

'That is correct,' agreed Miss Slatcher, and pursed her lips.

'And you really meant to sue him for breach of promise if he didn't marry your sister?'

51

'It would have been my duty.'

Dover sighed gently and sat staring at the dead girl's sister. He felt quite amiable towards her. After all, she'd just handed him, on a plate, exactly what he wanted – a nice fat juicy motive for Mr Rex Purseglove. She wasn't, Dover was quite sure, the kind of woman to back down, either. Rex Purseglove must have known exactly where he stood: either he had to marry Isobel or see his chances of becoming an officer in the Air Force trickle gently down the drain.

Violet Slatcher was older than Dover had expected. He guessed her to be in her early forties, although her greying mousy hair, make-up-less face and dowdy clothing would have made a less expert observer put her at over fifty. She had a thin, peaked face with a tight little mouth and sharp, slightly protruding eyes. She seemed very tense and on edge, a woman living on her nerves, but, allowing for a bit of religious fanaticism here and there, she'd told a coherent, and very acceptable, story.

Dover sighed again and picked up his bowler hat. This was a favourite trick of his. He liked to make his witnesses think the interview was over and then, as they relaxed and were perhaps slightly off their guard, he would fire a parting salvo – if he had one. He certainly had one for Miss Slatcher.

He rose heavily and reluctantly to his feet. Sergeant MacGregor and the Vicar got up too, and Miss Slatcher let her back come in contact with that of her chair for the first time since Dover had entered the room. She dabbed unconvincingly at her eyes with a small lace handkerchief, a gesture which failed to conceal the flinty triumph on her face.

Dover swung ponderously round on her. 'Why did you tell the *Custodian* that your sister was on the point of recovery?' he demanded.

Miss Slatcher's eyes protruded even further and she

was so astonished that it was a second or two before she could speak.

'Who told you that?' she asked in a faint, choked voice.

'Never mind who told me!' said Dover harshly. 'Why did you do it?'

Miss Slatcher looked helplessly at the Vicar, who avoided her eyes, and then back at Dover's unpleasantly scowling face. She found no help anywhere.

'Oh dear!' moaned Mr Bonnington plaintively. 'It wasn't you who put that ridiculous story in the paper, was it? That really was very wrong of you, Miss Slatcher. You know it wasn't true. How could you be so heartless?'

'Heartless?' repeated Miss Slatcher and took refuge in a trapped woman's last resort – tears. 'Heartless? You're the ones who are heartless. I just couldn't bear it any longer. There was my poor Isobel, lying unconscious in that hospital week after week, and outside everybody was going on just as usual, as though nothing had happened. You were all beginning to forget her. She was still alive but you were all beginning to forget her, what had happened to her, what she'd suffered. Oh, everybody was upset about it at first. They said it was disgraceful that nothing was being done to find the devil that shot her but nowadays, why some people who knew her quite well don't even ask me how she is. I couldn't bear it! Just to forget her, casually, like that – it was worse than killing her a second time.'

Sobbing almost uncontrollably now, Violet Slatcher swung back to Dover. 'I wanted to make them remember her again. I wanted to make them remember that the man who shot her was still walking about, unpunished! Dear God,' she almost shouted, 'I wanted revenge!'

'Oh dear!' said Mr Bonnington again. 'Dear lady, do try to reconcile yourself to what has happened and clear your heart of this bitterness. As Christians, we must resign ourselves to the will of God, you know.'

'She was my sister, not yours!' Miss Slatcher blew her nose and pulled herself together. 'And don't you accuse me of being a bad Christian! I know my Bible as well as you do and it says there – "An eye for an eye a tooth for a tooth" . . .'

'It also says – "Vengeance is mine, saith the Lord",' Mr Bonnington pointed out.

'It also says – "The Lord helps those who help themselves"!' retorted Miss Slatcher.

Mr Bonnington smiled helplessly and Dover broke in before he could produce another quotation.

'Miss Slatcher, you gave this completely fictitious story about your sister's recovery to the *Custodian* just to stir the whole thing up again? Is that it?'

Violet Slatcher nodded her head fiercely. 'Yes, I did. I am a poor helpless woman and I had to use what weapons the good Lord placed to hand. And after all,' she said complacently, 'my efforts have not been in vain. You are here!'

'Er, yes,' said Dover.

'He will hang, won't he? The man who did it, I mean? Shooting – that's capital murder, isn't it? All right, Vicar, you want me to resign myself to the will of God – well, on the day that murdering beast hangs, I will!'

The three men left Miss Slatcher's house together and all of them felt a wave of relief as the door was shut smartly behind them.

'She was very devoted to her sister,' Mr Bonnington observed. 'Very devoted. This has been a great blow to her, you know.'

'If you ask me,' said Dover unkindly, 'it seems to have knocked her clean off her rocker. Did she always go on like that?'

Mr Bonnington smiled apologetically. 'Well, she's always been a very fervent churchwoman – rather inclined to over-dramatize things a bit, but a sincere believer none the less and, in many ways, an example to all of us.'

'Humph,' grunted Dover sceptically.

'I felt I had to come round this evening to see her,' Mr Bonnington went on as he walked down the street with Dover and MacGregor. 'I knew she would be very upset after Isobel's death and, of course, with there being no other relations, I was afraid she would be alone in her grief.'

'The parents are dead, are they?'

'Oh yes, many years ago, I believe.'

'This one appears to be very much older than her sister,' said Dover.

'Yes, fifteen or sixteen years, I should guess. I suppose that partly explains Violet's devotion to Isobel. She seems to have been more like a mother to her than a sister.'

'What do you think of this business of her telling the *Custodian* that Isobel was going to wake up any minute?'

'Who knows?' The Vicar shrugged his shoulders. 'I imagine her own explanation is true in part and then, I think, she was reasoning to some extent like a child. Wishful thinking, you know. The idea that if you *say* a thing is true, then to a certain extent, it *is* true. Poor woman.'

'Where does the money come from?'

'The Slatchers'? Oh, well, Isobel was a librarian here in the town and Violet is manageress in one of these launderette places. I think there's a little money from the parents as well, but not much.'

'Do you know Rex Purseglove?' asked Dover, glancing sideways through the darkness at Mr Bonnington.

'Oh yes, he's one of my parishioners.'

'Miss Slatcher thinks he killed Isobel, you know. D'you think he did?'

'Good heavens, Chief Inspector, I hope not! What a terrible thing to suggest. I do hope you aren't taking what

Miss Slatcher said, or implied rather, in the heat of the moment seriously?'

'Did he want to marry Isobel?'

Mr Bonnington frowned. 'Chief Inspector,' he said evasively, 'one doesn't wish to speak ill of the dead, but Isobel Slatcher was a rather forceful, even bossy, young woman. She was, too, rather over-anxious to get married. A young man like Rex Purseglove might well find himself involved in a situation to a rather greater extent than he had anticipated. I don't honestly think he ever dreamed of marrying Isobel. After all, she was three or four years older than he is and not, I'm afraid, a very attractive girl.'

'Humph,' said Dover. 'And what about your relations with her, Vicar? Are you married, by the way?'

'I'm a widower, as it happens,' said Mr Bonnington stiffly. 'Though what that's got to do with the matter, I can't imagine.'

'Might have a lot,' replied Dover cynically. 'Well, was she chasing after you?'

'Certainly not! What on earth gave you that ridiculous idea?'

'Well, she was a regular visitor at the vicarage, wasn't she?'

'Once a week for an hour on Saturday nights. She very kindly came in to give me a hand with the clerical side of my work – she typed letters and things for me. I would have preferred her to come at some other time but, of course, she had her work at the library. Seven o'clock on a Saturday evening was not,' complained Mr Bonnington, 'a very convenient time for me.'

Since he had Mr Bonnington there, Dover decided to take him through his story of the shooting. Nothing much emerged that they didn't already know from the file. The Vicar had been in his study when, a few minutes after Isobel had said good night and left the vicarage, he had heard the sound of the two shots from outside. He had hurried out of his front door and along by the high wall of his garden. Just on the corner he had found the girl and, assuming that she was dead, had rushed back to phone the police. When he returned the second time he had found Rex Purseglove hovering uncertainly beside the girl's body.

'Was there anybody else about?' asked Dover.

'Not as far as I could see. I assumed that whoever had fired the shots had run away before I got outside.'

'But did nobody else hear the sound of the shots? I should have thought that in the middle of a town you'd have had a crowd round in no time.'

'Well, St Benedict's actually, Inspector, is in a rather quiet little backwater. The railway runs in a cutting on one side of Church Lane – that's where Isobel was shot – and on the other side there's the churchyard and the church itself, the vicarage garden which is on the corner, then the vicarage and then the church hall. It's really quite a distance away from any houses or from the main road. It was a coldish night and dark, and the sound of the shots didn't in fact carry as far as you might think. I wasn't really sure I'd heard them myself. Mr Ofield was practising on the organ in the church that night and he didn't know a thing about what had happened until he came in to Matins next morning.'

'You didn't *hear* anybody running away after the shots were fired?'

'No, I'm afraid not. Of course I'd started to rush outside myself as soon as I realized what it was I'd heard.'

'Hm,' said Dover. 'Oh well, I expect I'll be calling round at your place tomorrow some time – just to have a look at the scene of the crime. No doubt I'll see you again then. Good night.'

'Er, good night,' said Mr Bonnington, not sounding overjoyed, as Dover lumbered off into the darkness with Sergeant MacGregor tagging along behind him.

57

Dover was humming a merry little tune to himself as he ambled along, his bowler hat stuck jauntily at the back of his head.

'Where are we going now, sir?' asked MacGregor.

'To see Rex Purseglove, my dear boy,' beamed Dover. 'We've got the case tied up, near as dammit! On the scene on both occasions, knows how to use a revolver and now a lovely, lovely motive! Either he married the fair, if elderly, Isobel Slatcher or that damsel was going to sue him for breach of promise and that would probably cost him a packet in damages and his career. We've got him, my lad, we've got him!'

'But, sir . . .' began MacGregor.

'Now, don't start that damned carping of yours!' snapped Dover with a rapid return to his old manner. 'I know a hell of a sight better than you do what a court requires in the way of proof and in due course, if necessary, I'll get it. Should be a piece of cake now we know where to look. But we're going along now to have another little chat with young Purseglove. What with Violet Slatcher's story about his engagement to Isobel and a bit of the old Dover bluff, I'll be very surprised if we can't bash a nice little confession out of that toffee-nosed young whelp.'

'But, sir . . .' insisted MacGregor.

'And don't start quoting the Judges' Rules to me, either,' continued Dover like an irate steam-roller. 'You young coppers pay too much attention to what's written in books instead of using your own judgement. The only time you need bother about the Judges' Rules is when the accused person's likely to know more about 'em than you do. I don't think Rex Purseglove'll know much about 'em, so we'll be quite safe. Besides,' he added righteously, 'I have no intention of breaking 'em, you know' – he chuckled to himself – 'only of bending 'em a bit, eh?'

'But, sir,' said MacGregor, valiantly trying for the third

time, 'if we're going to the Pursegloves', there's just one thing you ought to know.'

'Well?'

'We're going in the wrong direction, sir. I did try to tell you.'

Dover stopped dead in his tracks and turned a black, furious face on his sergeant. He took a deep, deep breath.

'You bloody fool!' he said, and meant it.

CHAPTER FIVE

THE PURSEGLOVES had obviously not anticipated a return visit from Scotland Yard. Mr Purseglove had changed out of his best suit and was now more comfortably arrayed in a dilapidated pair of flannel trousers, brown carpet slippers and an old sweater. Highly ill-at-ease and clearly very puzzled, he showed the two detectives into the front room and then disappeared to get his son. The front room looked bleak. The curtains were not drawn and a one-barred electric fire leered inhospitably in the hearth. In the room next door, in which the Pursegloves obviously lived, the television was abruptly switched off in the middle of a cat-meat advertisement and there was a rustle of anxious whispering. A few moments later the family trooped in.

Dover wrinkled his nose. He was just about to turn Mr and Mrs Purseglove out of the room when he realized that they would only listen at the keyhole if he did, so he resigned himself to letting them stay. In their anxiety to protect their son they might well let something of value slip out. While Mrs Purseglove fussed around drawing the curtains (she didn't want the neighbours to see) and switching on the electric fire, Dover passed the time by staring fixedly at Rex Purseglove. That young man became more and more uncomfortable and more and more uncertain as to how he should behave. He had, after all, only been an officer and a gentleman for a couple of days and nobody had taught him how either of them could be expected to react when faced by a black-browed, bad-tempered, fat chief inspector from Scotland Yard. Dover noted with great satisfaction that Rex Purseglove didn't appear to think of relying on sheer innocence to guard and guide him.

When everybody had at last sat themselves down, Dover with great and ominous deliberation set about his questioning.

'Now, Mr Purseglove,' he began in a voice which was pregnant with menace, 'we have just been having a word with Miss Violet Slatcher.'

He paused dramatically. Rex Purseglove swallowed hard. His mother pursed her lips and his father started to sweat gently. Dover was delighted. He'd show 'em that Superintendent Percival Roderick wasn't the only flaming pebble on the beach!

'Miss Violet Slatcher,' he thundered ponderously on, 'had a slightly different version of your' (sneer) 'understanding with her deceased sister. She says that you and Isobel *were* engaged, that you wanted to break it off, and that Isobel told you that if you did, she'd sue you for breach of promise. Well?'

It was Mrs Purseglove who answered. 'The spiteful old bitch!' she said.

'Oho!' trumpeted Dover. 'So it's true, is it? Well, now, this puts a very different complexion on things, doesn't it?'

'What do you mean?' asked Rex in a cracked voice.

'I'll ask the questions!' Dover let out a roar which shook the plastic flowers on the mantelpiece. 'Did you or did you not attempt to break off your engagement to Isobel Slatcher? And,' he added nastily, 'I want the truth this time!'

Mrs Purseglove was about to chip in again but her son stopped her. 'It's no good, Mum,' he said miserably, 'I'll have to tell 'em. It's no good trying to hush it all up now. I'll tell you how it was, sir,' he spoke humbly to Dover, 'but honestly, you've got it all wrong, really you have. You see what happened was like this. Last year I was stationed at RAF Himus – it's only about forty miles from here and week-ends I used to come home. There was nothing much to do on the station at the week-end, and it wasn't all that much better here in Curdley. Well, Sundays I used to go to church – just to please Mum, really – and I got friendly with Isobel Slatcher. You know how it is. I didn't mean anything serious – she was just somebody to go around with. Well, after a bit she got more and more possessive and started talking about my future, and about how I ought to be trying to get on and how much a week was the marriage allowance. Well, I started to back-pedal. I'd no intention of settling down for a good bit and, you can take it from me, it wouldn't have been with Isobel if I had! I tried to cut things off gently like, I mean, I didn't want to hurt her feelings but, well, it wasn't all that easy. I mean, we'd got into a sort of routine and in a small place like this you can't just fade quietly out of the picture. You know how it is.

'Then this business of trying for a commission came up and, I dunno, I suppose it just made me bring things to a head. I tried to explain to Isobel as nicely as I could that, well, my future was uncertain and I'd be going away for a good bit and, well, this was the end of the line. My God, you'd have thought the end of the world had come! She stormed the place down and accused me of everything under the sun. She started crying and carrying on about how I'd trifled with her affections and God only knows what.

61

And I don't mind telling you, Inspector' – Rex shot an embarrassed glance at his mother – 'her affections were about all I got the chance to trifle with, if you see what I mean. She wasn't having no funny business. She made that quite clear.'

'Really, Rex!' His mother tossed her head in indulgent reproof.

'Well, that's all there is, really,' Rex went on. 'I came home and told Mum what Isobel had said and she said I was well rid of her because she was too old for me anyhow. Then her sister Violet waded in and told me that I'd given Isobel to understand that I was going to marry her and she expected me to go through with it. Mum told her I wasn't having any and then Violet started going on about taking me to court for breach of promise. I don't mind telling you, it fair put the wind up me! I could kiss my commission goodbye if I got hauled up on a charge like that. And Mum was worried about what all her friends at the church would say and, of course, it was awful.

'Well, when I came home the next week-end, the Saturday Isobel was shot, Mum and me went round to see Violet to see if we could get any sense out of her. But we couldn't budge her, could we, Mum?'

'She was like a raving lunatic,' agreed Mrs Purseglove. 'Of course, she's been trying to get Isobel married for years now. Our Rex isn't the first one she's tried to trap into leading her to the altar. Everybody knows the pair of 'em, Isobel and Violet, thought about nothing but getting a husband for that girl. They all used to say if they didn't try so hard, she might have had a bit more success. It puts a young chap off, you know, if people start talking about weddings the minute he says hello to a girl.'

'Whose idea was it that you should go round and meet Isobel from the vicarage?' asked Dover.

'It was mine,' said Mrs Purseglove. 'I thought he might

be able to talk Isobel round if he had her on her own – away from Violet.'

'But I didn't kill her, Inspector,' protested Rex. 'You must believe me. I wouldn't have dreamt of doing anything like that.'

'Wouldn't you?' asked Dover sceptically.

'No, I wouldn't, and you can't prove that I did!'

'Can't I?' said Dover truculently. 'Well, we'll see about that. The police aren't such fools as they look, you know. We found out right away, for example' – he watched Rex closely – 'that Isobel Slatcher didn't die a natural death on Friday morning. She was murdered!'

'Murdered?' cried Rex, what little colour there was left in his face draining rapidly away.

'Yes, murdered!' Dover hammered the word home. 'Somebody went to her room in the hospital on Friday morning and killed her. Somebody who'd read in the paper that she was going to get better and might be on the point of naming the man who shot her. You, in fact!'

'It's a lie! I never touched her!'

'You were alone with her in her room for three-quarters of an hour. Who else but you could have done it?'

'Oh my God!' moaned Rex, clearly on the verge of tears. 'It wasn't me! I never set foot in that damned room!'

'Wadderyermean?' snarled Dover, hoping his ears had deceived him.

'Look, I've told you what I thought about Isobel. She didn't mean a damned thing to me, and never had. You don't think I sat sorrowing by her bedside for three-quarters of a bleeding hour, do you? I only went to the damned hospital in the first place because Violet came round here on Thursday evening begging me to go. She was that upset and I felt sorry for her. After all, I knew she thought the world of Isobel and it seemed the least I could do.

63

And Mum wanted me to go because Violet said the chaps from the newspapers would be there and everything.'

'He put his officer's uniform on, you know,' said Mrs Purseglove proudly.

'But you told me yourself you were alone in that room with her!' bawled Dover, liking less and less the way things were shaping up.

'I know I did,' said Rex, 'but that was before all this malarky started, wasn't it? I didn't know she'd been killed then, did I? Well, I do now and you're not going to pin it on me, mate! I'll tell you what really happened and you can check it if you like.'

'Don't worry,' threatened Dover, 'I shall!'

'Well, you go and ask Mary Horncastle about it, then. She's the nurse who showed me up to Isobel's room. I've known her for years – we went to school together. She opened the door to Isobel's room and I just peeped in and then I went off with Mary to a little room where they keep all the dressings and things and she made me a cup of tea and I stayed chatting with her until it was time for me to go. She came down to the entrance hall with me and I was back home just before eleven, wasn't I, Mum?'

'You were, dear,' his mother nodded firmly. 'And Mrs Bootle from next door was here when you come in.'

'So there you are, Inspector! I don't know who killed Isobel in the hospital on Friday, but it damned well wasn't me, and I can prove it!'

To say that Dover was furious would be a most unwarranted understatement. He'd had the whole thing worked out so nicely and now all his lovely theories and deductions had been kicked to pieces before his very eyes – and before those of Sergeant MacGregor, which made it even worse. This young pup Purseglove had made him look a right old fool, and while this was no novel experience for Dover, it was still an unwelcome one. He stormed and raged and bullied and browbeat, but he couldn't shake Rex Purseglove. Of course, everything depended on whether Nurse Horncastle supported his story, but Dover knew his luck. She would!

In the end he reluctantly acknowledged defeat and was reduced to muttering dire threats about what happened to those who hindered the police in the execution of their duty – not much consolation for a man who'd been hoping to arrest a particularly callous and persistent murderer.

It was at this stage in the proceedings that the Purseglove family moved unexpectedly into the attack. Mrs Purseglove expressed herself freely and at length on the question of unfounded accusations, with particular reference to her only child, but it was Rex's father who put the cat amongst the pigeons. Joining in hesitantly to support his wife (he knew what reproaches he would have to face afterwards if he didn't), he brought up the question of the gun with which Isobel Slatcher had been shot.

'I don't know why you don't go and ask a few of your blooming questions off them as owned that,' he grumbled, ''stead of bothering a decent lad like our Rex what's serving his queen and country in the Raf.'

'RAF, Dad!' said his son crossly. 'I've told you before not to call it Raf!'

'The gun can't be traced,' snapped Dover equally crossly.

'Oh, can't it?' retorted Mr Purseglove sarcastically. 'Well, there's none so blind as them as won't see, is there?'

'And what do you mean by that?' demanded Dover.

'Only,' said Mr Purseglove calmly, 'that well nigh everybody in Curdley knows that them young hooligans in the Pie Gang had a Luger revolver round about Christmas last year. And,' he added significantly, 'they haven't got it now.'

'And who the devil are the Pie Gang?'

'They're a bunch of young Catholic layabouts on the

other side of town,' explained Rex. 'Hey, Dad, I'd forgotten all about them! You see, Inspector, when Isobel
was shot last February there was a lot of talk that the
Catholics were at the back of it – Isobel had quite a
reputation for letting fly at them, you know, whenever she
got the chance.'

'And there was that young girl who was raped, too,' said
Mrs Purseglove.

'That's right, Mum, so there was. It was about three or
four days before Isobel was shot. There was a girl, Inspector, one of the Daughters of Mary, who was raped. She was
only about fourteen and there was the devil of a row about
it. Of course, all the Catholics said it was a Protestant
who'd done it and there was lots of talk about reprisals.
When Isobel got shot a lot of people thought that this was
the Holy Romans getting their own back, especially, as
Dad says, as plenty of people knew these Pie Gang kids
had somehow got hold of a Luger.'

'Of course,' said Mrs Purseglove with a sniff, 'nothing
was ever done about it. You wouldn't catch our police
running another Catholic in for parking his car in the
wrong place, never mind committing murder.'

'Not them,' agreed Mr Purseglove, 'they'd get the priest
along and give 'em absolution, they would.'

'More likely give 'em a medal,' observed Mrs Purseglove spitefully, ''specially if it was some Protestant girl
they'd killed.' She turned to Dover. 'P'raps you'd do as
well to have a look at these Pie Gang boys,' she suggested,
'and leave our Rex alone. That is, unless you're tarred with
the same brush as the rest of the bobbies in this town.'

It was at this point that Dover took his leave with as
much dignity as he could muster. Not only had he been
most unfairly deprived of his rightful prey – Rex – but he
had also gathered a piece of information from the general
public which should have been imparted to him by his

brother officers in the local police. His temper was not improved by this hint of unprofessional conduct.

It was MacGregor who bore the brunt of his chief inspector's displeasure, after all that is partly what detective sergeants are there for. The long cold walk back to the Station Hotel did nothing to lighten Dover's mood. His feet were killing him and he blamed MacGregor for that, too. He sulked massively all through dinner and reduced the waitress to tears because the Lancashire hot-pot (which he didn't want, anyway) was off.

It was only afterwards in the bar that he began to calm down a little. Dover enjoyed his pint of beer, but only if somebody else was paying for it. There was a widely held, though erroneous belief amongst the junior ranks at Scotland Yard that only unmarried detective sergeants with private incomes were assigned to Dover because the expenses of providing him with free beer and cigarettes were so heavy. MacGregor, who had been chafing in double yoke with Dover for some time now, had often considered becoming both a teetotaller and a non-smoker, but had come to the conclusion that money wasn't everything. It was well worth a few bob to keep the chief inspector in a fairly reasonable state of mind.

Dover was half-way through his third pint before MacGregor judged that it was safe to mention the progress (for want of a better word) of the Isobel Slatcher case.

'What's our next move to be, sir?' he asked.

Dover stared despondently into the depths of his tankard. 'God only knows!' he said gloomily.

'I suppose we'd better check with Nurse Horncastle about young Purseglove's alibi, hadn't we?'

'I suppose so,' grunted Dover without much interest. 'You'd better go round by yourself to the hospital first thing tomorrow morning and have a word with her. I reckon I'll have to go and see Colonel Muckle.' He brightened up at the thought. 'He's going to have a bit of explaining to do, he is! I suppose there wasn't a word in the file about this Pie Gang, was there?'

'No, sir. There was just a note that they hadn't been able to trace the Luger. It looks as though it was a war souvenir that somebody had brought back from Germany. Must have been hundreds of 'em smuggled in by Servicemen after the war.'

'Hm.' Dover took a thoughtful pull at his beer. 'Still, it doesn't alter the fact – does it? – that the local boys must have known about this Pie Gang tie-up, and yet they haven't put a single blooming word about it in the report. Very naughty. The Chief Constable and I are going to have a very interesting chat, very interesting indeed.'

'You don't want me to come with you, sir?'

'Not bloody likely!' snorted Dover with a fruity chuckle. 'I shan't want any witnesses – and I'm damned well sure old Muckle won't!'

'If Nurse Horncastle bears out Rex Purseglove's story, sir, I suppose that means we'll have to cross him off the list completely, doesn't it?'

'What list?' asked Dover sourly. 'He's the only flipping one we've had on it so far. But if he can prove he didn't do the suffocating with the pillow, then I reckon he's in the clear. Pity, he was measuring up nicely. Still' – he made a half-hearted attempt at optimism – 'we've hardly started yet. Somebody else'll turn up, no doubt. Tomorrow afternoon we'd better go and have a look at where the girl was shot. That might give us a few ideas. There's one thing, you know, MacGregor – assuming that young Purseglove is innocent and is therefore telling the truth, it's funny that if he heard the shots, he didn't hear anybody running off, or see 'em, either.'

'Well, they may have cleared off in the opposite direction,' MacGregor pointed out, 'or hopped over a wall, or anything. In any case, neither Purseglove nor the Vicar seems to have thought of looking round for the attacker, do they? For all they bothered about him, he could have been standing in the shadows watching 'em. He may never have even tried to run away at all.'

'Yes, you may be right,' said Dover indifferently. 'Well, I'm going to bed.' He yawned widely. 'I've had a long day and I'm tired. You'd better write your report up before you turn in. Don't mention this gun business till we find out what Colonel Muckle's side of the story is. See you at breakfast.'

Although Dover came down next morning prepared to tackle his bacon and eggs in a fairly reasonable frame of mind, this benign mood didn't last for long. MacGregor had thoughtfully ordered a selection of Sunday papers and, at the sight of their screaming headlines, Dover's brow rapidly clouded over. Bigamous Bertie was in the news once again and, behind him, he dragged Superintendent Roderick to a bit more unsolicited publicity. Now that Bigamous Bertie had gone with a jerk through the pearly gates, the Sunday newspapers were in a position to reveal all. Only one, of course, had managed to get Bigamous Bertie's own story. They'd bought it long before he was even brought to trial and, what with hung juries, appeals and pleas for mercy, they'd had it on ice for a long time. Now they were going to get their money's worth.

The other newspapers did the best they could. One had got the life story of a 'wife' who had been spared the holocaust, and another had ghosted a sister's account of one of the four victims. There was even an article by an old man who had worked as a gardener in one of Bertie's bigamous establishments. Whichever paper one opened – even the 'serious' ones dragged Bertie's name in under the guise of a discussion on capital punishment – the sensational story of Cuthbert Boys was there for all to see. And, of course, you couldn't mention Bigamous Bertie without the name of Super Percy cropping up as well. There were nearly as many pictures of the 'most famous detective since Sherlock Holmes', as one paper put it, as there were of his victim.

Dover's breakfast was completely ruined. He told MacGregor to summon a taxi for him and he set off in a fine old temper for the Chief Constable's residence. He caught that gentleman just as he was setting off for Mass, and the two men retired back inside the house for what was no doubt a very spirited exchange of views.

By eleven o'clock Dover was back in the lounge of the Station Hotel, feeling much more cheerful. He had imperilled the Chief Constable's immortal soul by making him too late for church, he had received an abject apology for the prevarication of the local police in respect of the Pie Gang, and the Luger had been handed over to him. On the whole, a most satisfactory morning.

He was surprised to find that Sergeant MacGregor had got back before him.

'Well?' he demanded. 'How did you get on?'

'Piece of cake, sir,' said MacGregor. 'Nurse Horncastle supported Rex's story up to the hilt and begged me not to let Matron get a whiff of it, otherwise, I gather, the poor girl will be dissected alive. Her story that she was busy with an emergency case was just a bit of fiction made up for Matron's benefit. The truth is, I suspect, that she was too busy flirting with the gallant Purseglove to remember that she was supposed to be keeping an eye on poor Isobel. There doesn't seem a hope that Rex could have got into Isobel Slatcher's room after he'd just peeped in. Nurse Horncastle very kindly entertained me to a cup of tea in the same slop-place room that she'd taken Rex to. It's just a little sort of cupboard place on the other side of the main ward. Even if Rex had been left alone for a few minutes,

70

and Nurse Horncastle says he wasn't, he'd have had to go back through the main ward to get to Isobel's room. He was in uniform, sir. He could never have slipped through without somebody noticing it. The patients in there are rather lively. I got greeted with a chorus of wolf whistles myself when I passed through, both times. Nurse Horncastle said that the, er, ladies gave Rex the same ovation.'

Dover wrinkled his nose. 'Oh well,' he said, 'that's that. Exit Rex Purseglove as Suspect Number One.'

'Did you have any luck with the Chief Constable, sir?'

Dover permitted himself a complacent grin. 'Not too bad,' he admitted modestly. 'Colonel Muckle was good enough to clear one or two little points up for me.' He smirked broadly. 'Seems a very co-operative chap, really. Helpful, you know. Anyhow, I've got the Luger.' Dover dragged the gun out of his overcoat pocket and plonked it down on the table. 'They knew all about the Pie Gang, of course. It was pretty common knowledge that one of the young devils had got hold of a Luger and had been swanking about it all over town. I've no doubt that this one here is the same one. Colonel Muckle says his chaps went and asked them about it after Isobel was shot, but they all played the innocent and denied that they'd ever had a gun of any sort. Muckle says that's as far as his men could get but, as I told him, if his coppers don't know how to bash the truth out of a lot of crummy teenagers, it's about time they learned! I don't think' – Dover lovingly regarded his clenched and meaty right fist – 'that I shall have much trouble with 'em.'

'Do you think they shot Isobel Slatcher then, sir?'

'No.' Dover shook his head. 'They've got a cast-iron alibi, unfortunately. They were actually in police custody at eight o'clock that Saturday night. You remember about the Daughter of Mary who got raped – well, according to the Chief Constable, that was just her version of what

71

actually happened – anyhow, there was a great to-do about it and the Pie Gang evidently felt it was up to them to avenge the honour of Catholic maidenhood. A leading Protestant bigwig – a mason, too, apparently – had been buried that afternoon so these bright boys decided to take a trip out to the cemetery and dig him up again. What a town, eh? Well, the local police had been keeping a pretty close eye on the Pie Gang and they got wind of what the young devils were planning. They went out to the cemetery and waited for 'em. They copped the lot before a sod of earth was turned, and hauled 'em all off to the police station. There's no doubt about it, even if this is their gun they certainly didn't shoot Isobel Slatcher.

'Anyhow' – Dover picked up the Luger – 'you and me are going to have a word with 'em now. Seems they can't lie in bed on Sunday mornings because they've got to go to Mass, but they sit around afterwards all morning in a café until their mums have got their Sunday dinners cooked. The station sergeant told me where to find 'em.'

'Shall I get a taxi, sir?'

'No need to bother,' said Dover grandly. 'The Chief Constable has most kindly allocated us a car and a driver for the rest of our time here. Decent of him, wasn't it?'

CHAPTER SIX

THE POLICE car dropped the two detectives at the end of the street in which Elsie's Café, their destination, was situated.

'Freddie Gash, he's the one you want,' the police driver had told Dover. 'You'll find him in there all right. You can't miss him. He'll be the one with blackheads all over his face.'

Elsie's Café was to be found in one of the less salubrious quarters of Curdley and it was, as Dover had been warned, a somewhat greasy looking dump. Dover and MacGregor walked resolutely down the street to the near hysterical delight of the neighbourhood kids, whose ability to spot a copper at a hundred yards on a foggy day was innate. Dover strode magnificently through them, scattering snotty-nosed toddlers in all directions. MacGregor, who was a bit soft-hearted where children were concerned, tried pushing them gently out of the way with his hands. One angelic-faced little girl bit him severely on the thumb.

'I reckon that'll turn septic,' said Dover unsympathetically as he pushed open the café door. The door-bell pinged a cracked warning and three leather-jacketed youths sitting at one of the four wooden tables looked up. From the back a large fat woman in a grubby flowered overall shuffled sullenly in and rested her ample bosom on the linoleum-covered counter.

'Two coffees, please, miss!' ordered Dover, and moved across to sit down at one of the vacant tables. He inspected the top of the table he had chosen, decided that even he couldn't stomach it and moved off to another. It was better, but not much. Dover pulled out a wooden fold-flat chair, wiped it with his handkerchief and gently lowered his not inconsiderable bulk on to it. For a minute the issue was in doubt, but the chair was stronger than it looked and, creaking ominously, it successfully took the strain.

MacGregor came over to join him with two cups of coffee. Dover took one look. 'Ugh!' he said.

MacGregor sat down opposite him.

'I suppose that's them, is it?' he asked, glancing at the only other customers. The three youths had their heads together and were whispering amongst themselves.

'I reckon so,' said Dover. 'That looks like what's-his-name – Gash – with the blackheads. God, they look a right bunch of layabouts, don't they?'

The three lads decided to play it up a bit.

'Cor!' exclaimed the one with the blackheads loudly. 'Ain't there a pong in 'ere all of a sudden? Smells like rotten old socks, dunnit, Skip?'

'Yeah,' agreed Skip, tipping his chair back nonchalantly on two legs. 'Y'd think Elsie'd be a bit more particular about who she served in 'ere, wun't yer?'

The third member of the trio, who was cleaning the dirt from under his finger-nails with a flick knife, contributed his mite. 'If yer arsk me, Elsie's pies have got enough blue-bottles on 'em already without bringing any more in.'

This none-too-sharp witticism brought loud guffaws of laughter and the gang glanced sideways to see how the victims of their barbs were taking it. Both Dover and Mac-Gregor sat boot-faced and unresponsive, their coffee un-touched before them. Still propped up behind the counter, Elsie watched the proceedings with mild interest.

''Ere.' Gash, the leader, dragged, with some effort, a coin out of the pocket of his jeans and flipped it grandly on to the table. 'Let's 'ave some music, Pegtop!'

Pegtop shook his long blond hair out of his eyes and rose languidly to his feet. He leaned over a battered-looking juke box standing just by the far side of the table, put the coin in and hunted among the buttons for the air of his choice.

That was enough for Dover. He propelled himself across the room and clamped a hand like a vice on Pegtop's arm before the fatal finger could descend and let loose the sounds of hell.

Pegtop yelped with surprise and pain.

'Sit down!' snarled Dover, enforcing his behest with a well-directed thump between the teenager's thin shoulders.

74

Pegtop staggered in the right direction and, coughing pitifully, collapsed back on his chair. But Dover, who was not inexperienced in these matters, hadn't finished. Just before the two bottoms, or seats, made contact Dover's left foot shot out and jerked the chair aside. Pegtop crashed to the floor in an ignominious and painful heap.

His two friends, blessed with a primitive sense of humour, sniggered disloyally before raising their newly-broken voices in protest.

'Shut up!' barked Dover, and grabbed the remaining chair. Expertly he swung it round and sat down astride it, his arms resting crossed on its back. Teenagers weren't the only ones who watched cowboy films/on the telly. MacGregor caught the idea and with his hands poised just above his hips (ready for the draw) he sauntered across the café and leaned, relaxed but alert, against the juke box.

Pegtop, cursing in a subdued mutter, picked himself up from the floor, reassembled his fold-flat chair and sat down. The Pie Gang gazed at their uninvited guests with some apprehension and a little bewilderment. Both increased as Dover, with a wonderfully dead-pan face, slowly pulled the Luger from out of his overcoat pocket. The Pie Gang stared at it, fascinated. With a faint sniff, Dover took out his handkerchief – it was none too clean but MacGregor was the only one to be offended by this. With majestic deliberation Dover lovingly wiped the gun, tested its working parts – it was unloaded – and blew softly down the barrel. Having stretched out this performance as long as he could, he carefully, still without uttering a word, laid it down in front of him on the table.

After yet another pause Dover broke the silence. 'We're from Scotland Yard,' he announced grimly.

Freddie Gash dragged his eyes from the Luger and, as leader of the gang, undertook to make the first response.

'So?'

Dover glared moodily at him. 'We're investigating the murder of Isobel Slatcher.'

'Yeah?'

'We think you three may be able to help us.'

'Aw, get knotted!' mumbled Skip, and flinched as Dover looked at him.

'We don't know nothing,' yapped Pegtop nervously. 'The cops know that. It weren't nothing to do with us!'

Dover's eyes switched back to Freddie Gash's face. Gash, in spite of the blackheads and a noticeably weedy physique, was the leader of this lot and Dover didn't believe in dealing with underlings at any level of society.

It was to him that Dover drawled his next question. 'Wasn't it?' he asked.

Freddie Gash licked his lips and let his eyes flick for a moment to the gun. 'Naw!' he asserted. 'Yer can't touch us. We've got an alibi.'

'Really?' said Dover with apparent scepticism.

'Yerse! We was right on the other side of the town when she got shot.'

'Going to dig up a corpse, I hear,' mused Dover in an understanding tone.

Freddie Gash smiled rather proudly. All his front teeth were decayed. 'Yerse, we was. Only they nabbed us first. I reckon somebody squealed.'

'Charming,' murmured Dover.

'Gorn, he was only a bloody old Protestant!' retorted Gash contemptuously.

'He were a freemason, too,' said Skip. 'They all goes straight to 'ell anyway. Pope says so.'

'And it was them what started it,' added Pegtop, who had recovered his *savoir-faire*. 'They done one of our bints first, yer know!'

'Is that your gun?' asked Dover, changing the conversation abruptly.

Freddie Gash looked at it again, with longing. 'Naw,' he said regretfully, 'never seen it before in me life.'

'Pity,' sighed Dover. 'Oh well, looks as though we shan't be able to return it, after all.'

There was a puzzled silence while Freddie Gash, Skip and Pegtop ruminated over the possible implications of this remark. MacGregor had a livelier mind. His jaw tightened. Surely the old fool couldn't be going to . . .

'Return it?' asked Freddie Gash, his brow furrowed in unaccustomed thought. He picked nervously at a convenient blackhead.

''Sright,' said Dover blithely. 'Once I've got this case tied up and the murderer of Isobel Slatcher's been tried and had his neck stretched a bit further than Nature intended, we, the police, will have no further use for the' – he squinted speculatively at Gash – 'the murder weapon.'

The gang stared avidly at the Luger. As a prestige symbol it already stood pretty high, but as the instrument which had been responsible for the death of that Protestant tart – right here in Curdley . . . cor!

Dover picked the gun up and weighed it temptingly in his hand. 'Yes,' he went on, lying blandly, 'normally we'd give it back to the owner, but in this case, unfortunately, we don't know who the owner is. Do we?'

Freddie Gash wiped his hand nervously across his forehead as he struggled to work it out. Was it a trap? Did the police really give dubiously acquired guns back to young layabouts, even though they did attend Mass regularly and Confession once a month? The native cunning which had enabled him to live the life of Riley with no visible means of support (except his mother) ever since he left school, failed him dismally now. Recklessly he fell back on greed and self-interest.

'It were mine,' he croaked in a voice strangled by emotion and pride.

'Oh, it was, was it?' said Dover gently.

'Yerse, I gor it when Father O'Brien took us on a coach trip to London to see Westminster Cathedral. Cost me twenty bloody nicker, it did.' He stretched out his hand towards the gun.

Dover landed him a hefty crack across the wrist. 'You're not getting it yet, sonny boy!' he snapped. 'I want to know a bit more about it first. Now then, when did you go on this trip to London?'

''Bout a fortnight before Christmas last year,' said Freddie, sulkily rubbing his wrist.

'Did you get any ammunition with it?'

'Yeah. This same chap gimme four bullets.'

'Did you fire any of them?'

''Course I did! I fired one shot at old Mother Arnfield's ginger tom, but I missed the bugger. And then on New Year's Eve me and Skip went down t'railway line. Mate of mine's fireman on one of them goods trains and I took a shot at him as he went by in the cab. Him and his driver nearly wet their pants with fright when they heard the bang! Weren't half a giggle, weren't it, Skip?'

Dover broke impatiently through the gang's reminiscent chuckles. 'So, there were two shots left?'

''Sright.'

'And then what happened?'

''Ow d'you mean?'

'Well, did you lose the gun, or what? You hadn't got it in your possession in February, had you, when Isobel Slatcher was shot? Did you lend it to somebody?'

'Naw, I lost the bloody thing.'

'Where?'

Freddie Gash, very sensibly, put the brakes on. He exchanged glances with his two mates, stared longingly again at the Luger and raised his eyes dubiously to Dover's face. 'I can't remember,' he said with a sigh of disappointment.

'Don't give me that crap!' bawled Dover. 'Of course you can remember! Look, I'm only interested in this murder case, see? I don't give two tuppenny damns about anything else you and your little playmates have been doing. And,' he added significantly, 'I shan't pass on anything you tell me to the local police, either. Get it?'

Young Gash understood what Dover meant all right, but he wasn't sure if he believed him. He had imbibed a deep suspicion of the police with his mother's milk, and his subsequent contact with them had done nothing to remove this feeling. Of course, even he recognized that Dover was not what you might call a run-of-the-mill policeman, but he was still a flattie and, presumably, tarred to some extent with the same brush.

Dover gave an exasperated snort down his nose and made as if to put the Luger back in his overcoat pocket. That did it. Freddie Gash sang.

It was a rather incoherent story with some confusion as to times, dates and motives, but Dover gathered that the teenage element in Curdley were vigorously carrying on the Catholic v. Protestant warfare of their elders. While the adult members of the community restricted themselves in general to verbal thunderings from the pulpit and verbal sniping on committees and elsewhere, the youngsters went in for more direct action. They tossed bottles at each other's religious processions and broke the windows of each other's churches. From time to time one rival gang would beat up their opposite numbers and a retaliatory attack would follow in due course.

During the couple of months which preceded Isobel Slatcher's attempted murder, the pace had hotted up a little and the rape of the Daughter of Mary and the Pie Gang's attempt to dig up the deceased freemason were merely two of the more lurid skirmishes. Freddie Gash was now telling Dover of a third.

79

'We thought we'd go and bust up one of these mothers'
meetings things they have, see, just to give all them old
cows a bit of a scare, like. Well, we went along one night
to this parish hall place where they have their dos and we
all got us faces blacked up like commandos and I'd got me
gun and we was going to bust in on 'em all and do a sort
of hold-up, see? Well, summat went wrong or the buggers
had changed the night or something, because when we
kicked the bleeding doors open, the place were full of men.
There were about twenty or thirty of 'em and before we
knew what was happening they were coming at us like a
pack of bleeding wolves. There was only about six of us
and we hadn't a hope against that mob – so we beat it,
pretty damned quick. Well, everything got a bit mixed up
like and this little entrance hall was all cluttered up with
coats and chairs and hymn books and things and before we
could get out of the bleeding door into the street they was
on top of us. Well, we had a bit of a punch-up and this other
lot weren't too keen at coming close in because my mob
had all got coshes or bicycle chains or something and after
a bit we managed to get away. But some bleeder'd knocked
me gun out of me hand and I'd lost it. I weren't half
chocker, too. Twenty bleeding quid down the drain! And
that's it, mate. This were long before that bint got hers.'

'Hm,' said Dover. 'And the gun was loaded?'

'Yerse. I'd still got these two shots left, see?'

'What was the exact date? Can't you remember?'

Freddie Gash looked at Skip and Pegtop and then
shrugged his shoulders. 'Dunno,' he said. 'End of January,
beginning of February, p'raps.'

'We'll want it a bit closer than that,' said Dover. 'What
day of the week was it?'

''Ere, Skip,' said Gash with authority. 'Nip round home
and get me perishing press-cutting book. Me mum'll be in
the pub now, but the key's under the door mat.' He turned

to Dover as Skip hurried out. 'I think we got a write-up on that job,' he commented nonchalantly. 'That'll give you the date and everything, won't it?'

'Which parish hall was it?' asked Dover.

'That one off Corporation Road – what's it called, Pegtop?'

'St Benedict's,' said Pegtop with a sniff.

'St Benedict's!' yelped Dover. 'But that's near where Isobel Slatcher was shot!'

'Yeah, that's right,' agreed Freddie helpfully. 'I hadn't thought of that. She got croaked in Church Lane, didn't she? It'd be just round the corner from this church hall place of theirs.'

Dover leaned back complacently in his chair. 'Well, well,' he said, highly pleased with himself, 'just fancy that!'

While they waited for Skip to return with the press-cutting book Freddie Gash relaxed to such an extent that he pulled his cigarettes out and stuck one in his mouth. Being an ill-bred young lout he made the tactical error of not offering the chief inspector one. Dover scowled evilly, leaned across the table and plucked the cigarette out of Freddie's mouth. He crumbled it slowly to pieces in his hand. 'Don't push your luck, sonny!' he advised threateningly.

The press-cutting book, when it arrived, proved to be most useful. Freddie Gash had apparently been publicity conscious from a very early age and the first pages were devoted to reports of choir outings and Sunday-school football teams in which he had taken a prominent part. These were followed by write-ups of various incidents of hooliganism in which Freddie presumably had also had a finger, though his name was not actually mentioned. He was lucky in a way that the *Custodian* was a Protestant paper and tended to give more space to the wrongdoings of the Catholic youth than it did to those of its own faction. The account of the Pie Gang's raid on St Benedict's church hall filled two half-columns and ended with a biting indictment of the local police, who once again had failed to bring the perpetrators to justice. There was no mention of a gun being found on the scene of the crime.

'Hm,' grunted Dover as he read the story, 'Monday, twenty-ninth of January. Make a note of that, Sergeant!'

'Told you it were about then,' Freddie pointed out cheekily. 'See, it were two or three days before that Daughter of Mary kid got hers.' He jabbed a grubby finger at the next cutting. "Course, it was some Protestant bugger did her.'

'Garn!' sneered Pegtop, interrupting his nose picking to join in the conversation. 'It were that fancy man of her mother's what done her! Everybody knows that.'

His leader turned on him fiercely. 'You keep your bleeding trap shut!' he raged. 'I'll tell Father on you, straight I will! It were some Protestant bugger what done her, and don't you bleeding well forget it!'

Pegtop blinked, but Dover intervened curtly. 'Cut it out!' he snapped. 'Now, have you got anything else to tell me? No? All right, beat it!'

'What about me gun?' protested Freddie, sullenly watching Dover replace it in his pocket.

'I've told you. You'll get it back when the case is closed. It's all right, lad' – Dover leered unconvincingly – 'you can trust me. Now, hop it!'

The Pie Gang slouched disconsolately out of the café and Dover and MacGregor prepared to follow them. The proprietress, Elsie, who was still leaning on the counter and had listened to the whole conversation, spoke.

'I used to know the Slatchers,' she remarked conversationally.

'Oh?' said Dover.

"Sright! 'Course I've never spoken to 'em, but donkey's

years ago, when we was kids, they used to live in our street. On the other side, of course,' she added piously. 'They was all heathens what lived on the other side.'

'Really?' said Dover.

''Sright. We never had nothing to do with 'em, of course, but I remember Violet quite well. Stuck-up little bitch she were, too.'

'That's the elder sister?'

Elsie waggled a couple of chins. 'Sister?' she said sardonically. 'Well, I suppose you might call her that.'

'What do you mean, Mrs ... er ...?'

'Miss Leddicoat,' said Elsie obligingly. 'L,e,d,d,i,c,o,a,t – same as the martyrs.'

'Er, quite,' said Dover. 'Well, Miss Leddicoat, what's this about Violet Slatcher? She is the elder sister, isn't she?'

'Them,' responded Miss Leddicoat with a contemptuous sniff, 'as believes that'll believe anything.'

'But you know better?'

'I'll say I do! Stands to reason, doesn't it? You've only got to put two and two together, haven't you?'

Dover waited with growing irritation for her to continue.

'After all,' Miss Leddicoat obliged, 'I'd known the Slatchers all me life. He was a chauffeur in them days, though from the way him and his wife used to look down their noses at everybody else you'd have thought they was king and queen of England. 'Course, chauffeuring weren't a bad job in them days, and it were clean too, but that didn't give 'em no right to set themselves up like they did. They only had one kid too – that was Violet. There was fourteen of us at home and it makes a difference, I can tell you. 'Course, it's a mortal sin – birth control, I mean – and they're probably both in hell paying for it now, but it did mean Violet had a damned sight easier time of it than most of the kids in our street. When she left school she didn't go into the mill like the rest of us. Oh no, her ladyship

83

used to go off, tarted up to the nines every morning, to some job her dad'd got her in an office. Oh well' – she sighed massively and not without relish – 'they say pride goes before a fall.'

'And Violet fell, did she?'

'Not half! Nobody never knew who the chap was but he must have given Miss High and Mighty a fair old tumble in the hay. Well, she started getting a bit fatter, you know, but at fifteen or sixteen you put it down to puppy fat, don't you? None of us ever suspected that she'd got a pudding in the oven.'

'She was going to have a baby?' asked Dover with a bit more interest than he had shown so far.

''Sright. Not that they ever admitted it, you know. No, after a few months Mrs Slatcher – the mother, that is – let it get around that *she* was going to have a baby, see? Well, old Mr Slatcher, her husband, came in for a bit of leg pulling, I heard, because, God only knows, everybody thought he'd been well past that sort of thing for years. 'Course Mrs Slatcher was no chicken either, but everybody thought she'd been caught just before the change, you know. Well, two or three months before the baby was due, Mrs Slatcher clears out of town and takes Violet with her. I forget what reason they gave for that but it was something pretty slim. Anyhow, in due course back they came and Violet's had a little sister – I don't think! Bit after that they moved away to another part of the town.'

'I see,' said Dover. 'So Isobel was really Violet's own daughter. Tell me, did a lot of people know about this?'

'Oh yes. Well, everybody in our street knew, that's a cert. But it was only a nine days' wonder, you know. We all had a good laugh at the way they tried to cover it up, but what's one more kid born out of wedlock, eh? I've had three myself and you'd be surprised how quick people forget about it. 'Course, all this hooha with Violet Slatcher took place nearly thirty years ago. If it hadn't been for Isobel getting herself shot like that I don't suppose I should have given a second thought to the business. I mean, you can't remember everything, can you?'

Dover shook his head. 'No, I suppose not, madam.'

'Are you stopping for your dinner? Pie and beans we've got today.'

'No, thank you,' said Dover quickly, remembering the coffee. 'Come on, Sergeant, we've got a lot to do!'

They left the café and walked back down the street towards the waiting police car. They passed a group of little girls solemnly moving round in a circle and chanting in shrill, off-key voices the latest folk-song:

> 'Big'mous Bertie is me name!
> Marrying ladies is me game!
> When I'm tired of their charms and grace,
> I bash 'em with a hatchet in the face!
> Oh, Big'mous Bertie is me name!
> Marrying ladies is me game!'

Dover scowled at them and hurried on.

CHAPTER SEVEN

OVER LUNCH in the Station Hotel, MacGregor, who in spite of being so handsome and suave really was a bit of a prig, took it upon himself to remonstrate with his chief inspector about his somewhat unethical behaviour towards the Pie Gang. Dover's lower lip protruded more and more. He bitterly resented criticism from any quarter and to have some jumped-up little detective sergeant laying the law down to him – well, it was more than human nature could bear! The fact that this untimely rebuke was fully justified only made things worse.

'Whichever way you look at it, sir,' MacGregor pointed out, primly self-righteous, 'it was compounding a felony now, wasn't it?'

'I doubt it,' snarled Dover sulkily. His knowledge of the finer points of the law had some curious gaps in it but, just occasionally, he knew what he was talking about. 'From what I remember about compounding felonies, you've got to do it for some monetary gain. And I didn't!' He shovelled a large forkful of food into his mouth.

'Well, whatever heading it comes under,' retorted Mac-Gregor, 'it was an offence of some sort. You bribed those young beats by offering to return that gun to them, although they've no legal right to hold fire-arms and it's probably stolen anyhow, and you've promised to conceal the fact that they were the ones who made an armed attack, of all things, on St Benedict's church hall. It's really going a bit too far, sir!'

'Oh, don't be so bloody squeamish!' growled Dover. 'You young coppers are all the same – frightened of your blooming shadows!'

'But there'd be the devil of a row if it came out, sir,' protested MacGregor. 'Why, they might even give you the sack for it!'

'It won't come out! Not unless you start grassing.'

'I wouldn't dream of saying a word, sir, you know that. But the fact remains, you really shouldn't have done it.'

'Phooey!' Dover blew contemptuously down his nose. 'I got results, didn't I? You've got to sail a bit near the wind at times and the sooner you get that into your head, the better detective you'll be. If I'd gone in with kid gloves on and asked 'em a few polite questions, we'd have got the same answers as the local police did. And a hell of a lot of good that would have been to us! At least we know now where that gun was lost – right on the scene of the crime! It's worth a bit of fiddling to get information like that.'

MacGregor still looked puritanically unconvinced and Dover gobbled up his ice-cream with grim malevolence. When MacGregor produced his cigarettes, Dover very nearly refused one in a fit of pique. However, he decided to be magnanimous and grudgingly pulled one out of Mac-Gregor's elegant silver case.

'What do you think about Miss Leddicoat's evidence, sir?' asked the sergeant, thinking that a change of subject might now be wise.

'Dunno,' replied Dover grumpily. 'Interesting bit of background, but I can't see it makes all that much difference, really. It's not the first time a daughter's been passed off as a younger sister and I don't suppose it'll be the last. Might explain why the pair of 'em were so keen on wedding bells, though. Once bitten, twice shy, as you might say.'

'What are we going to do this afternoon, sir?'

Dover shot MacGregor a look of loathing. 'Well, you can go and write up your reports. I'll meet you down here at, oh, at three o'clock. I'm going to go and have a quiet think about things in my room. And I don't want to be disturbed.'

The two men parted, MacGregor to produce a suitably fictionalized account of the evidence they had received from the Pie Gang and Dover to have a peaceful post-prandial snooze, flat out on the top of his eiderdown.

At three o'clock they set off to view the scene of the first crime.

Isobel Slatcher had been shot on the corner of Church Lane where, for no apparent reason, it took a sharpish bend around St Benedict's vicarage and the vicarage garden.

The police car drove carefully and slowly – Dover didn't permit anything over thirty m.p.h. even on a motorway – down Corporation Road and then gingerly turned right

87

into Church Lane. Although Corporation Road was one of the main shopping streets in Curdley, Church Lane, lying at the far end and away from the town's centre, was a quiet little backwater. The surface of the road was still cobbled and the main railway line ran along the entire length of the left-hand side. The railway was in a cutting and a ten-foot-high blank wall with bits of broken glass set in the top effectively kept the general public off the tracks.

On the right-hand side, at the corner where Church Lane entered Corporation Road, was St Benedict's church-yard, now full and no longer used for burials except in one or two of the family vaults which still had spare accom-modation. Farther along Church Lane stood St Benedict's Church itself. It was a massive, blank-walled, Victorian building in a slate-grey granite. The stained-glass windows were set high and covered with wire netting, a reasonable precaution taken by every church and chapel of whatever denomination in Curdley. Next to the solid block of the church and still on the right-hand side of Church Lane came the vicarage garden. The Lane took a quite pro-nounced right-hand bend here and it was just on this corner that Isobel Slatcher had been shot. The vicarage garden, like the railway lines on the other side of the road, was boxed in by a high stone wall, embellished along the top with bits of broken glass and a strip of rusty barbed wire. Proceeding along Church Lane, round the wall of the vicarage garden, you came next to the vicarage itself, which was contemporary with the church. Then came St Bene-dict's church hall, a more modern brick building, with a fish and chip shop next to it on the far side. Beyond the fish and chip shop lay a row of bleak, small houses, most of which had broken out into an unfortunate rash of do-it-yourself front doors and chromium knockers.

The police car stopped outside the main entrance to St Benedict's Church and Dover and MacGregor got out with some reluctance to pursue their investigations. A light, soot-filled drizzle had begun to fall and every now and again there was a heavy rumble as an unseen train passed by on the other side of the wall. The two detectives walked to the bend in the road.

'Must have been about here, sir,' said MacGregor, tapping the pavement with his foot.

'Hm,' said Dover. 'Right under the wall of the vicarage garden, eh?' He looked around him and sighed. 'This curve's so shallow here that nobody coming from Corporation Road, or from the other way past the vicarage, would be able to see a damned thing if they were more than twenty yards or so away.' He looked up. 'No street light either,' he grumbled.

'I suppose that's why the murderer chose the spot,' said MacGregor brightly.

Dover scowled at him.

There was a pause while both men damply surveyed their surroundings.

'It's a bit depressing, sir, isn't it?' ventured MacGregor.

Dover ignored him and turned to face the direction from which they'd come. 'Now then,' he muttered, 'Rex Purse-glove must have been waiting down there, on the corner of Church Lane and Corporation Road – just by the grave-yard, in fact. Now, he hears the shots and after a few minutes, when he's worked his courage up – thank God we've got a Navy! – he comes walking along towards where we are now, past the graveyard and past the church.'

The chief inspector walked a few yards towards Cor-poration Road and looked round again. Sergeant Mac-Gregor trailed along behind him, thinking slightly more about what the rain was doing to his new shoes than about the as yet unsolved murder of Isobel Slatcher.

'Now,' Dover went on more loudly, 'assuming, as we unfortunately must, that Mr Rex Purseglove is not the murderer, we shall also have to assume that he was speaking the truth about what happened when his girl friend was shot, shan't we?'

'Yes, sir.'

'Right. Well, he said that he didn't see anybody coming away from the body towards him and Corporation Road, didn't he?'

'Yes, sir.'

'In that case, whoever shot the girl must have cleared off in the direction of the vicarage and the church hall, mustn't they?'

'Well' – MacGregor looked round for himself – 'I don't know about that, sir. They needn't have stuck to the road at all, need they? They could have nipped off somewhere else – hidden for a bit, perhaps?'

'Where?' sneered Dover.

'Over the railway wall?'

'Don't talk wet!' snapped Dover. 'Look at it, you fool! Nobody could scale that without a ladder, and I'll bet there's a sheer forty-foot drop on the other side.'

'They could have slipped into the church itself.'

'Bet you half a dollar that door's locked. Go and check it.'

It was.

'That's two and six you owe me,' said Dover. 'Hand it over. Thanks.'

'How about the churchyard? That wall's not all that high.'

'It's not all that low, either,' retorted Dover. 'Anyhow, it's too near to where Purseglove was standing. Even he would have his ears pricked after those shots. He'd have been bound to hear or see somebody as close to him as that.'

'Wasn't there a gate in the wall of the vicarage garden?'

Dover frowned. 'I didn't notice. Let's have a look.'

They walked back.

90

'There,' said MacGregor triumphantly, 'I thought I'd seen one.'

'All rusted up,' snorted Dover. 'Look at those hinges and the lock. Thing's not been opened for years.' He gave it a kick. 'See? It's stuck fast. That's out!'

MacGregor tried to open it without success.

'Well, there you are!' concluded Dover, displaying rather excessive satisfaction. 'Whoever shot her ran off in that direction, past the vicarage and the church hall.'

MacGregor suppressed a disloyal desire to ask, so what? After all, the old fool was doing his best.

'What time is it?' asked Dover. This was another of his annoying little habits. Although he had a watch (presented to him in gratitude by a multiple murderer who, thanks entirely to Dover's blundering, had escaped his just reward and now kept a betting shop in Bognor Regis), he never dreamed of using it, but expected his current sergeant to provide him with the time.

'It's getting on for four, sir.'

'Well, let's go and call on the Vicar. Might be able to scrounge a cup of tea off him.'

Mr Bonnington, however, was not in. He had not yet, so his housekeeper informed them, returned from the Sunday school which was held in the church hall. Dover intimated that in that case they would come inside and wait. The housekeeper eyed them suspiciously and didn't seem reassured when Dover announced that they were detectives from Scotland Yard.

'Well,' she said grudgingly, 'I suppose it will be all right, though what on earth you're doing detecting on the Lord's Day I can't imagine.' She swung back suddenly on them. 'You're not Holy Romans, are you?'

'No,' snapped Dover, pushing his way firmly inside. 'We're not!'

'No,' agreed the housekeeper unexpectedly, 'I suppose

91

coming from Scotland Yard you wouldn't be – otherwise that Bigamous Bertie man would never have been caught. He was a Catholic, you know. Hanging's too good for the likes of him.'

'I think he only posed as a Catholic,' said Dover, groping his way along seemingly endless dark passages in the housekeeper's wake.

'They got him in the end. Don't you read the papers? He was converted to Rome just before they hung him. Oh well,' she sighed grimly, 'we all know where he is now!'

She showed them into her kitchen. 'You'll have to wait down here where I can keep an eye on you. I can't take the responsibility of letting you loose all by yourselves in the Reverend's study. You can sit down over there.' She pointed to a couple of uncomfortable looking kitchen chairs. 'I've got to get on with my work. The Reverend'll want a good hot meal inside him before he starts the evening service.'

She began bustling around with pots and pans on the kitchen stove. The room was warm and there was a most marvellous smell of cooking in the air. Dover beamed hopefully, conscious of the fact that he'd not had a bite to eat since lunch and feeling sure that, in a Christian household, hospitality would be generous.

'Mr Bonnington's a widower, I understand,' he remarked.

'At the moment,' agreed the housekeeper. 'His wife died four or five years ago – just before he came here. He'd already been appointed and it was too late to change it, but they'd never have agreed to him if they'd known he was going to stay unmarried all this time.'

'Oh?'

'We see enough of celibacy with them Roman priests in this town. Scandalous, some of it is! We don't want anything like that going on *here*! I could tell you a tale or two about some of the things that lot get up to.'

'Really?' said Dover.

'They keep hinting to him that it's about time he found himself another wife, but he keeps putting it off. I warned him only the other day that it'll get to more than hinting soon.'

'I should have thought he'd be able to find himself a wife easily enough.'

'He could find a hundred! Every old maid in the parish has been setting her cap at him – and some of the young ones, too.' She inspected something cooking inside the oven. 'Mind you, he doesn't want to go getting himself one of these green young girls for a wife. Not at his age and with his position. I've said to him many a time, what he wants is a more mature woman, one who's had some experience of life, someone who can run his house for him and help him with the parish side of things. He wants a good respectable church woman, somebody his parishioners can accept.'

'H'm,' said Dover. 'Are you married, Miss ... er, Mrs ...?'

'Mrs Smallbone. I'm a widow.'

'I see,' said Dover. 'And do you live here?'

Mrs Smallbone was scandalized. 'I certainly do not!' She drew herself up. 'I've got my reputation to think of, and so has the Reverend. Not that it wouldn't be much handier all round if I did – obviously I could look after things much better – but I'm out of here every night by six o'clock or just after. This means he's got to make do with a high tea before I go instead of a proper dinner, but as I've told him many a time he can't have it both ways.'

'So you weren't here the night Isobel Slatcher was shot?'

'Oh, no. I'd always gone by the time she arrived. If you ask me' – Mrs Smallbone wiped her hands grimly on a towel – 'that was part of the idea. I warned the Reverend about it. "You'll only get talk," I said, "having a young woman like her coming here late at night when there's only the two of you in the place." He didn't care much for it himself but of course he hadn't the guts to stand up to her.'

'Are you suggesting that Isobel Slatcher was one of those who were setting their caps at Mr Bonnington?'

'I'm not one to speak ill of the dead,' retorted Mrs Smallbone self-righteously, 'but when you find unmarried women breaking their necks to do voluntary work for a parson who's not married either – well, they aren't always inspired by the welfare of the church. My guess is that if the Reverend had ever been such a fool as to ask Isobel Slatcher to marry him, she wouldn't have said no. Apart from anything else, she wasn't getting any younger, you know.'

'Was Mr Bonnington interested that way?'

'Not him! He could do a sight better for himself than Isobel Slatcher – and he knows it!'

Dover gazed moodily at Mrs Smallbone who was now energetically laying one end of the kitchen table for Mr Bonnington's high tea. She was, depressingly, only laying one place. Dover blew crossly down his nose.

'By the way,' he asked, 'do you remember, about a fortnight or three weeks before Isobel Slatcher was shot, some gang of boys raided the church hall one evening – a Monday, I think it was?'

'Indeed I do,' said Mrs Smallbone. 'It was some of those young Catholic hooligans – not that they were ever punished for it, but you get used to that in this town.'

'Do you know what happened?'

'Well, I wasn't there myself but I heard all about it. It was the Men's Bible Class and, apparently, they'd just got settled down when these teenagers came bursting into the hall. There was hundreds of 'em and they were all wearing masks and brandishing coshes and knives and heaven knows what. Mr Purseglove told me they all came in

94

whooping and screaming like a pack of wild Indians, smashing and breaking everything in sight. Well, the men in the Bible Class were a bit taken aback at first. After all,' she commented sardonically, 'it's one thing to read about being martyred for the faith, and quite another to volunteer for it. However, one or two of 'em were a bit more courageous than the rest and they led what I suppose you'd call a counter-attack. There was quite a bit of talk afterwards in the parish, I can tell you, about who was at the front and who was at the back. Charlie Bates, for example. He stands over six foot in his stocking feet and he's supposed to have been no end of a boxer in his day. He took to his heels and cleared off out through the back way. Said he thought there might be some more of those little devils coming in from the back – but there's not many who believe him. Mr Purseglove on the other hand, although he doesn't look as though he could pull the skin off a rice pudding, he collected a black eye and gave as good as he got by all accounts.

'Well, once they saw what they were up against, these young limbs of Satan beat a hasty retreat. Our chaps went tearing after 'em but they didn't catch anybody. Mr Ofield chased 'em down as far as Corporation Road – 'course, he's a good bit younger than some of the others – but even he couldn't catch any of them. The next day half the Bible Class were sporting bruises and cuts – and weren't they proud of 'em! The vestibule of the church hall looked like a battlefield – I can tell you that because I was one of the women who helped tidy it up. Oh, and the Reverend fell over a chair and sprained his ankle, so I'd him limping around like a wounded soldier for days afterwards.'

'I see,' said Dover. 'Er, this Mr Purseglove you mentioned – is that Rex Purseglove's father?'

'Yes, that's the one. He's been attending that Bible Class for years. I should think his wife's glad to get him out of the house.'

'And this chap, Ofield? I've an idea that Mr Bonnington mentioned his name.'

'Quite likely. He used to play the organ quite a bit for us. He was in the church practising the night Isobel Slatcher got herself shot, but of course he didn't hear anything. Funnily enough he and Isobel both used to work at the library. He's chief librarian, you know, though I did hear he was leaving to take a job somewhere else.'

'Is there any chance of getting a list of all the men who were at the Bible Class that particular evening?'

Mrs Smallbone looked at the chief inspector in surprise. 'I suppose so. I think they keep a register. Anyhow, you'd better ask the Reverend. That's him just coming in now.'

Mr Bonnington was not overjoyed to find that he had two visitors waiting for him in the snug warmth of his kitchen. After all Sunday was, as he pointed out rather testily, his busy day, and while he appreciated that the police had their duty to perform he would like to stress that he, too, had *his*.

'You're late as it is,' added Mrs Smallbone as she dished up a man-sized helping of cottage pie and placed it, steaming and odoriferous, before the Vicar.

Dover's mouth watered and his stomach rumbled quite audibly. MacGregor frowned slightly but neither Mrs Smallbone nor Mr Bonnington answered this *cri de cœur*. They didn't even offer Dover and MacGregor a cup of tea.

'I know I'm late,' Mr Bonnington went on, liberally daubing his cottage pie with tomato sauce. 'Oh dear, I sometimes wonder whether Sunday schools aren't really more trouble than they're worth.' He smiled to show that this was just his little joke.

Mrs Smallbone sighed and pushed a large plateful of bread and butter towards her employer. 'What's happened now?'

'It's that young Miss Beeby again. She's an excellent

96

worker and very devout but, really, she is a fool! She told her class last week that they could learn any six verses from the Bible they liked. I ask you, fancy telling a class of ten-year-old boys that! You can imagine what happened today. The class was in an uproar and she was in tears and it was ages before I could find out what had happened. She was far too embarrassed about the whole thing to give me a coherent story. I wouldn't have thought a girl of her age these days could be quite such a prude.'

'You'd better give her the girls' class next week.' Mrs Smallbone poured out another cup of tea for the Vicar and put the sugar in for him.

'I don't know,' said Mr Bonnington ruefully, 'what makes you think that the girls have any less knowledge of certain passages in the Bible than our young gentlemen have. Oh well,' he smiled bravely, 'I shall just have to work something out before next week. After all, that's what I'm here for.'

With a sigh of repletion he wiped his lips on his table napkin and pushed his chair back from the table.

'An excellent meal, Mrs Smallbone,' he beamed. 'As always. Well now, Inspector, what can I do for you? I'm afraid I haven't much time to spare. Evensong begins at half past six.'

'I'd just like you to show me, sir,' replied Dover grumpily, 'where you were and what you did the night Isobel Slatcher was shot. Just so we can get a picture of what actually happened.'

'Well, as I told you, I was in my study,' began the Vicar.

Dover rose ponderously to his feet. 'Perhaps you'd show us, Mr Bonnington,' he said.

Under the somewhat jaundiced eyes of the two detectives Mr Bonnington acted out his part. He sat down at his desk in the study.

'I was working here,' he said, 'when I heard the shots. I hesitated for a moment or two, not really being sure what it was, and then I got up and hurried outside.'

'Time it, Sergeant,' said Dover as he followed Mr Bonnington out of the study.

On the pavement outside the front door Mr Bonnington stopped again. 'I hesitated a bit here, too,' he said, 'trying to orientate myself. Then I hurried in this direction and found her just here on the corner.'

'Did you close the front door?' asked Dover, staring blankly at the spot where Isobel Slatcher had fallen.

'No, I never thought to. I left it open.'

'You examined the girl and thought she was dead?'

'Yes, I did.'

'But you knew who it was?'

'Oh, I recognized her, of course. Her clothes as well as her face. I'd only said good night to her a couple of minutes before, you know.'

'Then you went back inside and phoned the police. The phone's in your study? Hm, how long would all that take – three or four minutes? No longer, anyhow. Then you came back and found young Purseglove. Was he standing or kneeling by the body, or what?'

'He was just standing there, looking down at her.'

'You used the front door again, did you, the second time you came out?'

'Yes.'

'You didn't think of using this gate in the garden wall?'

'Oh, that? No, it hasn't been opened for years. I imagine it's completely rusted up by now. I've never used it myself. It's always kept locked.'

'I see,' said Dover, and sighed. 'And you didn't see anybody at all coming away from this corner in the direction of the vicarage?'

'No, nobody at all.'

'Just one more small point, Mr Bonnington,' said Dover, happy in the knowledge that if he was getting wet – the rain was falling quite heavily now – the Vicar, coatless and hatless, was getting absolutely soaked. It would serve the skinny old devil right! 'The church door – this one here leading out into Church Lane – is it kept locked?'

'Oh, dear me, yes. Always. Except when there's actually a service on.'

'Was it locked on the Saturday night when Isobel Slatcher was shot?'

'Definitely. The only key is kept in the vicarage and I would have known if anyone had taken it. And now, Inspector, if that's all, I really think . . .'

'Just a minute, Mr Bonnington,' said Dover blandly. 'Didn't you tell me that this fellow – what's-his-name? – Ofield was practising on the organ in the church that night? How did he get in?'

'He used the vestry door, of course,' snapped Mr Bonnington, turning his collar up. 'We've two or three keys for that – so that the cleaners and people can get in. It's round on the other side of the church. There's a path leading from Corporation Road through the graveyard. That's why Mr Ofield not only didn't hear the shots but didn't see the police and the ambulance and all the rest of it when he left the church. He didn't come out into Church Lane at all.'

'Hm,' said Dover, and sought desperately for some more questions. 'Is the church hall door kept locked?'

'When the building is not in use. Perhaps we could go back inside the vicarage, Inspector? I see no point in us standing out here in the dark getting soaked!'

Dover pulled MacGregor to one side. 'You got any questions to ask him?' he hissed. 'Because if so, now's your chance.'

As it happened MacGregor had a few theories of his own

and was delighted, and surprised, to be given a chance of exploring them. Usually Dover liked to do all the talking.

Mr Bonnington pointedly didn't ask them back into his study but remained, frequently consulting his watch, in the hall of the vicarage. Three small pools of water from their dripping clothes began to form on the polished linoleum.

'Mr Bonnington,' began MacGregor, throwing himself into his part with all the snap and decision of an American lawyer on the telly, 'can you tell us anything a bit more definite about the relationship between the deceased Isobel Slatcher and Rex Purseglove?'

The Vicar shot him a look of loathing mingled with a certain amount of surprise. 'What precisely did you want to know, Sergeant?' he asked with another impatient look at his watch.

'Were they engaged to be married?'

Mr Bonnington sighed. 'Rex certainly never gave me to understand that they were, as I think I told you before. However Miss Slatcher, Violet that is, did come round to see me with some rather vague preliminary inquiries about the ceremony. I intimated that I thought the whole business was a little premature and that the banns would naturally have to be put up by the engaged couple. She seemed rather annoyed and implied that I was being unnecessarily unhelpful.'

'When was this?'

'Oh, a week or two before Isobel was shot.'

'And Rex Purseglove never mentioned his engagement to you?'

'No, he didn't. But when Isobel was lying unconscious in hospital Violet Slatcher mentioned the matter to me again. She wanted to know if it were possible to marry the young couple by proxy, or while Isobel was still in a coma. Naturally I told her it was completely out of the question.'

'This was rather an odd request, wasn't it?' probed Mac-Gregor with a shrewdness worthy of a better cause.

'Quite ludicrous. But Miss Slatcher was really rather fanatical about getting Isobel married off. Her anxiety would have been amusing if, of course, it hadn't been so tragic under the circumstances. I don't know the reason for her attitude – perhaps some unfortunate experience in her own past. Naturally I have never inquired. And now I really must ask you to go. If I don't hurry I shall be late as it is.'

'One last question, sir, if you don't mind. When this story appeared in the *Custodian* about Isobel Slatcher being on the point of recovery, did *you* believe it?'

'Of course not, Sergeant. I happen to be the Church of England chaplain at the hospital and I was fully conversant with the state of Isobel Slatcher's health. I knew that, short of a miracle, she would never regain consciousness and that if she did, she would never be a rational person again. The brain damage was too severe. I didn't know where the *Custodian* had got its information from but as soon as I read the article I half suspected that Violet Slatcher was behind it. Grief can drive the best of us to do some very odd things.'

Thirty seconds later Dover and MacGregor were standing in the rain outside the vicarage front door which had been shut firmly in their faces.

Dover summed up his impression of their afternoon's work.

'I don't know about you, MacGregor,' he said, 'but I'm damned hungry!'

CHAPTER EIGHT

Dᴜʀɪɴɢ ᴛʜᴇ time they had been together MacGregor had blushed on many occasions for his impervious chief inspector, but never quite so rosily as now when he found himself following Dover into, of all places, a fish and chip shop. Remonstrations had proved in vain. Dover had scornfully. brushed aside his sergeant's genteel objections and had thumped resolutely into the shop. Mac-Gregor found a grain of comfort in the fact that they were the only customers. As he stood miserably at the high counter he wondered if that paragon of detectives, Super-intendent Roderick, had ever been so careless of his own social standing (and so indifferent to the finer feelings of his subordinates) as to set foot in such an establishment, unless of course it were in the strict line of duty.

'Two plates of fish and chips, with peas,' demanded Dover, who clearly knew his way around.

The man behind the counter shook his head. 'Sorry, mate,' he said, 'we haven't got a dining-room here. I only sell 'em to take out.'

MacGregor blenched and began to think hopefully about the ground opening up and swallowing him.

'But,' the fish and chip man went on, 'you're welcome to eat 'em here at the counter, if you don't mind standing up.'

'All right,' agreed Dover amiably, 'we'll do that.'

The two detectives peered in silence over the high counter as the proprietor bustled about, dipping slabs of white fish in batter and tossing them into the near boiling oil, neurotically shovelling the chips about as they cooked and restlessly sliding the roll-top covers backwards and forwards over his smoking cauldrons. Dover licked his lips.

MacGregor, his face set and his expression grimly blank, prayed quite hard that nobody would come in.

When they had been somewhat unceremoniously turfed out of the vicarage, Dover, in a rush of enthusiasm which did not occur very frequently, decided to have a look at the church hall which was just next door. There wasn't much to be seen. The windows which gave out on to Church Lane were small and set high in the otherwise blank wall. They were also barred. The front door was locked and what with the rain and the poor street lighting Mac-Gregor felt that they could well have saved themselves their twenty-yard walk. Dover stopped and contemplated the building with a damp, disparaging sniff, and it was then that his nostrils caught the unmistakable aroma of fish and chips. From then on there was no holding him.

Two large newspaper bundles were slapped down on the counter.

'Four and sixpence, if you please, sir!'

Dover immediately became engrossed in unravelling his packet and MacGregor, with a resigned shrug, handed the money over. Fastidiously he watched his chief inspector scattering salt and vinegar with an expert hand over the compressed pile of smoking fish and fat pale chips. With a delicate shiver he saw him grab a handful, curse because they burnt his fingers, and stuff them with a grunt of satisfaction into his mouth.

'Come on, lad.' Dover spoke through a mouthful of chips. 'Don't let 'em get cold!'

The proprietor of the shop leaned companionably on the counter.

'You the chaps they've had sent down from London?' he asked.

'We are,' admitted Dover grandly and dashed Mac-Gregor's last hopes of remaining anonymous.

'Scotland Yard, isn't it?'

103

'It is,' said Dover.

'I suppose you know this big detective fellow – Super Percy?'

'We do,' replied Dover with a marked lack of warmth.

'Well, I reckon it's about time they called the experts in up here,' remarked the fish and chip man, thoughtfully wiping his vinegar bottle. 'Our lot couldn't solve a crossword puzzle in a kids' comic – not even if you give 'em a dictionary. Stupid lot of bastards they are! Do what the priest tells 'em, you know, and that's all. Soon as we heard what had happened to that Slatcher girl I says to the wife, well, I says, that's one crime Curdley police'll never solve – that's for sure. With her being strong Church of England, you know, and always letting fly about confessions and indulgences and worshipping the Pope. They'd got it in for her all right!'

'You're a Protestant, I take it?' said Dover, manoeuvring a large lump of fish into his mouth.

'I'm a free thinker, I am!' The fish and chip man drew himself up proudly. 'I don't hold with any of that superstitious twaddle, meself.'

'Really, Mr, er . . .?'

'Dibb's my name. Alfred Dibb.'

'Really, Mr Dibb? Well, I imagine you're rather an odd man out in this town?'

'Not half!' agreed Mr Dibb sadly. 'You can say that again, mate! I've got both lots of 'em against me. Affects me trade too, you know. Why, if I was to sacrifice me principles I could make a fortune in this town. But, as I always says to the wife, a man's got to be true to his beliefs.'

'Oh, quite,' said Dover.

'You wouldn't credit the prejudice in this town against a chap who thinks for himself, you wouldn't really. Take the night this Slatcher girl was shot. Only happened just round the corner, but did they ever come and ask *me* if I'd heard anything? Not bleeding likely, they didn't! Not Curdley cops! All right, I says to the wife, if that's the way they want it, that's the way they can have it. I'm not the sort to go pushing meself in where I'm not wanted. I'm probably the only impartial witness in the whole bleeding town, the only man who's got the guts and intelligence to think for himself, but if they can't come to me I'm buggered if I'm going to them!'

Dover nodded absentmindedly, his attention absorbed by MacGregor's pile of fish and chips.

'Aren't you going to eat those, Sergeant?' he asked.

'I'm not really very hungry, sir,' said MacGregor primly.

'Oh well' – Dover reached out an eager hand – 'there's no point in wasting 'em. Now then, Mr Dibb.' He turned back to the fish and chip shop owner. 'So the local police didn't question you about the shooting of Isobel Slatcher?'

'No,' said Mr Dibb resentfully, 'they didn't.'

'Well, you're dealing with Scotland Yard now. Suppose you tell me what happened.'

Mr Dibb beamed happily. 'I should be very glad to tell *you*,' he said pointedly. 'At least I know that *you* won't be reporting every word I say to Rome or Canterbury.'

'Quite,' said Dover. 'Now then, what did happen? Did you hear the shots?'

'Well, it was like this. I was here in the shop getting everything ready like, because we get the rush round about nine o'clock on Saturdays.'

'You were alone? There weren't any customers in?'

'No, I was here by meself. The wife was in the back. Well, I'd got the door open because it was quite warm in here with all the cooking and so on and I heard the London express go by. I just glanced up like you do, you know, at the clock and I see he was dead on time – same as usual. Very reliable that train is.'

'And what time was it?'

'Eight five – on the dot. And that clock of mine's a very good time-keeper. Well, just after he'd gone through I heard these two bangs, you see, one after the other. For a minute I thought it was those fog signals they put on the lines sometimes, but then I says to meself, no, I says, that can't be right because there isn't any fog, see? And then I thought to meself, in any case, I thought, the bangs came *after* the train had gone through, you see, which they wouldn't have done if they'd been fog signals.'

'Quite,' said Dover, finishing off the last of MacGregor's chips and wiping his face and hands with his handkerchief. 'And then what did you do?'

'Well, I thought it over for a minute or two, you know, wondering like, and then I went outside and had a look down the street.'

'Which way?'

'Well, both ways, really, though I thought the shots had come from up the vicarage direction. Well, everything seemed quiet and there was nobody about and I was just going to come back inside again when I saw Mr Bonnington come rushing out of his front door. I could see his dog collar quite clearly because, of course, he'd left his hall light on. Well, I thought there must be something up because he left the door open and usually he's a great one for keeping everything locked up because we've got some wild young devils round here that'd pinch a hymn book if they couldn't find anything else. Well, I see him rushing off round the corner so I hung on for a minute to see if anything else was going to happen. In a bit he comes rushing back and tears inside the vicarage again. Never seen him move so fast all the time he's been here. Doesn't shut the door this time either, so I says to meself, you hang on a bit longer, Alf, I says, because sure as eggs is eggs he's going to come out again. Well, sure enough, two or three minutes later out he comes again, looking all hot and bothered, and off he nips

106

round the corner again. Well, I was getting a bit cold, standing about outside with no coat on, so I came back inside.'

'You didn't go and see what had happened?' asked Dover.

Mr Dibb shook his head. 'Weren't none of my business. I've never been one for pushing my nose into other people's affairs. Live and let live, that's my motto. If there had been a shooting or something like that, it was nothing to do with me and I wasn't going to get mixed up in it. Later on, of course, I saw the ambulance drive off and there was police cars all over the place, so I knew something had happened. Besides, I couldn't just leave the shop wide open with nobody here and money in the till and everything. I've got my business to think of, you know.'

'When did you find out what had happened?'

'Well, some of my customers later on had heard about it. They said some girl or other had been killed but nobody knew who it was at first. 'Course, it turned out later that she hadn't been killed at all, but even so, as I said to the wife, there might have been some bleeding maniac hanging around and supposing he'd taken a pot-shot at me, eh? Where would I have been then? There wouldn't have been no public subscription opened for my wife and family, not in this town there wouldn't.'

'Now, just a minute,' Dover broke in. 'After these shots were fired, did you see or hear anybody coming from the vicarage direction this way, past your shop?'

'No, I didn't, because nobody did.'

'Rubbish!' snorted Dover crossly. 'Somebody shot Isobel Slatcher and they must have cleared off before Mr Bonnington arrived.'

'Oh, I grant you that,' said Mr Dibb generously. 'But they must have gone the other way – past the church to Corporation Road. They certainly didn't come past here.'

'They might have slipped by on the other side of the road, perhaps, without your noticing them?'

'They might,' conceded Mr Dibb with sarcastic condescension, 'if I'd just been getting on with my work in here same as usual. But I wasn't, was I? Soon as I heard those shots I was on the qui vive, see? I was half expecting somebody to come by. Everything was dead quiet and I'd got the door open. Even the other side of the street's not a hundred miles away, is it? Nobody came down this way, you can take my word for that. I couldn't have missed 'em, and then it was only a few seconds before I went outside to have a look-see meself.'

He looked offended and started chipping potatoes vigorously in a sort of guillotine. 'You can take it from me straight,' he insisted, rapidly immolating one potato after another, 'nobody went past this way! And, apart from the Vicar, I didn't see a living soul until the police and the ambulance arrived.'

And on this point Mr Dibb refused to be budged. He insisted that Dover and MacGregor test for themselves that it was impossible for anyone to slip by the shop while someone behind the counter was staring out of the window. MacGregor was sent out into the rain to enact the part of the fugitive assassin while Dover took Mr Dibb's place behind the counter. After five minutes in which MacGregor walked, ran, and even crawled on his hands and knees past the fish and chip shop, Dover acknowledged defeat. With Mr Dibb alerted by the sound of the shots, nobody could have got by him, even before he actually went and stood outside.

All the good humour which a stomach full of fish and chips had brought to Chief Inspector Dover was dissipated as if by magic. He shouted and bawled at Mr Dibb and browbeat him quite unmercifully, but the only self-confessed exponent of rationalism in Curdley stuck resolutely to his guns. No one had gone past his fish and chip shop

108

and he would face martyrdom rather than admit the slightest possibility that they could.

'Nobody went by here,' he insisted. 'I'll take my Solemn Declaration on that!'

'Obstinate old fool!' snarled Dover as he and Mac-Gregor made their way back to where they had left the police car. 'Blithering idiot!' he snapped as MacGregor held the door open for him.

The police driver, who'd been sitting waiting for nearly three hours wondering where his superiors were, hastily stubbed out his cigarette and started the engine.

'What the hell do you think you're doing?' yelped Dover furiously. 'I'll tell you when we're ready to go. Turn that bloody thing off!'

'Yes, sir,' said the driver meekly.

MacGregor surreptitiously opened a window, but the smell of fish and chips remained overwhelming. The police driver couldn't fail to notice it, and draw his own conclusions.

'Give us another fag, MacGregor,' said Dover grumpily, 'and let's try and sort this thing out. Right, now three people heard the shots: Rex Purseglove on the corner of Corporation Road and Church Lane, the Vicar in his study and this gibbering lunatic, Dibb, in his blasted fish and chip shop. The Vicar gets to the girl first. He doesn't see anybody hanging about. Rex Purseglove comes along Church Lane from Corporation Road and he doesn't see anybody. Dibb swears that nobody came down Church Lane past his shop. Whoever shot Isobel Slatcher couldn't have climbed that wall by the railway – even if he had a ladder or something, one of the three would have been sure to see him. He couldn't have taken cover in the vicarage garden or in the church or in the church hall because all the doors were locked and there's no other way in. The vicarage wall's too high to climb and he'd have had quite a job to climb into the graveyard because that wall's getting

109

on for six foot high, and he'd be too near to Rex Purse-glove in any case. So what are we left with? Isobel Slatcher was shot by the Invisible Man!'

'One of them might be lying, sir.'

'Of course one of 'em's lying, you damned fool! Any idiot could have worked that out! The point is, which one?'

'Yes, sir,' said MacGregor.

'All right, Sergeant,' said Dover generously, 'which one do you think's lying?'

MacGregor sighed gently, pretty certain that whatever he said would be wrong. 'How about Mr Bonnington, the Vicar, sir?' he asked.

'Mr Bonnington, the Vicar?' Dover's voice rose to a near scream of astounded refusal to believe the evidence of his own ears. 'For God's sake, MacGregor, try and use what little intelligence you've been given! What's Bonnington got to lie about, for Christ's sake?'

The police driver sat, straight backed, staring through his rain-swept windscreen, and listened avidly to every word.

'Well, sir,' said MacGregor defensively, 'he was on the scene of both the crimes, wasn't he? We've only got his word for what happened when Isobel Slatcher was shot. He could have killed her himself, couldn't he? And then he was one of the men in the church hall when that Pie Gang lad lost his gun. He could have picked it up as well as anyone else.'

Dover sneered a terrible sneer. 'My God,' he remarked pleasantly, 'don't you ever listen to anything that's said? In the first place, Dibb at the fish and chip shop saw the Vicar leave the vicarage *after* the shots were fired, didn't he? He saw him leaving quite clearly. So that puts Bonnington *out*!'

'Yes, sir,' muttered MacGregor.

'And what's this about him being on the scene of the second crime? Was he in the hospital?'

'Yes, sir. Nurse Horncastle mentioned that he goes round

110

the wards every Friday morning, so at least he was in the hospital.'

'As it happens it wouldn't even matter if he'd been right in Isobel Slatcher's room. Whoever killed Isobel Slatcher killed her because he believed that newspaper story. He'd attacked her once and all but killed her. There was no point in risking a second attempt unless he thought she was going to recover. Now Bonnington knew that there was no hope of recovery at all. If he was the one who attacked her in February – which he wasn't – he, of all people, would know that there was no use risking his neck to keep her mouth shut. He knew she'd never get better.'

'But he could have found the Pie Gang's gun, sir.'

'Ah yes, but he wasn't the only one in the church hall that night, was he?'

'No, sir.'

'Well, have you got any more bright ideas, Sergeant?'

'Well, sir, if it wasn't Mr Bonnington who's been lying, I suppose it must be Mr Alfred Dibb.'

'Dibb? What the hell has Dibb got to lie about?'

'I don't know, sir' – MacGregor shook his head help-lessly – 'but since we've cleared Rex Purseglove he's the only one left, isn't he?'

'And who says we've cleared Rex Purseglove?' demanded Dover truculently.

'Why, you did, sir. He's got an alibi for the second attack in the hospital and so, naturally, if he didn't do that one he didn't do the other one either.'

'I think,' said Dover slowly, 'that he is responsible for both attacks. That hospital alibi with Nurse Horncastle or whatever-her-name-is is a put-up job. There's a flaw in it somewhere you must have missed.'

'But, sir . . .'

'Just keep your trap shut and listen to me for a few minutes! Take this shooting business in February. Neither

Mr Bonnington nor Dibb saw anyone about at all down their end of Church Lane. That means that whoever shot Isobel Slatcher must have gone off in the other direction, unless you're assuming some collusion between the two of them which is just damned ridiculous. Now, at the Corporation Road end of Church Lane was Rex Purseglove – even he admits that. He must have shot her, rushed back to the corner, waited a minute or two and then gone back again all innocent like. He's got a damned strong motive, he's admitted that he believed that newspaper article and he was on the spot in the hospital when she was finally killed. What more do you want?'

'But what about the gun, sir? He couldn't have found that. He wasn't even there in the church hall that night.'

'No,' agreed Dover triumphantly, 'he wasn't, but his father was! Look at it this way. Young Rex has got himself involved with Isobel Slatcher. His mother and father think the world of the little rat – they'd do anything to help him. Suppose in the shindig at the church hall his old man finds that gun. It'd be like a gift from heaven! If they can't get Isobel and Violet to see sense, somebody's got to do something drastic or young Rex is well and truly up the spout! What better weapon than a gun like that – especially when nobody knows you've got it! It's a cinch, I tell you! This case fits Rex Purseglove like a, er . . . like a glove. Motive, opportunity and the weapon!'

MacGregor shrugged his shoulders – not too obviously. You could drive a coach and horses through the holes in this analysis, but once Dover got an idea fixed in his mind it would take more than the arguments of a mere detective sergeant to get it out again. And, in any case, it so rarely happened that the chief inspector ever had any ideas at all that it would be dangerous, and even unkind, to deprive him of this one.

'What's the next step then, sir?'

Dover frowned. He'd had a long day but, convinced that he had the solution of Isobel Slatcher's death within his beefy grasp, he very much wanted to get the whole thing tied up as soon as possible. In some obscure way he felt that a speedy conclusion would be a slap in the eye for Superintendent Roderick. Spurred on by sheer green jealousy he decided to do a bit more work before calling it a day.

'Let's see if we can get a bit more on Rex Purseglove's movements round here just before Isobel was shot. He went to see Violet with his mother, didn't he? And then he came away to try and tackle Isobel by himself. Didn't he mention calling in some café or other to waste a bit of time?'

MacGregor dragged out his notebook and hunted through it in the feeble light provided in the roof of the car.

'Yes, here we are, sir! He went to a place called Los Toros in Corporation Road.'

'Right!' said Dover. 'We'll try there first. Get a move on, driver!'

The driver did. The car shot away from the kerb with a powerful roar. Dover was flung back in his seat as they leapt forward and then was flung forward as the driver slammed through an impressive change into second gear. Before Dover had time to draw breath the car had swung left on two screaming tyres into Corporation Road and he and MacGregor were struggling helplessly against the centrifugal force. There was another forward and backward thrust as the driver changed into third gear and then, before anyone could collect his wits, a heavy police boot descended on the brake. The car stopped dead.

'Los Toros, sir,' announced the driver.

In a grim silence Dover retrieved his bowler hat from the front seat and got shakily out of the car. The driver politely held the door open for him.

Dover scowled. 'I'll deal with you later!' he growled through clenched teeth. 'You . . . you homicidal maniac!'

113

He tottered inside the café and collapsed on a small round stool standing near the wall. A narrow shelf not more than six inches wide was fastened to the wall at a convenient height. Dover regarded it dubiously.

'Shall I get a couple of coffees, sir?' asked MacGregor.

Dover nodded. 'Yes, and get me a bun or a cake too.'

While MacGregor was collecting the order, Dover, still somewhat dazed, looked round. Los Toros was Curdley's concession to the coffee-bar trade. It was about the size of a spacious bathroom and possessed one minute table surrounded by three miniature imitation milking stools. Down one side of the room was the little shelf next to which Dover had established himself, and four high stools covered in red plastic. At the far end was a tiny counter mostly occupied by an Espresso coffee machine and a plate of sandwiches covered by a glass dome. On one wall was a fake bullfighting poster and fourteen advertisements for American-style soft drinks.

''Strewth!' groaned Dover when MacGregor placed a glass cup and saucer before him. 'I can't stand this frothy muck!' He bit disconsolately into a large Bath bun. 'Who's behind the bar? The owner? Get him over here!'

The proprietor of Los Toros was a fat, greasy-looking little man with side-whiskers and an ample bald patch. As he had no other customers he was quite willing to come out into the open and have a few words with the gentlemen from Scotland Yard. He was not unknown to the local police but felt quite confident that none of the little sidelines he ran was likely to engage the attentions of such top brass as a chief inspector. He smiled engagingly and admitted that his name was Pedro.

'You own this dump, do you?' asked Dover, who could spot Pedro's sort a mile away. 'How long have you been here?'

'A couple of years, Inspector.'

114

'Business doesn't look very brisk,' observed Dover sourly.

Pedro hesitated. He had the business man's natural desire to complain that times were hard and that he barely made enough to keep body and soul together, but he knew the dangers of admitting to the police that your legitimate business didn't pay. The nosy bastards then started rooting round for whatever you were doing that did give you a fair return for your time and trouble.

Pedro played it safe. 'Oh, it livens up later on,' he said smoothly, 'when the flicks come out.'

Dover snorted sceptically. 'Were you here the night that girl was shot round by St Benedict's?' he asked.

'Isobel Slatcher? She finally kicked the bucket, didn't she? Yes, I was here, same as usual. February, wasn't it?'

'Do you know Rex Purseglove?'

Pedro looked shrewdly at the chief inspector. 'Oh, so that's the way the wind's blowing, is it? Yes, as a matter of fact, I do. He used to come in here quite a lot at one time. He brought Isobel Slatcher in once or twice.'

'You've got a good memory,' snapped Dover suspiciously.

'Well, it's not every day one of your customers gets shot, is it? Sort of gives you something to remember 'em by. Besides, Isobel Slatcher wasn't the usual type of tart I get in here. She was a good ten years older, for one thing. I'm blowed if I can make out what Rex was up to. I mean, when a young fellow goes round with a woman damned near old enough to be his mother, well, you generally know what he's after. But if that was his idea with La Slatcher, he'd put his money on the wrong horse.'

'Did he come in here the night Isobel Slatcher was shot?'

'Aw, turn it up, Inspector, you damned well know he did.'

'Can you remember what time?'

The café door opened suddenly and a young girl stood on the threshold. Her skirt was well above her knees and she made as if to teeter forward on high stiletto heels.

'Not now, dear,' said Pedro quickly, 'I'm busy for the moment. You come back a bit later, dear.'

The girl stared blankly at him, her jaws rhythmically masticating a lump of chewing gum.

'Come back in about an hour, there's a good girl,' said Pedro, trying hard to establish contact, 'I might have something for you then, dear.'

With a completely expressionless face the girl backed out and closed the door. They could hear her heels tapping on the pavement as she tottered off down the street.

Dover wrinkled his nose and Pedro shrugged his shoulders helplessly. 'Thirty years ago,' he remarked sadly to no one in particular, 'my dad would have dropped down dead before he'd have let a moron like her get one foot in the business. Don't tell me standards aren't going down! Still,' he sighed philosophically, 'I suppose it's the same in every profession. Now then, what was you asking? Oh yes, what time was Rex Purseglove in here. Well, half past seven – quarter to eight maybe. I can't put it closer than that.'

'Hm,' said Dover. 'Do you remember what he looked like? Did he look upset or worried or anything?'

'Worried? He looked worried stiff! I've never seen him in such a state. Couldn't sit still for a minute and kept looking at his watch every thirty seconds. I did wonder whether he'd come in to ask my advice about anything – you know. Sometimes these young chaps'd sooner come to me for a spot of help rather than bother their parents. It's a bit less embarrassing all round and then, of course, I've got the right sort of contacts. Anyhow, before I could get over and have a quiet word with him he'd cleared off. Didn't finish his coffee, either.'

'You haven't seen him since then?'

'Not a hair of him. I heard he'd got his commission all right so I reckon my little diagnosis was wrong, eh? Still, he was dead chocker about something.'

116

And that was that. Not very helpful.

Outside Los Toros Dover stood for a moment, tossing a furious scowl at the police driver, and looked up and down the dreary, damp expanse of Corporation Road. MacGregor stood and looked too. They both spotted the pub at the same time. It stood on the other side of Corporation Road, just opposite Church Lane and St Benedict's graveyard.

Dover sighed. 'Might as well try,' he said despondently. 'It's the only place that'd be open at the right time. We'll walk,' he added quickly. 'You tell that dangerous lunatic to follow us with the car. And tell him he'd just better watch it! Another trip like the last one and I'll get him booted out of the Force before he knows what's hit him!'

The public bar looked the best bet from the outside. From the inside it appeared to be a dead loss. There was only one customer, a dirty-looking old codger huddled in an ex-army greatcoat. His eyes lit up hopefully when he saw a couple of strangers walk in.

MacGregor ordered two beers.

'Rotten evening,' he observed chattily to the barmaid.

She looked at him sourly and slapped his change down in a pool of beer.

MacGregor turned the charm on. 'You been here long?' he asked with a winning smile.

'Me and me husband took over last week. D'you want anything else?'

'Just get me one of those pork pies, MacGregor,' said Dover, carrying his beer away to one of the marble-topped tables.

As soon as MacGregor sat down, the old codger came over and joined them.

'Welcome to the William and Mary,' he said, grinning toothlessly.

Dover looked him up and down. 'Beat it!' he said curtly.

'Here,' protested the old man, 'there's no need to be

117

like that! I was only trying to be friendly like. My old dad. was a policeman,' he added shrewdly.

Dover sighed and unwrapped his pork pie.

'Cor!' said the old man. 'You're not going to eat that, are you? They've had that on that there plate for five years to my certain knowledge. You'll get food poisoning, that's what you'll get.'

'Have you been coming here for five years?' asked Mac-Gregor, always the optimist.

'Five years? I've been coming here every night for fifteen years, I have. Here, how old d'you think I am?'

'Seventy-five,' said Dover, who was pretty accurate in these matters, 'and you look ninety!'

The old man shot him a glance of utter loathing and turned back to MacGregor as being the more sympathetic, and generous character. 'My name's Harry Twitchin,' he said.

'Well now, Mr Twitchin,' said MacGregor, hoping that Dover would refrain from interrupting this delicate interrogation, 'do you remember the night that girl was shot round by St Benedict's?'

''Course I do!' retorted the old man. 'First bit of excitement we've had round here since Fred Birtwistle's wife come after him with an axe. Saturday, seventeenth February, it was. I remember it clear as yesterday.'

'You were in here that night, were you?'

''Course I was. I was sitting over there by the window, looking out, same as I always do when there's nobody else in the bar. That graveyard's quite a place for courting couples, you know,' he added with a chuckle. 'Beats me what attracts 'em, but some nights they're well nigh queueing up to get in there.'

'Do you know a young man called Rex Purseglove?'

''Course I do. Known his father for years, I have. And I saw him that night his girl friend was shot. She used to go

118

round to the vicarage for about an hour every Saturday night, regular as clockwork, and this night she got herself shot I saw young Rex hanging about on the corner there, waiting for her. He's waiting for his light-o'-love, I says to myself, but what good it'll do him Gawd only knows because she never looked like much of a one for a bit of slap and tickle as far as I could see.'

'I suppose you didn't happen to notice the time, did you?' asked MacGregor.

'Of course he didn't!' snorted Dover. 'The old fool's making it all up!'

'Here, who do you think you're talking to?' Harry Twitchin drew himself up with senile pride. 'I'll have you know that I've been a decent working chap all my life, and a good churchgoer too. I may be an old age pensioner but there's no call for you to start insulting me! Some of you young whipper-snappers want to watch your manners. If your memory's half as good as mine is when you're seventy-four, you'll be damned lucky! I can remember seeing Rex Purseglove standing over there on that corner the night Isobel Slatcher was shot as well as I can remember my own name.'

'Of course you can,' agreed MacGregor in a soothing voice. 'We know he was standing there for a few minutes, but we want to establish exactly what time it was, if we can. Now, did you by any chance hear the shots?'

Mr Twitchin shook his head. 'No,' he admitted. 'All the doors and windows were shut. I didn't hear no shots.'

Dover broke in. 'Did Rex Purseglove stand on the corner for a second or two, and then go off down Church Lane, and then come back again a bit later on and wait on the corner again?'

'No, he didn't. He was only hanging about by the church-yard the once. You ought to know that. While he was waiting there he heard these shots and that's when he set off

119

down Church Lane and found this Slatcher girl lying on the pavement. His dad told me himself what happened.'

Dover grunted. 'That's what's supposed to have happened,' he said, stuffing the last lump of his pie into his mouth.

'Are you hinting Harold Purseglove's a liar?' demanded Mr Twitchin ferociously.

'Of course not, Mr Twitchin,' said MacGregor hastily. 'It's just that we've got to check everything. I suppose as you didn't hear the shots you wouldn't have heard the train going by either?'

Mr Twitchin grinned. 'No, I didn't *hear* the train going by, but' – triumphantly – 'I felt it! That London express is a great big heavy train and he goes through here at a fair lick, I can tell you. Nearly shakes the glasses off the bar some nights. He usually blows his whistle just after he's gone through here and you can hear that if the wind's in the right direction.'

'I suppose you can't remember,' asked MacGregor very delicately, 'whether Rex Purseglove had already left the corner and set off down Church Lane before the London express went by?'

Harry Twitchin withdrew, somewhat dramatically, into deep thought. He closed his eyes and let his mouth drop open. It wasn't often that anybody took such an interest in him – certainly not a couple of bigwigs like these fellows from London – and he was determined to stretch out his moment of glory for as long as possible. He opened one eye and observed with satisfaction that both the detectives were waiting expectantly for his answer.

He opened both eyes and closed his mouth. In spite of themselves, Dover and MacGregor leaned forward.

'Very thirsty work, all this remembering,' said Harry Twitchin saucily.

Dover gritted his teeth. 'Oh, get the old . . . gentleman a

120

pint of beer, Sergeant.' He turned to Mr Twitchin. 'And it had better be worth it,' he threatened, 'otherwise I'll squeeze every last flaming drop out of you again!'

'Right,' began Mr Twitchin, clutching his pint happily and dribbling slightly on his ex-army greatcoat, 'well, as it happens I can remember everything quite clearly – just like it was yesterday. I've got a good memory, I have. Inherited it from my dad. I told you he was a policeman, didn't I?'

'You did!' growled Dover.

'Well, there I was watching young Rex Purseglove this night we're talking about and the reason I was concentrating on him, as you might say, was because there weren't nobody else about at all. Rotten, nippy sort of night it was. Well, I guessed he was waiting for his lady friend coming out of the vicarage and he was getting a bit impatient like, dithering about, you know, and looking at his watch. Well, then he suddenly lifts his head and listens.'

'The shots?' demanded Dover.

'No, the train! He sort of turned towards the railway line as it went by, not that he could see anything, of course, and then he looked at his watch again. 'Course, I felt it rumbling past, shaking everything in here, and I knew it was the old London express going through.'

'How long after that was it before he went down Church Lane?' asked MacGregor.

'Oh, a couple of minutes, I should think. He looked down the Lane, peering sort of, and then he looked all around as if he was looking to see if there was anybody else about. He looked a bit puzzled like and he seemed to be trying to make up his mind – you know how it is. And then he set off, not hurrying, mind you, towards St Benedict's. 'Course, as soon as he left the corner there I lost sight of him. It was too dark to see him going down Church Lane.'

Dover fought to the last ditch. At first he refused to

believe it and then he refused to admit that he believed it. He vented his spare wrath on the police driver, who submissively· drove back to the Station Hotel at a hesitant fifteen miles an hour and listened with great interest to the two nebbies from Scotland Yard bickering away in the back like a couple of fractious kids.

'Look, sir,' said MacGregor for the tenth time, 'there's really no getting away from it. If Rex Purseglove was standing on that corner when that train went by he couldn't have shot Isobel Slatcher. He just wouldn't have had the time. Mr Twitchin says he was there for a couple of minutes after the London train went through and . . .'

'I don't give a damn what that old rag bag said!' snapped Dover. 'He's making the whole thing up. His sort'd say black was white if they thought they'd get a free jug of beer out of it. And the way you asked the questions he knew damned well what you were after and said what he thought you wanted to hear. And it wouldn't surprise me if the Purseglove gang hadn't got together and bribed him.' He leaned forward and bawled down the driver's ear. 'Is that pub Protestant or Catholic?' he bellowed.

'The William and Mary, sir? Oh, Protestant, of course.'

'There you are!' crowed Dover triumphantly, as though this decided everything.

'But, sir!' MacGregor tried again. 'Nobody else could know about Mr Dibb's evidence, could they? I mean, it's the two statements taken together, isn't it, which are really significant? Mr Dibb said he heard the shots just *after* the train had passed him. Now I know it wouldn't take long for the train to go along the side of Church Lane and past the William and Mary, but it would take some time and if Rex Purseglove was still there on the corner when it did, he couldn't have got right down to the vicarage garden in time to fire those shots. Even if he left immediately he couldn't – and we know from Mr Twitchin's evidence that

122

it was another minute or two before he even set off – and then he wasn't hurrying.'

'Twitchin is a bleary-eyed, drunken, lecherous old sot!' snarled Dover. 'And if you believe that he can remember all this a year after it happened, you're as big a fool as he is!'

'Eight months, sir,' corrected MacGregor.

Dover glared at him and snorted furiously down his nose.

'I don't care if it was only eight bleeding minutes,' he howled. 'Rex Purseglove attacked Isobel Slatcher in February and killed her last week in the hospital! I'll stake my professional reputation on that! This isn't the first murder case I've been on, Sergeant,' he added sarcastically.

Unfortunately MacGregor was not in a position either to query the value of the chief inspector's professional reputation as a gambling stake or to point out that, although he had indeed been involved in a number of murder cases, Dover had brought embarrassingly few of them to a successful conclusion. The sergeant had to restrain himself to more acceptable arguments.

'But surely you don't think that Mr Dibb is lying, do you, sir?'

'Might be,' said Dover darkly.

'But what about Rex Purseglove's alibi at the hospital? Nurse Horncastle is quite prepared to swear he was never alone with Isobel Slatcher for one single second.'

'I reckon that's been fixed too,' said Dover sulkily.

The police car slithered to a sedate halt outside the Station Hotel and Dover hurried inside. In spite of his bad temper, he ate a hearty dinner.

CHAPTER NINE

Monday mornings are pretty dreary at the best of times and this one was no exception. Dover had had a sleepless night which he attributed to strain and worry about the case, but which was more likely caused by an overladen stomach. He came down to breakfast more boot-faced than ever and lost no time in burying himself in the morning paper. He now accepted, reluctantly, that Rex Purseglove was probably not the murderer – even Dover occasionally had to face up to facts – but he saw no reason for informing Sergeant MacGregor of his change of mind.

MacGregor quietly got on with his own breakfast having learnt by painful experience that there was no future in trying to jolly the chief inspector out of one of his black moods. The sergeant was not surprised to hear a snort of baffled fury from behind the newspaper. It just meant that Bigamous Bertie and Super Percy had once again forced themselves on to Dover's attention. Three women had demonstrated outside the prison when Bertie had been hanged and had been hauled up in front of the magistrates the following morning. One of them had made quite an exhibition of herself in court too, and the papers had devoted a fair amount of space to reporting her somewhat incoherent remarks.

Dover flung the paper aside with a pungent comment on the probable motives of these women – all unmarried – who apparently wanted to preserve Bigamous Bertie as a national institution.

'Half a loaf,' he remarked enigmatically and maliciously, 'is better than no bread.'

This idea that a man, any man, was automatically regarded by the opposite sex as a valuable and attractive item seemed to cheer him up a bit, and he glanced round the dining-room at the female breakfasters with the air of a pasha inspecting potential candidates for the harem. The choice presented to him was not an embarrassing one and, with a virile sneer, he turned his attention back to his bacon and eggs.

MacGregor judged it now safe to speak. 'What's the programme for this morning, sir?'

Dover regarded him with a jaundiced eye. Nag, nag, nag! Could he never be left in peace and quiet for a moment? Everything was always pushed on to his shoulders. He'd got to make all the decisions, work out all the plans, carry the whole bloody burden! He sighed deeply with self-pity and wondered, somewhat despairingly, what indeed their next step was going to be. If he couldn't have Rex Purseglove, he thought sulkily, he damned well didn't want anybody!

MacGregor was still waiting.

'We'll go round to the library,' said Dover, suddenly inspired. 'Might get a lead there. Some of her fellow-workers might know something.'

'We ought to have a chat with this fellow, Ofield, too,' agreed MacGregor. 'After all he was right on the spot when she was shot. He could have nipped out of the church door, shot her and popped back in again.'

Dover glared at his sergeant crossly. He hadn't thought of that possibility. Dover didn't like his sergeants getting too smart. He thought quickly of something to demolish MacGregor's theory.

'The key!' he said with ignoble triumph. 'There's only one key to the main door of the church and the Vicar had got that. He said so.'

MacGregor looked disappointed. 'Maybe it's one of those

125

locks like a Yale – you know, you don't need a key to open them from the inside?'

'No.' Dover squashed the idea. 'That's not very likely. Too modern for St Benedict's. But,' he added generously, 'you can check it some time if you like.'

The Curdley public library, formerly known as the Mechanics' Institute and Cocoa Rooms (this sonorous title is still carved irremovably in stone over the door) stands in Curdley's main square, opposite the bus station. It is a perfect specimen of Victorian Gothic. Inside everything was very sombre and gloomy. Stained-glass windows depicting Labour, Science, Education and the Domestic Arts cannot be expected to provide much passage for mere daylight. Every item of furniture – the shelves, desks, step-ladders and chairs – seemed to have been carved out of mahogany for a race of giants.

Mr Ofield, as head librarian, had a private little office which he shared with those books which were not considered suitable for general consumption. If any inquiring student could summon up enough nerve to invade Mr Ofield's sanctum he might, if Mr Ofield considered his motives pure enough, actually get what he asked for. This is not to imply that Mr Ofield himself was either a prude or excessively interested in the moral health of other people. He was in fact rather a progressive young man, but he had to live with his library committee. As part of the town's endless bargainings, all the members were Protestants. (Sewage and waste disposal, on the other hand, were acknowledged Catholic enclaves.) They were also somewhat puritanical in their outlook but very conscientious: they personally read all the doubtful books before banishing them to Mr Ofield's private office.

Dover took an instant dislike to Mr Ofield. He loathed all witnesses, whoever they were, because they were associated in his mind with work, and Dover was highly allergic

126

to work. But Mr Ofield was a rather good-looking, slick young man who obviously thought himself vastly superior to the rest of Curdley. And, of course, he was. He clearly thought himself vastly superior to Chief Inspector Dover as well, but he wasn't quite sure where he stood in relation to Charles Edward MacGregor, which was annoying for him.

Dover treated him to a preliminary hostile scowl.

Mr Ofield smiled thinly back at him through his stylish, prestige-bestowing, horn-rimmed spectacles.

'Well, Chief Inspector, what can I do for you? We have several books in our collection here dealing with criminology.' He smirked at his little joke.

Dover glowered at him. 'We've come to take a statement from you, sir' – his words were heavy with innuendo – 'about your relationship with the deceased Isobel Slatcher.'

No one was more surprised than Dover to see Mr Ofield go, quite suddenly, completely white, and then a painful scarlet. The chief inspector had just been indulging in a typical bit of spite, designed to take Mr Ofield down a peg or two and here he had, right out of the blue, hit the jackpot.

'You realize, Mr Ofield,' Dover went on, 'that we're dealing with a case of murder. A case of capital murder. Whoever murdered Isobel Slatcher will hang by the neck until he is dead.'

MacGregor, who had glanced at Dover with something like admiration as his stray shot had landed plumb on target, felt a familiar twinge of anxiety. He hoped the old fool wasn't going to ruin everything by overplaying his hand. Oh God, he was! With one podgy hand Dover was clasping his own neck as if to prevent a ligature from tightening around it. Luckily Mr Ofield was too unnerved to notice this performance.

'Yes,' said Dover, gloatingly, 'capital murder! Now then, are you going to give us a frank, straightforward account or' – hopefully – 'have I got to, er, take other measures?'

'My . . . my dear Inspector!' Mr Ofield made a valiant effort to pull himself together. 'I really don't understand what on earth you're talking about.'

'Don't you?' said Dover with an unpleasant grin.

'No, I'm afraid I don't. It's true that Isobel and I were, well, quite friendly at one time, but it was never anything more serious than that. And in any case, all this happened some considerable time ago.'

'Oh, you jilted her, did you?'

'No, I did not! Nothing of the kind. You're trying to make out that a perfectly innocent relationship – I might almost use the word "platonic" – was much more serious than, in fact, it was. Two or three years ago Isobel and I used to go to concerts together occasionally – the Hallé and things like that. The odd foreign film, and a couple of times we went together to the ballet.'

'In Curdley?' asked Dover sceptically.

'Of course not. In Manchester usually. There's quite a good train service.'

'And what brought these little cultural trips to an end?'

'Well, it's a bit difficult, really. After all the poor girl is dead and . . . Well, I realized after a bit that Isobel was, well, keener on me than she was on chamber music – if you follow me. Oh, you know what some women are like. They start getting possessive and looking in furniture-shop windows and asking how on earth you can manage without some blasted woman to look after you, and do you think church weddings are more romantic than registry ones. You know how it is. I could see the jaws of the tender trap opening and, well, frankly, I didn't find the cheese attractive enough.'

'So you broke it up?'

'I made a tactful but strategic withdrawal. It wasn't too easy, I can tell you, with both of us working here in the library. At one time I seemed to spend most of the day dodging out of sight behind the book stacks.'

'And how did she take it?'

Mr Ofield frowned. 'Not too well, I'm afraid. And, of course, when she found out a bit later on I was engaged to be married to someone else she got, really, quite spiteful.'

'Jealous, eh?'

'Well, not only that. My wife's Austrian, you see. And she's also a Catholic. No doubt you know, Inspector, what that means in this town. As far as Isobel was concerned anything Catholic was like a red rag to a bull. We got engaged, Trudi and I, unofficially, last Christmas. We tried to keep things as quiet as possible because I knew there'd be a devil of a row when it got out and I wanted to try and break people in to the idea first. Well, somebody let the cat out of the bag! My parents nearly had fifty fits and the people at church started treating me as though I'd got an infectious disease. The chairman of the library committee came to see me. He'd had an anonymous letter of all things, and for a bit I really thought I was going to get booted out.'

'And you think Isobel Slatcher was responsible?'

'I'm damned well certain she was! My fiancée got an anonymous letter too, hinting at all kinds of filthy things about me and my past and I'll stake my oath on it, Isobel wrote that. She damned nearly broke up my engagement. Of course, I've no proof that she was behind it all, but most of the furore seemed to die down after she was shot.'

'Indeed?' said Dover, glancing significantly at MacGregor.

Mr Ofield intercepted the glance. 'But that doesn't mean that I tried to kill her,' he protested. 'Good God, I wouldn't dream of doing anything like that!'

'Of course not, sir,' said Dover blandly. 'But you were on the scene, weren't you, when Miss Slatcher was shot outside St Benedict's?'

'I was practising in the church, but I didn't even know

anything had happened until I came in to work the next morning.'

Dover sniffed, not very reassuringly.

'Were you attending the Men's Bible Class when the Pie Gang raided it in January?'

'Those young Catholic hooligans? Yes, I was. But what's that got to do with it?'

'Where were you on Friday morning last week, Mr Ofield?'

'I was here.'

'In this room?'

'Well, here and in the library – you know, just like any other day.'

'Can you prove it?'

'Prove it?' yelped Mr Ofield, now really worried. 'Look here, you don't seriously suspect me . . .?'

'You're on my list, Mr Ofield,' said Dover smugly. 'You're on my list.'

'But why?'

'You've told us yourself! Isobel Slatcher, for various reasons, was out to make trouble for you. Thanks to her you might have lost your job, and your Austrian fiancée. Miss Slatcher was, most effectively, put out of action with a couple of bullets in her head and here you are – married, I think you said, and still Curdley's head librarian. You haven't got much of an alibi, have you, either for the first attack last February or for Friday's more successful attempt?'

'Oh my God!' bleated Mr Ofield, clutching his head in bewilderment. 'You can't be serious! I tell you I wouldn't have hurt a hair of Isobel's head! She was a nuisance, yes I grant you that – but so are lots of people and you don't go around trying to blow their brains out.'

Dover sniffed. 'Is it true,' he asked, trying another tack, 'that you are on the verge of leaving Curdley?'

With some reluctance Mr Ofield admitted he was. He

wasn't at all happy about the way the interview was developing, and had now reached the stage when he would have
been suspicious if Dover had asked him what time it was.

In spite of Isobel Slatcher's disappearance from the
scene, Curdley, or that section of it which mattered, was
not prepared to forgive and forget the unholy alliance which
Mr Ofield had contracted. All the town's social life, from
golf to bingo, was strictly segregated, except for the annual
reception which the mayor traditionally gave in the town
hall at the end of his year of office. Here all parties gathered
together and congratulated each other on the growing
tolerance and co-operation which had been observed in the
previous twelve months. Nobody believed, or was expected
to believe, a word of all this twaddle and everybody went
cheerfully home, mentally girding up their loins for the
next round in the battle.

'Curdley's an intellectual backwater,' explained Mr
Ofield, polishing his spectacles with an air. 'There's no
cultural life here at all. You can't find anyone to have a
serious conversation with about fundamentals – or about
art or literature, or even good food, if it comes to that. I
want to get somewhere where people really think and talk
about something besides last night's programme on the
telly. I've gone to a lot of trouble building up a really good
collection of progressive literature here – but do you think
anyone reads it? Not on your life! All they want is books
on breeding racing pigeons or do-it-yourself home decorat-
ing. No, I decided it was time to get out.'

'And where are you going?' asked Dover.

'Er, Welwyn Garden City, as a matter of fact. Of course
we shall be able to get up to London from there and see all
the shows and exhibitions and things. Besides, Trudi
doesn't like the climate up here.'

'Hm,' said Dover. 'By the way, did you see the report
in last Thursday's *Custodian* about Isobel Slatcher?'

131

'Yes, I did.'

'What did you think about it?'

'Well, I know it sounds awful but, to tell you the truth, I'd really half forgotten she was still alive. Such a lot seems to have happened recently what with me getting married and then going after this job in the South and the move and everything. Rotten shame, of course, somebody killing her like that just when there was a chance she might recover.'

Dover began to get bored. Out of sheer bloody-mindedness he made MacGregor write out Mr Ofield's statement on the spot and amused himself while this was going on by examining Curdley's collection of restricted library books. He found them a disappointing lot.

When the statement was ready, and there wasn't all that much of it, MacGregor passed his one-and-sixpenny ball-point pen over to Mr Ofield. Mr Ofield refused it with a surprised, but kindly smile, and pulled an expensive-looking Sheaffer out of his waistcoat pocket. MacGregor's face fell. It wasn't often he got caught out on things like that.

Mr Ofield read the statement through carefully, corrected one or two minor punctuation mistakes and scribbled an impressive signature underneath in jet-black ink – Antony Victor Ofield, F.L.A.

The two detectives returned to the Station Hotel for lunch, both agreeing for different reasons that, all things considered, they'd as soon see Antony Victor Ofield hanged for the murder of Isobel Slatcher as anybody else.

'Still,' admitted MacGregor regretfully, 'he doesn't really look a very strong candidate, does he, sir?'

'Oh, I dunno,' said Dover through a mouthful of Yorkshire pudding. 'He'd got a motive, you know, probably a damned sight stronger than he led us to believe. Isobel Slatcher could have done him quite a lot of harm and busted his marriage up as well. He strikes me as the kind of chap who'd go quite a long way when it came to looking after his own skin.'

'And he could have got the gun.'

'Yes, he could. And he could have nipped out of the church and shot Isobel and nipped smartly back in again. That'd explain why nobody else was seen in Church Lane after the shots were fired.'

MacGregor had a vague idea that somebody already had propounded this theory and had it pooh-poohed, but it was no good worrying about that now. 'But why should he kill her last Friday, sir? He's nothing to fear now. He's got married and he's on the point of leaving Curdley – why worry about Isobel Slatcher?'

'If he shot her in the first place, you damned fool, he'd have plenty to be afraid of, wouldn't he? If I've told you once I've told you a hundred times, MacGregor, whoever finished our Sleeping Beauty off in the hospital did it to stop her identifying him as the man who shot her last February. There can't be any other motive! My God, if you can't keep a few simple deductions like that straight in your head you might as well sign for your helmet and whistle and get back on the beat!'

'Yes, sir,' said MacGregor, meekly turning the other cheek.

'Now,' Dover went on, 'after lunch you get back to the library and see if you can find anything out about Ofield's movements last Friday morning. See if he could have slipped out over to the hospital and croaked Isobel Slatcher.'

Privately MacGregor thought that it might have been better to have conducted such an investigation before lunch, and before Mr Ofield could have had a chance of coaching a few witnesses, supposing he had any inclinations that way.

'Then,' said Dover, 'you'd better go round to St Benedict's and check the lock on that front door. If it can be opened from the inside without the key . . .' He popped a lump of cheese into his mouth – 'we'll have another chat with Mr Ofield.'

Dover munched and thought. He'd already made up his mind as to how he was going to spend the afternoon but he wanted to be sure that MacGregor wouldn't find time hanging on his hands.

'While you're at the library, Sergeant, you'd better ask the other girls there if they've got any revelations on Isobel Slatcher's love life. There might be one or two more unwilling swains that we haven't heard of yet. After all, she was twenty-eight, she must have had more than two near misses. And you might do a bit of tactful probing and see if they know any more about her relationship with Rex Purseglove and this Ofield squirt.' Dover yawned unpleasantly and scratched his head. 'You might turn up something. You never know.'

MacGregor hurried off happily like a dog let off the lead on a country walk, and Dover lumbered upstairs. Much to his annoyance he found that hordes of elderly women were pushing vacuum cleaners all round his room and those of his neighbours. There was no hope of having a quiet think up here. He lumbered back downstairs again and found a secluded corner in the writing-room. He settled himself luxuriously in one armchair and, having thankfully removed his boots, put his feet up on another. With a sigh he loosened his collar and undid the top button of his trousers. Thirty seconds later Chief Inspector Wilfred Dover, his mouth sagging open, was fast asleep.

He slept soundly until half past three. Most of the hotel staff and some of the other guests had been in to have a look at him – it was, after all, not a sight to be missed. However, their twittering mutters of shocked disapproval didn't disturb Dover.

What did rouse him was the piping squeaks of a small child who had been brought into the near-by lounge for

134

afternoon tea by an over-indulgent mother. While waiting for the tea to arrive – service was not rapid at the Station Hotel – the moppet grew impatient and fretful. After a short period of whining that she was hungry and a few tentative attempts at bawling (for which she received a sharp slap on the behind) she amused herself, and infuriated everybody else, by starting to recite poetry. Her repertoire was not large but her lungs were powerful and Dover groped back to consciousness to the accompaniment of a sketchy version of 'The Owl and the Pussy Cat'.

'"The Owl and the Pussy Cat went to sea In a beautiful pea-green boat."' The child's shrill voice was barely within the range of the human ear. Dover scowled. '"The Owl and the Pussy Cat went to sea In a beautiful pea-green boat."'

With a groan of rage and despair – Dover didn't approve of audible children – he closed his eyes and tried to shut the noise out, but the voice piped on, penetratingly if inaccurately.

'"Wrapped up in a five-pound note."'

Dover opened his eyes and glared in the direction of the disturbance.

'"And they sailed away for a year and a day."'

The needle stuck.

'"And they sailed away for a year and a day,"' repeated the child. '"And they sailed away for a year and a day. And they sailed away for a year and a day."'

'Hush, dear.' That was the mother. Even her indulgence was becoming exhausted.

'"And they sailed away for a year and a day!"' bawled the infant gleefully. Dover reached grimly for his boots. '"And they sailed away for a year and a day! And they sailed away for a year and a day! And they sailed away for a year and ..."'

The sound of a smack rang joyously through the hotel.

There was a moment's delicious silence while the child drew breath, and then there came the outraged scream of pure fury.

Dover smiled. The scream was ear-shattering but, remembering the slap which had preceded it, and caused it, it was bearable.

The chief inspector finished tying his boot laces and, with difficulty fastened the top button of his trousers. Near by things quietened down as the tea at last arrived.

Suddenly Dover paused. His hands dropped in astonishment from his tie which remained twisted under one ear. 'My God!' he exclaimed aloud in a voice of reverent awe. 'My God!'

He sat, staring vacantly into space, occasionally repeating his call to the deity in a hushed voice.

MacGregor, arriving hot foot from his solo mission, thought, with hope, that the old fool had gone off his rocker at last.

'Oh, here you are, sir,' he said brightly. 'I thought you'd be in your room. Well, sir, I'm afraid I haven't spent a very profitable afternoon. I went to the library first and I ...'

'Never mind all that twaddle!' said Dover and added proudly, 'I've had an idea!'

MacGregor shuddered. 'Really, sir?'

'Yes,' said Dover nodding his head sagely. 'Came to me in a flash, it did. We ... you've been on the wrong track, my lad. You'll have to watch yourself. I've warned you before about jumping to conclusions before you've hardly got your teeth into a case. Just let this be a lesson to you. Now, where does Violet Slatcher work?'

'She won't be there now, sir,' MacGregor pointed out officiously. 'She's not going back to work until after the funeral.'

'I don't want to see her!' snapped Dover. 'I want to see

136

where she works — and if you don't know where that is, find out! And get the car round. We're going there right away. Come on, man, move!'

Ten minutes later the two detectives stood outside the Snowite Launderette.

Dover wrinkled his nose as he surveyed the scene. 'How far is it to the hospital?' he demanded.

MacGregor dragged out his street plan and calculated rapidly. 'Three or four minutes' walk, sir,' he said, frowning as he tried to work out what his superior officer was up to. Dover was indulging himself in a bit of master minding and had no intention of divulging his Great Idea to a mere sergeant before he had to. If MacGregor was such a clever devil he could work it out for himself.

'Come on,' he said. 'Let's go inside.'

Ten pairs of feminine eyes which had been intent on the circumvolutions of their own and other people's washing switched in astonishment to the two men who came barging in.

A female battle-axe, standing on guard by the cash desk, examined them suspiciously, noting with displeasure (she worked on commission) that they hadn't brought any dirty washing with them.

'Well?' she said. 'What do you two want?'

'We just want to ask you a couple of questions,' began Dover, hopefully raising his bowler hat one-eighth of an inch from his head in a conciliatory gesture.

The battle-axe picked up the telephone. 'Get me the police,' she said.

'For God's sake!' snapped Dover. 'We *are* the police. Show her your pass thing, MacGregor.'

The battle-axe perused MacGregor's identity card with scrupulous care, reading every word of it. 'All right,' she admitted grudgingly, 'you're a policeman. What about him?'

137

'I'm a policeman, too,' protested Dover. 'I'm a detective chief inspector!'

The battle-axe silently held out her hand.

Dover hunted furiously through every pocket he possessed. He was almost certain that someone at some time had duly provided him with proper authorization, but since never before in his entire career had he been called upon to produce it, it wasn't surprising that his knowledge of its present whereabouts was, to say the least, hazy.

At last, to the surprise of everybody, he found it. It was crumpled and stained with what looked like tea, but it satisfied the battle-axe, who directed on it the same scrutiny that she had afforded MacGregor's.

Once assured of her visitors' bona fides the battle-axe unbent a little. She took them into a small side room where they could talk in private, and informed them that her name was Mrs Kyle. She and the elder Miss Slatcher ran the launderette between them.

'Wasn't it dreadful about poor Isobel?' said Mrs Kyle, her eyes popping with excitement. 'First her getting shot like that and then dying on Friday. I did hear' – she shot a sly glance at the two detectives – 'I did hear that was murder, too.'

'Then you heard aright, madam,' said Dover, firmly sitting down on the only available chair.

'Really?' Mrs Kyle's eyes grew even rounder. 'What do you know about that, eh? Somebody must have had it in for her all right, mustn't they? 'Course Violet used to think the sun shone out of that girl, though I could never see it myself. Still, there's no smoke without a fire, is there? She couldn't have been such a little angel as all that, could she? Otherwise all this wouldn't have happened, would it? I mean, respectable, decent people just don't go around getting murdered, do they?'

Privately Dover thoroughly agreed with these sentiments,

138

but he was in no mood to waste precious time on them at the moment. He had had an idea and he wanted to pursue it with as much dispatch as possible.

'Did you know Isobel Slatcher well, Mrs Kyle?' he asked.

She shook her head, regretfully. 'No, as a matter of fact I've only spoken to her once or twice. She never came in here, you know. Wasn't posh enough for her ladyship, I suppose.'

'But her sister works here?'

'Violet's the manageress, Inspector – not quite the same thing as working here, you know. Anyhow, she always used to pretend that she only did it for pin money and just to help pass the time. Always gave you to understand that she didn't need to work for her living. Lucky for some, I always say.'

'Are you and she always here together?'

'Well, not quite. We're open six days a week, you know, so I usually take all day Tuesday off and Violet usually takes Monday afternoon and Wednesday morning. We're always busier towards the end of the week, so we're both in together then. 'Course, now I'm having to manage on my own. I don't suppose Violet'll be back for a bit yet. I reckon this business has clean bowled her over.'

'How often did she visit her sister in the hospital?'

'Oh, twice a day, at least. She used to pop out sometimes for half an hour or so when we weren't too busy. They were very good to her at the hospital – they didn't bother about visiting hours or anything like that. They just used to let Violet pop in for a few minutes more or less whenever she felt like it. I mean, it didn't do any harm, did it? She could only just go and look at her lying there.' She shuddered a little. 'Oh, fair gives you the creeps, doesn't it, even to think of it? Her just going on and on and never waking up. What you might call a living death. Mind you, Violet keeping popping out like that, it made a lot more work for

139

me and, of course, I never expected it would drag on for all these months or I wouldn't have been quite so obliging. But in a case like that there's not much you can do, is there?'

'What about last Friday morning? Were you both in here together then?'

Mrs Kyle's eyebrows shot up. 'Last Friday morning,' she repeated. 'You mean when Isobel was killed in the Emily Gorner?'

'That's right.' Dover glanced at MacGregor's puzzled frown with satisfaction. Thought himself such a young clever devil, did he? Well, let him sort out this one for himself.

'Ooooh!' said Mrs Kyle doubtfully. 'You don't think Violet had anything to do with it, do you?'

'Never you mind what I think!' said Dover shortly. 'Were you both here together?'

'Well, yes, we were.'

'Did Violet leave the place at all during the morning?'

'Well, yes,' admitted Mrs Kyle, not sure she liked the way things were developing, 'as a matter of fact she did, but only for about ten minutes or so.'

Dover's nose twitched ecstatically. 'Where did she go, eh? To the hospital?'

'Oh no.' Mrs Kyle's head shook firmly. 'She went to the bank. She always goes round as soon as they're open on Friday morning. She likes to be the first customer for some cock-eyed reason. Still, you know what some of these old maids are like, sort of pernickety. And she'd always got to go herself. Even when she was half dead with a bad cold or something, she'd never let me go for her. Didn't trust me, I suppose.'

'And which bank do you use?' asked Dover.

'The District.'

'And where is it?'

140

Mrs Kyle gulped and went a bit pale. 'It's nearly opposite the Emily Gorner,' she said faintly. 'On the other side of the road.'

'I see,' said Dover.

MacGregor's jaw was hanging slightly open. Surely he didn't seriously think that Violet Slatcher, of all people . . .

'Just one last question, Mrs Kyle,' said Dover comfortably. 'I see you're wearing a white overall. Did Violet Slatcher wear one, too?'

'Oh yes, definitely. We've got to look hygienic, you know.'

Dover nodded his head wisely. 'Quite,' he said. 'And when Miss Slatcher goes out to the bank, does she take her overall off?'

'Oh no, it wouldn't be worth it just for a few minutes, would it? She just pops her coat on top.'

'Thank you,' said Dover and, for once in his life, really meant it.

On the way to the bank Dover refused to answer any of MacGregor's questions. 'I haven't got time to spell it all out for you in words of one syllable,' he snapped. 'Good God, you're supposed to be a detective, aren't you? You bloody well work it out for yourself. Be good practice for you!' He laughed unpleasantly.

The bank was closed but Dover kicked impatiently at the huge, impressive double doors until they were opened. There was some unfortunate confusion at first as the bank staff mistook Dover's brusque intrusion for a raid and one dear old wizened bank clerk made a valiant attempt to sell his life dearly. Two of the girls tried to have hysterics, but Dover soon put a stop to that.

At last he got his hands, figuratively speaking, on the man he wanted, the teller with whom Violet Slatcher habitually conducted her business on a Friday morning.

He smiled wryly when Dover mentioned her name. 'Oh

141

yes,' he said, 'I've been dealing with her for years. Very pleasant sort of woman, but she likes things just so, always checks everything very carefully. You'd be surprised,' he added with a rather superior air, 'how many people *are* like that where money's concerned. Last Friday? Oh, much the same as usual. She wasn't actually waiting on the doorstep when I unlocked the door, like she usually is, but she was just coming across the road so I knew the world hadn't actually come to an end. I pulled her leg about it a bit, you know, said something about having her put on jankers if she was late again. She just gave me one of those tight, we-are-not-amused, little smiles, so I didn't pursue the matter. Come to think of it, she probably didn't know what the hell I was talking about, anyway.'

Outside the bank Dover paused, reverently removed his bowler and mopped his brow. 'Well,' he said, screwing his hat firmly back on his head, 'I reckon that's that. I think we'd better go and get a warrant.'

'A warrant?' gasped MacGregor. 'For Violet Slatcher? You must be out of your mind, sir!'

'Who the hell d'you think you're talking to, Sergeant?' demanded Dover, who expected his subordinates to show a proper respect.

'I'm sorry, sir, but you can't really think Violet Slatcher murdered her own sister?'

'Daughter,' corrected Dover.

'Well, that only makes it worse. Do you mean to say that she shot Isobel outside St Benedict's Church, let her linger on like that for eight months and then suffocated her last Friday morning with her own pillow?'

'Of course not!' said Dover crossly. 'She'd nothing to do with the shooting part of it at all. She thought the world of her sister – daughter. Everybody says that. What on earth should she want to kill her for?'

MacGregor took a deep, deep breath. 'I'm afraid, sir,'

he said carefully, 'I'm not quite with you on this. If Violet Slatcher didn't kill Isobel, what do you want the warrant for?'

'Oh, wake up, for God's sake, MacGregor!' Dover's patience was wearing thin. 'I said she didn't *shoot* Isobel. Somebody else did that. But Violet did finish her off, that's perfectly obvious. Look at the timing and everything. Friday morning she puts her coat on over her white overall and goes out to the bank – same as usual. I expect she left a minute or two earlier, but Mrs Kyle wouldn't notice anything like that. She gets to the hospital, let's say about five to ten. She knows Rex Purseglove won't arrive till ten and he'll probably hang about a bit waiting for the newspaper photographers to come and take some snaps of him in his brand-new officer's uniform. Violet slips her coat off, and there she is in a white overall. You know what hospitals are like – look at "Emergency Ward 10" – they're all wearing white coats. She'd be practically invisible. And don't forget she's been popping in and out of that hospital any old time for the past eight months. She'd know her way around perfectly. If anybody spotted her on her way to Isobel's room they wouldn't have thought twice about it. And if she thought she'd been noticed, well, she could always call the whole thing off. She goes into Isobel's room, pulls the pillow from under her head and smothers her. Then she puts the pillow neatly back in place again – very feminine touch, that. What would it take – a couple of minutes? Then she goes out again, puts on her coat and leaves the hospital. Straight across the road to the bank only a few seconds later than she'd been every Friday morning for years. Remember what the bank clerk said? He saw her coming *across* the road. If she'd come straight from the launderette she'd have been on the same side of the road as the bank all the way, wouldn't she?'

'Yes,' admitted MacGregor unhappily. 'But I thought

we were working on the hypothesis, sir, that one person was responsible both for the shooting and the actual murder in the hospital?'

'Ah,' said Dover with a lordly wave of his hand, 'that's where you went wrong, isn't it, my lad? I've warned you before about jumping to conclusions before you've got all the facts. It's a bad failing of yours.'

'But, this changes everything, doesn't it, sir? I mean, if you're right' – Dover scowled blackly at this – 'if you're right, sir, and Isobel was killed in the hospital by Violet, then all this business of eliminating people because they couldn't have made both attacks – well, we were just wasting our time, weren't we, sir?'

'Well,' said Dover sourly, 'I wouldn't have put it quite like that myself, but I see what you're trying to get at. Anyhow, now we – I've solved the second attack we shouldn't have much difficulty in pinning down the joker who actually started the whole business off by shooting Isobel Slatcher in Church Lane. Now, come on, we can't hang about here all day. We'd better go and get this bit over with.'

'There's just one thing I'm still not clear about, sir.'

Dover gave a sceptical snort. 'Well?'

'Well, why did Violet Slatcher kill Isobel? I mean, I just can't see any reason for it. Was it one of these mercy killings?'

'No, rather the opposite, in fact.' Dover decided to be all enigmatic and irritating. 'I'll give you a clue, MacGregor.' He chuckled. 'Try "The Owl and the Pussy Cat", my lad, try "The Owl and the Pussy Cat"!'

CHAPTER TEN

MACGREGOR'S FOOT itched to kick his chief inspector where it would do most good. He didn't consider it very good form for a senior police officer to be facetious about murder cases. Naturally he restrained himself from physical assault – Dover wasn't worth sacrificing his career for – but he did try to point out that while the case against Violet Slatcher did, of course, sir, look very convincing, there wasn't what you might call over much in the way of proof.

This implied criticism enraged Dover, as any form of criticism always did. 'I don't need proof,' he blustered. 'She'll confess, you'll see. Once she knows we've got the facts she'll collapse like a pricked balloon. Good grief, if you wait for *proof* every time, nobody'd ever get arrested!'

When Dover and MacGregor finally arrived at Miss Slatcher's house neither of them was actually looking forward to the encounter. They were both somewhat relieved when, once again, Mr Bonnington opened the front door in answer to MacGregor's ring. He seemed very surprised to see them.

'Is Miss Slatcher in?' asked Dover brusquely.

'Well, yes, Inspector, she is, as a matter of fact. Er, naturally.' He smiled rather nervously. 'I've just called round to see if there is anything I can do for her, poor woman. It's a very trying time, you know, what with the inquest and the funeral and everything. Did you want to see her? Couldn't it be left until a bit later? She's really not herself, you know.'

'I'm sorry, sir, but I must insist on seeing her now,' said Dover, and stepped resolutely across the threshold.

Violet Slatcher evinced neither surprise nor pleasure when she saw who had arrived. She was sitting bolt upright in a chair by the fire, her hands folded placidly in her lap.

'Well,' she demanded sharply, 'have you arrested him yet?'

'We're still pursuing our investigations, madam,' said Dover smoothly, nodding to MacGregor to get his notebook out.

Violet Slatcher sniffed contemptuously and turned her head away to stare into the fire.

'We would like to ask you a few more questions, madam,' Dover went on, taking the seat opposite her.

Mr Bonnington was still hovering uncertainly in the doorway.

'Perhaps you would like me to go?' he asked without much enthusiasm.

'No,' said Dover quickly, 'I think you'd better stay.'

'Whichever you do,' snapped Miss Slatcher with tart indifference, 'I wish you'd close that door. You're letting all the cold air in.'

There was a pause while Mr Bonnington settled himself unobtrusively at the back of the room and Dover wondered where to begin. Violet Slatcher seemed to have more self-control and toughness than he had expected, and he was not so sure now that she was going to break down and confess all at the first rattle of the handcuffs. He sighed deeply.

Violet Slatcher glanced impatiently at him. 'Well, get on with it! I haven't all day to waste, if you have.'

'All right, madam. Well, first of all I'd like to clear up a few points about the exact nature of your relationship to Isobel.'

This time Violet Slatcher's eyes didn't return to the heart of the fire. She watched Dover with a bitter, mocking smile on her pale lips.

146

'Perhaps, after all,' said Dover, 'you'd prefer Mr Bonnington to go?'

Violet shrugged her shoulders. 'What does it matter now.'

'So Isobel really was your illegitimate child, and not your sister?'

'She was.'

There was a gasp of astonishment from Mr Bonnington. The woman turned viciously on him. 'Well, what about it? She was my daughter and I loved her! Is that a crime? I made a foolish mistake when I was a girl – well, I've paid for it since. I only half knew at the time that what I was doing was wrong. In those days girls were left in ignorance until the night before they were married. At least, my mother never told me anything. I suppose she thought it wasn't nice. Well' – she laughed without humour – 'she was right about that! I found out the hard way what beasts men are.'

'My dear Miss Slatcher . . .' began Mr Bonnington, feeling it incumbent upon him to offer some words of consolation and Christian forgiveness.

'You don't have to be sorry for me!' she snorted. 'God punished me for my wickedness, but He sent me consolation, too, in His infinite mercy. I had Isobel. I didn't betray my trust where she was concerned. You know that, Vicar! You know I brought her up to fear God and live a clean and decent life.'

'Yes, yes, of course,' murmured Mr Bonnington. 'Er, Inspector, is this all you came to discuss? I fail to see that it has much bearing on your investigations and it is obviously a topic which is extremely painful for Miss Slatcher, under the circumstances.'

Violet Slatcher broke in. 'Oh, it doesn't matter now,' she said. 'I've tried to keep it a secret all these years. I've been afraid every single minute that some Nosy Parker' – she glared at Dover – 'would find out. But I wasn't bothered about myself, I'll have you know. I had sinned, and if the

Lord wished to punish me by public shame – well, I must bow my head and submit to His will. That's what the Bible teaches us, isn't it? But I didn't want Isobel to suffer. She was innocent. I didn't want fingers of scorn pointing and mocking at her. Well, now she's gone and I don't care if the whole world knows of my shame.' She drew herself up resolutely. 'But I want her murderer caught and tried and hanged! That's what I pray to God for on my knees every night!'

Dover cleared his throat uncomfortably. 'Miss Slatcher,' he said, 'if we catch the man who shot Isobel when she left the vicarage, you do know that he won't be hanged, don't you?'

Violet Slatcher stared at him, her eyes bright and feverish. 'Won't be hanged?' she repeated. 'Why not? It's capital murder. I know it is because I looked it up. Of course he'll be hanged. All you've got to do is go out and arrest him.'

Dover shook his head. 'We shall only be able to charge him with attempted murder, you know,' he said gently. 'In a murder case the victim must die within a certain specified time, from the results of the attack.'

Miss Slatcher tossed her head. 'Good heavens, man, I know that! It's a year and a day. I looked that up too. I'm not a fool, you know.'

MacGregor glanced up from his notebook and caught Dover's eye. So that's what he was getting at with his 'The Owl and the Pussy Cat' hint. 'They sailed away for a year and a day . . .' Well, well, who'd have thought the old man had so much subtlety in him? Still, MacGregor felt extremely annoyed with himself. He shouldn't have missed an obvious point like that, not a bright and up-and-coming young detective sergeant like Charles Edward MacGregor.

Dover sighed again. He really wasn't enjoying this at all.

'So you knew that too, did you, Miss Slatcher?' He took a deep breath. 'Is that why you killed Isobel in the hospital on Friday?'

'My God!' That was Mr Bonnington whose mouth fell open in sheer astonishment.

Violet Slatcher reacted in a peculiar manner. She looked extremely annoyed. 'What absolute nonsense!' she snapped crossly, and tossed her head again. 'If that's all you can produce it might have been as well if you'd stayed down in London where you were. You're obviously wasting your time up here, and the taxpayers' money.'

'No,' said Dover, 'I haven't been wasting my time, and you know it. You loved Isobel and you wanted the man who shot her caught and punished, didn't you? At first you thought she might recover, after all she was still alive. But then, as time went on, you realized that she was never going to get better. And you realized too, didn't you, that people had just stopped bothering? The police seemed to have lost interest in the case and even your friends kept forgetting to ask you how she was.'

'A nine days' wonder!' Violet Slatcher nodded her head bitterly. 'That's all she was to them, a nine days' wonder. But I didn't forget!'

'No, but the doctors at the hospital finally made you realize that Isobel would never regain consciousness. She was condemned to a living death, and she might linger on like that for years and years.'

Violet Slatcher wasn't listening to him. When she spoke she seemed to be talking to herself. 'She was already dead,' she whispered. 'Her soul was with God. It must have been. Only flesh and bones were left, but Isobel wasn't there. I could do nothing more for her, nobody could, except to see that she was avenged. I saw Rex Purseglove's mother. She told me that he was coming home on leave. She said it might be months before he got back to Curdley again.

They'd posted him somewhere a long way off – I can't remember where. I knew I had to act quickly, for Isobel's sake. I got them to put that story in the *Custodian*. I knew Rex would see it when he came home. It must have scared the living daylights out of him, the cowardly little rat! I did wonder at first if that would be enough. If he'd be so frightened that she'd betray him and ruin his beautiful career that he'd sneak round to the hospital and finish off the job he'd already bungled once. But I daren't risk it. I didn't think he'd have the nerve to go through all that again. I had to do it all myself. I persuaded him to go round to see Isobel at the hospital. I knew he wouldn't be able to miss a chance of showing himself off in his new uniform. I went to Isobel's room just before he was due to arrive. Nobody noticed me. I held the pillow over her face. She didn't suffer. I put the pillow back and left everything nice and tidy. Then I went to the bank as usual.'

The room was quiet. Mr Bonnington mopped his brow.

'Well,' said Dover, 'that's that. Did you get it all down, Sergeant?'

Miss Slatcher gave herself a little shake. 'Would you like a cup of tea?' she asked in a bright, unconcerned voice.

'Not just now, thank you, madam,' said Dover. 'Sergeant, nip outside and bring that policewoman in. I think the sooner we get Miss Slatcher down to the station the better.'

Mr Bonnington went over to her and took her hand. He spoke softly to her but she didn't seem to understand. He looked questioningly at Dover. 'I'm afraid . . .' he said.

'I reckon it's the shock, sir,' said Dover. 'We'll get a doctor to her. All things considered, she's probably better like that for a bit. I don't think she really understands what she's done.'

Mr Bonnington shook his head. 'She's certainly been very queer and withdrawn lately, but I never suspected she was

150

carrying a burden like this. Poor soul.' He swallowed hard. 'They won't hang her, Inspector, will they?'

'No, sir,' said Dover. 'By the look of her I don't imagine she'll ever even come to trial. And I can't see the judge being very severe, even if she does.' There was the sound of people coming into the hall. 'Thank God, they're here at last. We'll get her away as quickly as we can. Don't worry about her, sir. She'll be looked after all right.'

Things in fact went off quite smoothly. MacGregor fetched Miss Slatcher's coat and she put it on calmly. She seemed to take quite a fancy to the young policewoman who had been brought to escort her and actually appeared pleased to have her support as they left the house and got into the waiting police car.

Back in the sitting-room Dover pushed his bowler hat back on his head. ''Strewth!' he said. 'Thank God that's over!' He sat down heavily in his chair.

'You were lucky, sir,' MacGregor said.

'You're telling me!' agreed Dover. 'I never thought she'd just give in quietly and admit the whole thing like that.'

'Well, at least she's got it off her conscience,' said Mr Bonnington piously. 'I still can't really believe it. She still thinks that Rex Purseglove did the original shooting, I take it?'

'That's right,' said Dover. 'She was trying to frame him really. She was quite convinced he was the fellow who'd shot Isobel and she realized that he wouldn't pay the full penalty of the law unless Isobel died within a year and a day. The law's quite clear. If you linger on for a year and two days it might be grievous bodily harm, but it ain't murder. Violet just wanted to make sure that this was a murder case, both to stir up the police investigation and to see Purseglove swing for it. Simple, really. Whichever way it turned out, whether we thought Isobel died from

151

her injuries or whether we found out there'd been a second attempt to kill her, she hoped to see young Purseglove hang for it. Might have worked, too,' he added thoughtfully. 'Naturally, nobody'd expect that the girl's own devoted sister – or mother – would kill her like that.'

'And just to get a fellow creature hanged, too,' said Mr Bonnington. 'Dreadful, quite dreadful! Oh well, Inspector, I suppose you'll want to get off now. You must have a lot to do. I'll stay and lock the house up.'

'No, that's all right, thank you, sir,' said Dover with a tremendous yawn. 'I want to have a look round here first. Case isn't closed yet, you know. We'll see everything's left safe and secure before we go. But there's no need for us to detain you, sir. I don't mind saying I was very glad you were here, but it's all over now. There's nothing more you can do for her tonight.'

With some reluctance and repeated offers of help, Mr Bonnington finally took his leave. When the front door had at last closed behind him, Dover got to his feet.

'Well, the first thing you can do, Sergeant,' he announced, 'is get into that kitchen and make us both a cup of tea! I don't know about you, lad, but I could damned well do with one.'

MacGregor fumbled around in the kitchen and finally produced a pot of tea with an air which stated quite firmly that this was not the kind of chore which a detective sergeant should be asked to undertake. He was not entirely displeased when Dover commented unfavourably on the thin, straw-coloured liquid which came dribbling out of the pot.

'What are we going to do now, sir?' asked MacGregor.

'Well, technically,' said Dover, 'we've found the murderer, and I suppose that's all we were expected to do. Still, I think we'll stretch our brief a bit. I'm damned if I'm going back without clapping the bracelets on the chap who was really responsible for that girl's death. I don't suppose they'll be able to pin anything more than attempted murder on him, but I'll have him behind bars for that if it's the last thing I do!'

MacGregor glanced curiously at Dover. He'd never seen the chief inspector in what you might call a crusading mood before. Catching criminals was just a job he was paid to do. But on this occasion he seemed to have been touched by the tragedy of Violet Slatcher, who had felt herself forced to kill her own daughter in order that the real criminal should not slip away scot free.

'Do you think Miss Slatcher was right, sir? I mean, did Rex Purseglove do the shooting outside St Benedict's – in spite of everything?'

'Dunno,' said Dover grumpily. 'I suppose we'll have to go through the whole damned thing again from the beginning – now that we don't have to bother about what happened in the hospital any more. Still, I don't see how Rex Purseglove can have done it, even so. Anyhow, there's not much more we can do tonight. We'll have a look round here and see if there's anything that'll give us a clue. There might be something in Isobel's past life that we haven't cottoned on to yet.'

'Hm,' said MacGregor doubtfully, 'but she's not likely to have been able to keep much secret from Violet, is she, sir? I mean, if it was anything serious enough to lead to murder, surely the older woman would have found out about it, and she'd have been able to put two and two together, same as us. She wouldn't have picked on Rex Purseglove so firmly if there'd been another candidate in the field.'

'Violet Slatcher may have *thought* she knew everything about her daughter's life,' Dover pointed out wisely, 'but that doesn't mean that she actually did. When you've had a bit more experience, my lad, you'll realize that there's nobody to equal nicely brought up young ladies when it comes to living double lives. You get it all the time with these disappearing cases. Sixteen-year-old Mabel disappears one day and Mum tells the police, in all good faith mind you, that her daughter's never had a boy friend in her life. And what do you find? Nine times out of ten she's hopped it with the local butcher who she's been having an affair with for the last two years. Parents don't know everything about their kids, not even when they think they do.'

When the two detectives had finished their tea and Dover had polished off a large piece of slab cake which he'd found in a tin – as he said, there was no point in letting it go mouldy – they set about their work.

The Slatcher household didn't appear to have been a wildly exciting one. Nobody had kept a diary or bundles of old love letters – or, indeed, any letters at all. MacGregor found a box of old receipts which went back about fifteen years and he unearthed the bank accounts of both women. Their expenses appeared to be highly reasonable in view of their income, and neither of them was overdrawn at the bank. The family photograph album came to an abrupt halt when Isobel was about ten – 'Probably lost the flaming camera!' commented Dover grumpily.

They moved into Isobel's bedroom, which Dover had half unconsciously been saving to the last, as a treat. If they were going to find anything it would surely be here. At the sight of the small, bleakly furnished room, his heart sank. He directed MacGregor to have a look through the chest of drawers and the wardrobe while he tackled the only remaining piece of furniture, apart from the narrow bed and an upright chair. With a grunt he sank on his knees by the small bookcase and peered at the books.

'Well, well,' he said, 'she may have been a staunch Protestant, but her reading was what you might call Catholic!' He squinted up at MacGregor to see if this witticism had been appreciated. It hadn't. Dover sighed crossly. 'Come and look at this lot, MacGregor! Some old children's books, and not a mark on 'em, about half a dozen prayer books and four Bibles. Then we've got all these pious books – dear lord, the things people spend their money on! But take a shufty at this lot. Oh dear me! *Married Love* cheek by jowl with *The Sexual Behaviour of the Human Male* – and well thumbed too. She wasn't going to be caught napping on her wedding night, was she?'

He pulled himself to his feet. 'Look through all that lot, MàcGregor, just in case she's slipped a letter or something in one of 'em.' He sat down on the bed with a sigh. 'Then I think we might as well be getting back to the hotel. We aren't going to find anything here.'

But they were luckier than they had expected, or than Dover had any right to be. In one of the Bibles MacGregor did find a letter. Dover grabbed it before the sergeant had a chance to read it. After all it had been Dover's idea to search through the books and he'd got the right to first look at whatever was found.

The letter was written on a single sheet of cheap note-paper. There was no address and the date, 'Jan. 10', gave no indication of the year. The handwriting was rather sprawling and none too easy to read.

Dear Vic,

I expect you will be surprised to hear from me after all these years but blood is thicker than water and I have nobody else to turn to. They have tracked me down at last and now they have got me. I expect you have read about it in the papers. You probably think I deserve all I have got coming to me but you can't forget that however much has come between us, you are still my brother. I need money and I need it desperately. I know you are not a rich man but you

155

must have some put away or be able to borrow some. What's the good of being respectable if you can't do that?

I would like to see you again but I realize this may be asking too much. Do try and send me the money, as much as you can. If I ever get out of this mess I swear to you I will go away abroad somewhere and you will never hear of me again. This is a matter of life and death.

Yours with love

Dover puzzled for a minute over the signature. 'What do you think this is, MacGregor? Cuth?'

'Looks more like Cath to me, sir.'

Dover wrinkled his nose. 'Yes, it does, doesn't it?' He frowned. 'A woman? Well, I suppose there's no reason why not.'

'Do you think it's important, sir?'

'Well, it's odd, isn't it? It's the only thing we've found that's in any way out of the ordinary. Why should Isobel Slatcher be hiding a letter like this, written to a man called Vic?'

'Perhaps she found it in one of the books at the library?'

'In that case, why preserve it so carefully in her Bible?'

'Some people are like squirrels. They'll hoard anything.'

Dover shook his head. 'Not the Slatcher women!' he said firmly. 'They don't keep bits and pieces of rubbish just for the sake of keeping them. You've seen that for yourself, MacGregor. Nothing's wasted in this house, but there's no old junk lying around either.' He scratched his head. 'No, if Isobel had found this letter somewhere and kept it to make paper spills or hair-curlers with I could understand it. But she didn't. She kept it, presumably where Violet wouldn't find it, as a letter. It must mean something.'

'Perhaps she just slipped it absent-mindedly in her Bible – you know how you do, sir – and forgot about it.'

'No.' Dover shook his head again. 'Look, she's got four Bibles. This one's a school prize. Look at the condition it's in. She's never used this one – why the thing's hardly ever been opened.' He cracked back the pages to prove his point. 'No, she put it in here deliberately. She hid it here. Point is, why? It's not her letter, that's for sure.'

MacGregor examined it again. 'Pity the signature's so badly written. Cath? Cuth? Leith, perhaps? Ceith? Will? Drat it, it might be anything.'

Dover peered at it himself. He really needed reading glasses, but preferred to think that people were using smaller print these days. 'Could be Cath,' he said gloomily. 'That'd be a woman, I suppose. Oh well,' he sighed crossly, 'I reckon a woman could have written it. Be just like a woman,' he snorted, 'to leave the year out of the date. Thing might have been written twenty years ago, damn it!'

'We can get the lab boys to check on that, sir. They'll probably be able to tell us whether it was written by a man or a woman.'

Dover sighed again and handed the letter back to Mac-Gregor. 'All right, get 'em to run a check on it.'

'Finger-prints?'

'Might as well. Though Gawd knows what good it'll do. We might try asking Violet Slatcher about it tomorrow. If she's not gone completely round the twist she might know something about it, though I doubt it. I wish we'd got the envelope.'

Dover sat sullenly on the bed while MacGregor had another hunt around to see if he could find anything else. He couldn't.

The two men returned to the Station Hotel and Dover permitted his sergeant to buy him a celebratory drink. After all, Dover had solved a murder case.

CHAPTER ELEVEN

WHEN DOVER came down to breakfast the next morning he had the unusual pleasure of finding himself a minor celebrity. News travels fast in Curdley and the word had flashed around that that fat old blighter from London had, against all the betting, actually solved the murder of Isobel Slatcher. The Protestants basked in the reflected glory of one of their co-religionists (C. of E. supporters played down the hero's Methodism) and the Catholics were delighted that the heinous crime had not been committed by one of them. It was, they pointed out smugly, only likely that a heretic would be guilty of killing her own child.

As Dover passed through the hall there was a flattering murmur as people knowingly pointed him out to their friends. The receptionist coyly asked him to autograph last night's menu and then, oh joy of joys, the Press burst in, excitedly demanding the inside story and would Chief Inspector Dover, sir, mind handing the menu back to the receptionist again while they took a picture. Dover smirked and obliged, only too willingly. He'd like to see Smartie Alec Roderick's face when he got an eyeful of this in his morning paper!

It was highly unlikely, though, that Superintendent Roderick subscribed to the *Curdley and District Custodian*. And, however much professional bustle and verve Ralph Gostage and his part-time photographer/wedding reporter put into it, there was no disguising the fact that the *Custodian* was the only organ of the Press anxious to photograph and interview the great man.

But Dover played his part to perfection. It might have been an everyday occurrence as far as he was concerned.

In curt, manly monosyllables he acknowledged the Press's congratulations on the successful outcome of his investigations and modestly attributed his latest triumph (like all his others) to 'hard work'. Sphinx-faced but eagle-eyed, he regretted that he could not divulge further details at this stage. And, yes, he intended to pursue resolutely and without fear or favour the dastardly perpetrator of the original cowardly attack on Curdley's Sleeping Beauty. No, he would not be attending the funeral, adding, meaningfully, that he would be otherwise engaged. The Press were delighted at such generous co-operation. Dover posed for another photograph, chins up and stomach in. It is impossible to guess how long all this would have gone on if Dover hadn't spotted MacGregor pushing his way through the admiring throng of guests and staff. That did it! Dover was the last one to share the limelight with anybody, never mind his own sergeant. Pausing only to request three dozen free copies of that week's *Custodian*, he bustled Mr Gostage rapidly out of the hotel before he could get a glimpse of the highly photogenic Charles Edward.

MacGregor came panting up, pink with excitement. 'Sir,' he began.

Dover held up a lordly hand and glanced significantly at the gaping crowd, happily prepared to drink in every confidential word.

'Not here, Sergeant!' said Dover, doing his Sherlock Holmes act. 'Walls have ears.'

Luckily breakfast tables have not, and once Dover had got a double helping of bacon and eggs (a modest tribute from the cook) in front of him, MacGregor was permitted to speak.

'That letter, sir,' said MacGregor, dropping his voice to a whisper just to be on the safe side. 'You remember, the one we found last night?'

'Yes, I remember, laddie,' Dover spoke absent-mindedly. He was wondering whether he ought to start smoking a

159

pipe, or taking snuff. The public liked that sort of thing and one had to think of one's image, didn't one? A pipe, perhaps? He frowned doubtfully. With his dentures? Some of MacGregor's words filtered through. Dover switched smartly back to reality.

'What's that?' he snarled.

'I think I've solved the letter, sir,' hissed MacGregor.

'For God's sake, speak up, Sergeant! Lost your flaming voice or something?'

'No, sir,' said MacGregor, reverting to his normal tone.

'Well, what's all this about the letter?'

'I was thinking about it last night, sir, and trying to puzzle out the signature when, all at once, it hit me!'

Dover gave a disparaging sniff.

'It just came to me in a flash, sir. The signature – it's Cuth.'

Dover shovelled a forkful of egg rather unsuccessfully into his mouth. 'So what?'

'Cuth – that's short for Cuthbert, isn't it?'

'Probably,' said Dover, anxious not to commit himself too far.

'Well, if it is Cuthbert, can't you see what that means, sir?'

'No!' snapped Dover. 'I can't. For God's sake, get on with it, man!'

'Cuthbert! Cuthbert Boys, sir!'

Dover munched his bacon. 'Who's he?'

MacGregor's jaw tightened and silently, to himself, he said the same rude word ten times. Somehow, it helped.

'Cuthbert Boys, sir! Bigamous Bertie! The chap Superintendent Roderick caught!'

'Oh!' Dover scowled horribly. 'Him! Well, what's he got to do with it? Pour me out another cuppa, will you?'

MacGregor picked up the teapot, wondered for a moment

if he dared, decided he didn't and meekly filled his chief inspector's cup.

'I think, sir,' he said, watching Dover spoon the sugar in, 'that the letter we found in Isobel Slatcher's Bible might have been written by Cuthbert Boys. As far as I can remember the date would fit in all right. Bigamous Bertie was run to earth some time after Christmas last year. This letter's dated the tenth of January and I reckon that might be just about when Bertie was arrested. Now, Super Percy's just run him in, on a capital murder charge too. Bertie must have been feeling pretty low. He can't have had any friends or anybody he could turn to for help – not after the kind of life he'd been living. So, what does he do? He turns to his family and writes to the brother he's not seen for donkey's years.'

Dover reached for the last piece of toast. 'Hey, wait a minute,' he said, always ready to pick holes in other people's theories. 'How do you know the letter was written to a man? It might have been sent to a woman.'

'No.' MacGregor shook his head firmly and produced the letter which he had carefully sealed in a transparent envelope. 'Look, it says here, "But you can't forget that however much has come between us, you're still my brother." The letter was written to a man all right. Cuthbert Boys's brother.'

Dover screwed up his nose and read the letter through again. 'Well,' he observed grudgingly, 'I suppose it might fit – if the signature is Cuth and if the date's right. But, I dunno, it might fit dozens of things, mightn't it? No, I think it's a bit thin, MacGregor, it's a bit too far fetched.'

'But we could check it, couldn't we, sir?'

'How do you mean?'

'Well, surely the lab could find out for us how old the letter is. They can check the ink, can't they? They should be able to give us some idea how old the ink is at the very least. And we can check the handwriting too, can't we? There must be some specimens of Bertie's handwriting somewhere. And the date – we can easily find out whether Bertie would be likely to have written a letter asking for help in January this year. It's my guess he wanted the money to pay for his defence, probably didn't realize the newspapers'd see to all that in return for his life story.'

'All right,' said Dover. 'But what's it going to prove, even if Bertie did write it?'

'Don't you see, sir? It could be a motive for Isobel Slatcher's murder.'

'Motive for murder?'

'Yes, sir. Suppose Isobel found this letter somewhere – in a returned library book, perhaps. She puts two and two together, like I did, and realizes that it was written by Cuthbert Boys to his brother. The brother of Cuthbert Boys is somebody here in Curdley. Suppose she knew who the letter was written to? Suppose she tried a bit of the old blackmail? The victim gets fed up with it and shoots her.'

''Strewth!' observed Dover contemptuously. 'You're letting your imagination run riot a bit, aren't you? Isobel Slatcher a blackmailer? Blimey, that's coming it a bit strong, isn't it? There hasn't been a hint of blackmail anywhere, and you damned well know it. Oh no, this is building a bit too much on a signature we can't blooming well even read!'

MacGregor was disappointed. 'But, if we don't follow this letter up, sir,' he asked pointedly, 'what are we going to do next?'

It was a good question. Dover scowled. He hadn't the least idea. He took a large mouthful of hot tea and thought deeply. Young detective sergeants were, in his considered opinion, the lowest form of police life, and he spent long hours complaining happily about their shortcomings and inadequacies. But, however scathing he might be about the present generation of young detectives, the last thing he wanted was to have a really bright one working for him. That would be murder!

Detective sergeants should be seen rarely, and heard never at all. They should be humble and admiring witnesses of the brilliant feats of detection carried out by their superiors. Any contributions which they felt it incumbent on them to make should be proffered modestly and hesitantly. They shouldn't, thought Dover, twitching his nose crossly, discover something which, right out of the blue, might solve the whole bloody case. It put Dover in such a dilemma. If he followed up MacGregor's line of thought and it turned out, oh horror of horrors, to be right, it would be very difficult (though not impossible) to deny his sergeant at least a share in the glory. And on the rare occasions that Dover actually managed to bring one of his cases to a successful conclusion he liked the limelight to play exclusively on him.

On the other hand, if he refused to have anything to do with his sergeant's latest bright idea what, as MacGregor had so pertinently asked, the hell were they going to do next. It was all very annoying.

Dover's underlip stuck out unhappily and he pushed his tea-cup forward again for a refill. It really was very difficult. Still, he sighed pathetically, these things were sent to try us. With a bit of luck he might still be able to pick MacGregor's brains while retaining the lion's share of the credit, if any, for himself. He had, after all, frequently done it before. He reached for the sugar.

'All right,' he said, 'we'll follow up this letter. Remember I told you last night it was significant, key to the whole case, I reckon. In fact I can't think why you haven't sent it to the lab already. Now then, I've got to go and see the Chief Constable this morning about Violet Slatcher, so you can get on with the routine stuff. Get them to try and establish how old that letter is – they ought to be able to tell us if it was written less than a year ago. And get it checked for finger-prints. It should have Isobel Slatcher's on it, and Bigamous Bertie's, if he wrote it, and a third set – the brother's. Check whether we've got any record of those in the files. If Bertie's brother's anything like Bertie was he should have passed through our hands at some stage or another.'

'OK, sir,' said MacGregor.

'Then get on to London and find out exactly when Bertie was taken into custody. See if anyone can remember whether he wrote a letter shortly after his arrest. And get a photostat copy of our letter down immediately for a comparison of the handwriting.'

'OK, sir,' said MacGregor again, happily making notes in his notebook as Dover fed his own suggestions back to him.

'Then you'd better start checking on all the people called Boys in Curdley and' – Dover was a great one for piling the work on to other people – 'the surrounding districts. You can get the local police to give you a hand there,' he added generously. 'You might as well get them started on that right away. It'll save time.'

'I could have a word with Superintendent Roderick too, sir,' suggested MacGregor. 'He got quite chummy with Bertie. He might know whether he had any relations in this part of the world.'

'He might,' sniffed Dover.

'Anything else, sir?'

Dover looked at the letter again. 'The chap it's written to looks as though he's called Vic. I suppose that's short for Victor. Might narrow the field down a bit when you're checking on the Boys clan. Victor Boys – shouldn't be too difficult to find.'

MacGregor rushed eagerly away, delighted to be able to pursue his own line of investigation and delighted not to have Dover breathing down his neck all the time. The chief inspector took his time and eventually strolled into the Chief Constable's office to receive the sincere congratulations which awaited him there. It was all most satisfactory. Colonel Muckle took him out to lunch at his club and introduced him to all the leading Catholic dignitaries of the town. They were flatteringly generous with their praise and hospitality.

It was nearly three o'clock when Dover got back to his hotel room, his cheeks flushed with victory and alcohol. With his boots still on – he didn't quite feel up to the bending down required to take them off – he flopped happily on top of the eiderdown and sank into a blissful sleep.

At seven o'clock MacGregor, dog-tired after a hectic day, came in to wake him up. At first Dover didn't feel too good. He hadn't exactly got a hangover and he hadn't exactly got indigestion, but he felt like somebody who had eaten and drunk far too much in the middle of the day and had then tried to sleep it off in the afternoon. He washed his face grumpily, peering into the mirror with bloodshot eyes. He stuck his tongue out, winced, and hastily withdrew it back into his mouth.

MacGregor took him down to the bar and after he'd sunk half of his first pint of beer the chief inspector felt strong enough to listen to his sergeant's account of his day's work. It was, like the curate's egg, good in parts.

'We were right about the letter at any rate, sir,' began MacGregor, sensibly associating Dover with the original idea.

Dover nodded wisely. 'Ah yes,' he said complacently, 'I thought I was on the right lines there. Bigamous Bertie did write it then, did he?'

'Yes, sir. The boys in the lab up here checked the ink and paper and they were pretty definite that it was written in January this year. They said it couldn't possibly be more than a year old. I got on to London then but, unfortunately, Superintendent Roderick is away on leave, so I couldn't speak to him, but I think I've managed to clear most of the points up. Bertie was arrested on the ninth of

January all right, though I couldn't find anybody who remembered whether he'd written any letters or not. Pity they don't keep a record because that might have given us the brother's address. Anyhow, I got a photograph of the letter wired to London and the experts down there are pretty certain Bertie wrote it. Of course they can't be a hundred per cent sure till they've seen the original but, assuming it's not a deliberate forgery, they're pretty confident Bertie wrote it.'

'Umph,' said Dover, 'and what about the finger-prints?'

'Not much good, I'm afraid, sir. There were several belonging to Isobel Slatcher – incidentally, sir, it's a good thing they've not buried her yet. You see, she's not touched anything for eight months, with her being unconscious, and I think we'd have had quite a job finding any of her dabs in her room even. Violet's kept it quite clean and tidy and she's probably wiped off most of the prints on the furniture and things.'

'But there must have been other prints besides hers on the letter?'

'Well, there are traces of other prints, sir, but they're too blurred and indistinct to be any good. We couldn't even identify Bertie's positively.'

'Blast it!' said Dover. 'Well, go on.'

'That's about all as far as the letter's concerned, sir. Bigamous Bertie definitely wrote it, presumably from the police station the day after he was arrested, but we aren't any nearer as to who he wrote it to. I've got people in London still checking as to whether he ever mentioned having a brother, but it's a bit of a job trying to track his contacts down after all this time. However, neither his solicitor nor the barrister who defended him ever remember him talking about his family, and the newspaper reporter who ghosted his life story says that Bertie wouldn't even reveal where he was born, or even exactly when. They did

166

think of searching the records at Somerset House but decided it wasn't worth it. There might have been complaints to the Press Council if they'd started trying to drag Bertie's family into it. I suppose we could do that ourselves – try Somerset House, I mean – but, of course, even if we found a brother it wouldn't tell us where he is now. However, we may have to resort to that to get a lead because, so far, we've drawn a complete blank up here.'

'Have you checked all the people called Boys?'

'We've checked 'em all, sir,' said MacGregor sadly. 'It isn't a very common name so luckily there weren't all that many of them, but as far as we can tell there isn't one who fits the bill.'

'Were any of them called Victor?'

'Two, sir. One was a little boy of about seven and the other was a sailor. He's been at sea for the last eighteen months according to his mother. South Pacific or somewhere. I'm having his exact whereabouts checked with the shipping line he works for, but I don't think he's our man.'

'Hm,' said Dover.

'I'm afraid we've come to a bit of a dead end, sir.'

'Hm!' said Dover again. 'What about the other Boys? The ones who weren't called Victor? Did any of them look a likely candidate? Vic might just have been a nickname, you know, though I must admit it doesn't sound a very likely one.'

'There wasn't anybody who seemed to fit the bill, sir.'

Dover frowned. 'I wonder,' he said thoughtfully, 'if Bigamous Bertie changed his name at any stage.'

'Well, he used a lot of aliases, sir. He got married under half a dozen different names, if I remember correctly. But he was tried as Cuthbert Boys so I presume that was his real name. I don't know how far they check on these things.'

'I wasn't thinking of him just assuming another alias,' said Dover, 'I was wondering if he'd changed his name properly, by deed poll. He seemed to have had a fairly decent background, didn't he? And he was quite concerned about keeping his family out of the limelight. It's just possible that early on in his career of crime he changed his name to keep his family out of the newspapers. See what I mean? We're looking for Cuthbert Boys's brother up here, but he may not be called Boys.'

MacGregor nodded his head. 'Yes, I see what you mean, sir. I'll go and phone the Yard and see if I can check it.'

'Yes, you do that.' Dover slid heavily off his stool. 'I'll go on in and have my dinner. You can join me when you've got through.'

MacGregor phoned the Yard and was promised an answer as soon as possible. By half past eight he got it. It was pretty definite that Cuthbert Boys had not changed his surname. Further checks would be made in the morning but Boys's name had been carefully checked when the police finally got their hands on him and it was not thought that something so obvious as a legal change of name had been overlooked.

Dover grunted crossly and looked as though he was on the point of blaming MacGregor for this setback. Gloomily the two men got on with their meal.

'Perhaps,' said MacGregor after a bit, 'instead of Cuthbert Boys changing his name, it was the family that did it. That'd be more logical, wouldn't it, sir? I mean, Bertie started going off the straight and narrow pretty early on in life. The family might well have wanted to dissociate themselves from him and so they were the ones to do the name changing.'

Dover scowled. 'I'd already thought of that!' he snapped. This was a barefaced lie but the chief inspector was getting a bit fed up with MacGregor. It was all right for him to come up with one bright idea, but Dover didn't want the thing to start becoming a habit. It was, after all, *his* case and he'd solve it or not in his own sweet way. MacGregor could flaming well keep his nose out of things which didn't concern him. Young Charles Edward was in danger of getting too big for his boots, but Dover was just the man to cut him down to a more amenable size.

'It's perfectly obvious,' he went on, wiping the strawberry ice-cream off his moustache, 'that if Bertie didn't change his name, the rest of the family might have changed theirs. Any fool could see that! But where does it leave us? We'd have to check every blessed man in Curdley and see whether at any time he'd ever changed his name from Boys. And it needn't necessarily be a local man, come to that. Might just have been somebody staying temporarily in the town round about January and February this year. 'Strewth! It'd be an impossible task!'

'Couldn't we check at Somerset House, sir, and try it from that end? We could find out if anybody had ever changed their name from Boys. There shouldn't be all that many of 'em.'

'But we don't know that the change-over was a legal one. It's no crime just to call yourself by another name, is it? You don't have to go through all that legal fuss and palaver if you don't want to.'

Dover helped himself to a large piece of cheese.

'Anyhow,' he went on, anxious to get it in before Mac-Gregor thought of it, 'we've still got a bit of a lead to follow up. If our chap's changed his surname it's quite possible that he's kept the same Christian name. People often do.'

MacGregor's heart sank. Was Dover going to expect him to check all the men in Curdley called Victor? It would take years! He opened his mouth to suggest, deferentially of course, that this was going to be rather a big job but once again Dover forestalled him. There was a splutter of crumbs as the chief inspector spoke through a mouthful of water biscuit.

169

'Luckily,' he said indistinctly, 'we've already come across a fellow called Victor.' He squinted at MacGregor to see if Scotland Yard's white hope had thought of that one. Most satisfactory. Judging by the puzzled look on his face, he hadn't. Mentally Dover chalked up a small victory to himself.

'Really, sir?' said MacGregor, frowning in an effort to remember. 'Who was that?'

There was a small snag here because Dover, whose memory was by no means phenomenally good, was blowed if he could remember. He had a vague idea that the name Victor had cropped up somewhere but where, precisely, still eluded him.

'My God, MacGregor,' he sniffed pompously, 'you'll really have to pull your socks up, you know, if you want to get on in this game. A good detective should take note of everything, every tiny detail no matter how insignificant it may seem at the time. He's got to store it all away in his brain, just in case it may come in useful later on. I've warned you about this before. You're still learning the job, you know. You've got a wonderful chance, working with me on these cases. You ought to be studying how I tackle a case and then when you get one of your own, if you ever do, you'll know how to set about it. I'm doing the best I can to give you a good training and show you how to deal with an important investigation, but you've got to show a bit of initiative and know-how yourself, haven't you? I shan't always be here to hold your hand and spell every-thing out for you, shall I?'

'I see what you mean, sir,' said MacGregor politely, 'But which one of the people we've seen *is* Victor?'

'You get your notebook out,' snarled Dover, 'and bloody well find out for yourself! You got all the statements signed, didn't you?'

'The statements?' MacGregor laughed ruefully. 'Of

170

course, sir, I remember now! His middle name was Victor, wasn't it? Fancy you spotting that, sir. Funny, isn't it? Once you've got it, you can't imagine how you ever overlooked it in the first place.'

Dover's face took on a more petulant look than usual. This was a fine state of affairs. Now MacGregor knew who Victor was and he didn't. Luckily Dover was spared the humiliation of actually having to ask as MacGregor supplied the answer.

'Antony Victor Ofield, F.L.A.! Signed with a flourish in jet-black ink!'

'Precisely!' agreed Dover, just as though he'd known all along. 'I was wondering how long it would take you to spot him.'

'Do you think he's a likely candidate, sir?'

'Why not? He and Isobel were working together in that library. She might well have been in a position to get her hands on his private correspondence. If she'd just found that letter in a returned library book, she might not have known who it belonged to. But if it was Ofield's, well, she'd be sitting pretty, wouldn't she?'

'And she may not have been blackmailing him for money, either, sir,' contributed MacGregor, who was beginning to get quite excited about the possibilities. 'We know she was dead keen on getting married and she'd been on pretty friendly terms with Ofield. He meets this Austrian girl and starts cooling off, so Isobel says, either you lead me to the altar, Antony Victor, or I'll tell the world that your brother is the notorious Cuthbert Boys, that well-known bigamist and multiple murderer!'

'But in that case,' objected Dover, 'why was she trying to ruin him if she'd got hopes of marrying him herself?'

'Ah, but we don't know for certain that it was Isobel who was stirring up all the trouble, do we, sir? That was only Ofield's guess. Or maybe it was just her way of letting him

171

know she wasn't kidding. You know – just giving him a foretaste of what she was prepared to do if he didn't come across.'

'Yes,' said Dover, 'you may have got something there. Anyhow, it's not all that important. What does matter is that we can tie up Ofield with that gun. He was at the Men's Bible Class when Freddie Gash and the Pie Gang raided the church hall. Ofield could have found that gun and kept it, just as well as anybody else. Then, the night Isobel was shot, he was right there on the spot. He'd know all about her visiting the vicarage every Saturday night, and how long she stayed, and which way she'd be likely to go home. He could have slipped out of the church, waited for her and shot her, and then popped back to his organ playing. My God, it's as easy as falling off a chair. He's an intelligent chap, too. He'd probably realize right from the start that Isobel was never going to recover, so he goes ahead and marries this foreign bit of fluff. He waits a bit, hanging on here in Curdley, until he thinks things have quietened down, and then he calmly applies for a job somewhere else. That's quite smart, you know. It might have looked suspicious if he cleared out right after Isobel was shot – but this way it looks all innocent and natural like.'

'He's quite a possibility, isn't he, sir?'

'Possibility!' snorted Dover. 'He's a dead bloody cert! I didn't like the look of him the first time I clapped eyes on him, but he didn't seem to have all that much in the way of a motive, but now, well, now it's a horse of a different colour! What time is it?'

There was a clock right opposite him on the dining-room wall but Dover didn't believe in keeping a dog and barking himself.

'Just gone nine, sir.'

'Right! Well, we'll just have our coffee and a cigarette

172

and then we'll go and see our friend, Mr Ofield. With a bit of luck we can get him under lock and key tonight.'

MacGregor was uncomfortably aware that all this had happened before. He tried to preach a bit of caution. 'Don't you think we'd do better to wait until morning, sir? After all, the Yard's still looking into this Cuthbert Boys side of things. They may turn up something by morning which will change the whole picture.' He looked unhappily at the chief inspector. 'We've really not much to go on, sir, have we? It looks pretty certain that the letter in Isobel Slatcher's Bible was written by Bigamous Bertie, but it's only speculation that she was using it to blackmail anybody. She may never have made any use of it at all. And we're only guessing, really, aren't we, sir? We don't know that Bertie's brother is actually here in Curdley. And we're guessing still more, on very slim evidence, that if Bertie's brother is in Curdley, he's actually Mr Ofield.'

MacGregor shot a wary glance at Dover and was not reassured by that lowering brow and pouting bottom lip. He pressed on, however. Somebody had to stop the blundering old idiot from making a bigger fool of himself, and the police, than usual.

'And even if we're right all along the line, sir, and Ofield is Bertie's brother and the letter was written to him, we can't really jump straight from that to arresting Ofield for the attempted murder of Isobel Slatcher' - there was one final, hopeless appeal - 'can we, sir?'

It was the voice of reason. Dover unhesitatingly turned a deaf ear to it.

'What the hell's the matter with you, MacGregor?' he demanded pugnaciously. 'You're the biggest bloody wet blanket it's ever been my misfortune to meet! I can't for the life of me see what the devil you're jibbing about. If Ofield didn't shoot Isobel Slatcher, I'd like to know who the hell you think did! I know that, so far, the evidence is

173

all based on deduction but, damn it all, it's logical deduction! Once we face Ofield with the facts he'll crack like one of those eggs with little lions on it. He'll give himself away somehow, you'll see.' Dover flapped a negligent hand. 'Anyhow, I've got a feeling in my bones that he's our man. It's a matter of instinct, and it's never let me down yet!'

'Are you going to get a warrant for him, sir?'

Dover thought for a moment. 'No,' he said warily, 'I don't think there's any need for a warrant at this stage. We'll just go along and question him – see what happens. Play it off the cuff, you know. He looks a bit of a cissy to me. I reckon if we push him around a bit, we'll get the truth out of him.'

'He's no fool, sir,' warned MacGregor, looking with a shudder at Dover's massive fists. 'He's probably got a pretty good idea of his rights as a citizen, and of yours as a police officer.'

'Oh, I shan't hurt him,' retorted Dover blithely. 'I know how far I can go, don't you worry. And we've got to do something, haven't we? If we don't get cracking we'll be up here for the bloody winter! I don't know about you, my lad, but I want to get back to London and my own bed as soon as possible. I've had enough of this dump!'

CHAPTER TWELVE

IT WAS nearly ten o'clock when Dover rammed a fat index finger into Mr Ofield's front-door bell and held it there. He was bitterly indignant that the only result was the strangled tinkling of some blasted chimes, instead of the long, menacing buzz that he had every right to expect. He

174

had just raised his fist to beat on the door panel when the door opened and Mr Ofield peered out into the darkness.

Mr Ofield was not overjoyed to see his visitors and seemed reluctant to let them into his home at such a late hour, but Dover had a specially trained right boot to deal with such contingencies. Almost before he knew what was happening Mr Ofield had two large, broad-shouldered detectives overcrowding his hall. From behind a closed door came the strains of a very erudite piece of chamber music. Dover sneered gently. He liked something with a bit of tune to it himself.

'Perhaps we'd better go in here,' suggested Mr Ofield, opening another door and switching the light on, 'I don't want to disturb my wife.'

The room was chilly and uninviting. The walls and paintwork were a bleak, dead white, relieved only by a striking example of modern art which appeared to portray a nude woman in what Dover could only call a compromising situation. Had it not been for the rather sophisticated subject matter, comparisons with the work of backward four-year-old children would inevitably have arisen in Dover's somewhat traditional mind.

Dover and MacGregor were just trying to work out how you were supposed to sit in a couple of ultra-modern chairs while Mr Ofield moved across to draw the curtains over the black, blank slabs of window, when the door opened again and a woman came in.

MacGregor stared and repressed an incipient wolf whistle as being unworthy of a Scotland Yard detective on duty, though the object of his admiration certainly merited a tribute of some sort. Even Dover, not particularly susceptible to feminine charm, blinked. Trudi Ofield was what he classified as a hot bit of stuff, and no mistake. He couldn't help shooting a somewhat bewildered glance at her husband. There must be more about Curdley's head

175

librarian than he had given him credit for. No wonder Isobel Slatcher had been tossed aside like an old glove. If this was the competition, she just wasn't in the same class, not by a long chalk.

Mrs Ofield smiled shyly, but with devastating charm at her husband's guests. 'Tony, darling,' she said with a delightful Austrian accent which made the most trivial comment tingle with an almost sad, romantic undertone, 'why don't you bring these gentlemen into the other room? It is so much warmer there and more comfortable.'

'They're only staying for a couple of minutes, Liebchen,' said Ofield, 'it's not worth disturbing you.'

Dover, however, was already on his way to the door. 'Thank you very much, madam,' he said. 'I think we may be here rather longer than your husband anticipates, so we might as well make ourselves at home, mightn't we?'

A few moments later Dover was snugly installed in Mr Ofield's armchair next to a roaring fire. The record-player had been switched off and Dover had been offered – a rather unexpected touch of hospitality in Curdley – a glass of wine and, since this was apparently all he was likely to get, had accepted it. This room, too, was extremely modern in its furnishings, but Dover's attention was caught not by the examples of peasant pottery carefully placed here and there, nor by the futuristic lamp standard peering aggressively over his left shoulder, nor by the broad green leaves of some twenty potted plants which were banked up against one scarlet papered wall. He stared expressionlessly at a row of silver cups and plaques which filled two long shelves.

Trudi Ofield who had curled up, kitten-like, on the settee saw the direction of his eyes.

'Those are Tony's,' she said, revealing small, even white teeth as she smiled. 'He won them, but I have to clean them.'

MacGregor grinned besottedly. Mrs Ofield really was a honey. What a voice, what a face, what a figure! Wow!

Dover, however, was long past the stage when a pretty woman could absorb the whole of his attention. He turned, unsmiling, to Mr Ofield.

'So they're your trophies, are they, sir? May I ask what you won them for?'

Mr Ofield turned a bright red. 'Pistol shooting,' he muttered unwillingly.

Dover's eyebrows rose. 'Pistol shooting?' he repeated thoughtfully, and looked at the cups again. 'You must be quite a crack shot.'

'I've given it up now,' said Mr Ofield hastily. 'I don't seem to have the time to spare any more.' He smiled intimately into his wife's large brown eyes. MacGregor felt like kicking him. What a bloody waste!

Dover said nothing. He just sat, a mean-looking mass of a man, slumped in his chair. He wasn't quite sure how to begin.

Mr Ofield was no fool. He saw that Dover was trying to get him to open the interview and he was determined not to oblige. The silence grew longer and longer. Mrs Ofield seemed rather bewildered, but since she was far from certain exactly what was going on she didn't want to make a *faux pas* by breaking the ice herself with some conventional remark about the weather. MacGregor was quite content to sit gawping at Mrs Ofield, and in any case he knew better than to open his mouth when his chief inspector was interrogating a prime suspect. Dover himself was quite happy. The chair was comfortable, the room warm, and this wine stuff didn't taste at all bad once you got used to it. He closed his eyes gently just for a moment, to rest them.

Mr Ofield acknowledged defeat. Against a police inspector who was prepared to drop off to sleep when he was supposed to be investigating a murder case, a mere head librarian didn't stand a chance.

'Er, had you got some more questions you wanted to ask me, Inspector?'

Dover opened his eyes reluctantly, and scowled.

'That's right, sir,' he said. 'I'm not entirely satisfied with the story you gave me yesterday. As you've probably heard, there have been considerable developments since then and we've received a great deal of fresh information.'

Dover's eyelids drooped down again and he seemed to have lost all interest in what he was saying.

'Well,' said Mr Ofield sharply, not wishing to have Dover sitting in his chair all night, 'I did hear that Violet Slatcher had been arrested for Isobel's murder and I must confess I am slightly at a loss to know what you're doing here. Isn't the case closed?'

'There's still the minor question of finding the fellow who shot Isobel Slatcher outside the vicarage,' murmured Dover, opening one eye to squint thoughtfully at Mr Ofield. 'Attempted murder – you could get twenty years for that.'

'And in what way do you imagine I can help you?'

'You can't help me, sir.' Dover shook his head regretfully. 'I've had all the help *I* want from, er, other sources. No, I came along here tonight, sir, to see if I could help *you.*'

'I'm afraid I don't understand you.'

Dover sighed and helped himself to some more wine. 'Well, it's this way, sir,' he said. 'When it comes to passing sentence a judge has a great deal of latitude, you know. He can't, naturally, dish out more than the maximum, but there's nothing to stop him being lenient, very lenient, if he feels that way inclined. Now then, if this chap who shot Isobel Slatcher was prepared to, shall we say, collaborate with the police, it might save us a lot of trouble. And we might – I only say might, mind you – put in a good word with the judge and it's possible . . .'

He wasn't allowed to finish. Mr Ofield leapt to his feet, his eyes ablaze with indignation. MacGregor didn't blame him. At times Dover really went too far. Maybe, thought MacGregor hopefully, this time he's met his Waterloo. He gazed expectantly at Mr Ofield.

Mr Ofield spluttered speechlessly for a few seconds, crimson in the face with fury. 'How dare you!' he choked. 'How dare you! I'll . . . I'll report you to the Home Secretary for this! How dare you force your way into my house in the middle of the night and accuse me of trying to murder Isobel Slatcher! How dare you!'

'I haven't accused you of anything, sir,' said Dover suavely, quite pleased with the way things were going. 'I told you that certain new facts have come to our notice and it's my duty to clarify the situation.' He looked slyly at Mr Ofield. 'I'm sorry if you took my remarks as an accusation, but I think you'd do better to calm down a bit, sir. Losing your temper won't do any good.'

'I am not losing my temper!' screamed Mr Ofield 'I just want to know what the hell you think you're getting at!'

'The truth, sir,' said Dover with irritating smugness. 'The truth, sir.'

Mr Ofield's fists clenched ominously.

'Tony, darling!' His wife spoke in a soothing voice.

Mr Ofield breathed deeply through his nose.

'Would you mind explaining, Inspector,' he said carefully through gritted teeth, 'precisely what you are getting at.'

Dover frowned. As a matter of fact he did mind explaining, very much indeed. He wanted Mr Ofield grovelling pathetically on the carpet at his feet, confessing all. Dover sighed deeply. Mr Ofield, blast him, wasn't going to oblige.

'All right,' he said at last, heaving himself a little more upright in his chair, 'the situation is simply this. I'm not satisfied with your story. No!' Dover held up a hand. 'I've given you a chance to come clean but you wouldn't take

179

it. Now you can listen to me for a change. Just look at the facts. Shortly before her death you were on very friendly terms with Isobel Slatcher. Just how far things had gone between you we don't know. Isobel Slatcher is dead and we've only got your word as to the extent of the relationship. Still, you and she not only worked together but you spent a certain amount of your free time in each other's company. Then things began to cool off, didn't they? At least on your side.'

'I've already explained to you about that!' snapped Ofield. 'And in any case there was nothing between Isobel and me which could cool off, as you put it. We were just good friends!'

'Ho! Ho!' said Dover sarcastically. 'Well, we've all heard that phrase before, haven't we? But you've already admitted that not long before she was shot, you and Isobel Slatcher became less "good friends" than you had been. She knew you wanted to marry Mrs Ofield here, didn't she? And she didn't like the idea, did she?'

Ofield looked contemptuously down his nose and didn't deign to answer.

'Let's just leave it at that, for the moment,' said Dover urbanely. 'She felt you'd jilted her and she was out to make trouble for you. You could see yourself losing your job and possibly your fiancée as well. Isobel Slatcher was out to ruin you, so you began to take steps to protect yourself.'

'Rubbish!' said Mr Ofield, not quite so resolutely as he would have liked.

'Your first bit of luck came,' Dover rumbled on, 'when that gang of young Catholic layabouts attacked the church hall one night. You were there, weren't you? One of them had a loaded gun with him. He lost it in the skirmish. Somebody found it. Somebody found it, kept it and later shot Isobel Slatcher with it.'

Mr Ofield licked his lips. 'Well, it wasn't me! It's the

first I've ever heard about a gun. There were dozens of other people there that night – I wasn't the only one.'

'Round about the time Isobel Slatcher was shot you were still one of the leading lights at St Benedict's, weren't you? You must have known that she used to go round to help Mr Bonnington with his paper work for an hour or so every Saturday evening. You did know that, didn't you, Ofield?'

'Of course I knew it. But so did plenty of other people. There was no secret about it.'

'But there weren't plenty of other people playing the organ in St Benedict's Church that night, were there? Might have been better for you if there had, eh?' Dover grinned unpleasantly. 'If there'd been somebody else with you while you were searching for the lost chord, you might have had an alibi, mightn't you? But then, if there had been somebody else there, you wouldn't have been able to sneak out of the church by the main door, wait until Isobel Slatcher came round the corner – as you knew she would – and shoot her twice with the gun you'd found after the to-do at the church hall.'

'You don't really believe I shot Isobel?' gasped Ofield, a look of horror dawning on his face.

'Don't I?' sneered Dover. 'The man who shot her got away from the scene of the crime without passing either the corner of Church Lane and Corporation Road or the fish and chip shop in the other direction. You know round there well enough. Suppose you tell me how he did it?'

Ofield shook his head helplessly. His wife was staring at him.

'Well, I'll tell you.' Dover was having a wonderful time now. 'He nipped back into the church and went on playing the organ while a girl bled to death on the pavement outside!'

'This is absurd,' muttered Ofield. 'It's absolutely ridiculous. You can't be serious, Inspector?'

181

'I don't usually joke about things like this, sir,' said Dover pompously. 'You may as well face the facts. You're in a very sticky position – don't let's have any mistake about that. You didn't want to bring me into this room tonight, did you? Could those cups over there be the reason? You'd be surprised, sir, how very few people know how to handle a gun. Did you know that? But you're an expert, sir, you're very familiar with fire-arms. You'd know how to use one all right, wouldn't you?'

'You're damned well right I know how to fire a gun,' retorted Ofield with a bit of a rally. 'I am a crack shot, but I'm hardly likely to miss twice at point-blank range, am I?'

'A lot of murderers aren't quite so calm and collected as they'd like to be,' growled Dover. 'Their hands often shake when it comes to the actual point of killing. It's the choice of the weapon that's significant. Nobody'd choose a gun unless they knew how it worked and whether it was loaded or not. And only an experienced shot, like yourself, would realize how little noise in fact a gun actually makes.'

'But you can't really believe I tried to murder Isobel just because I thought she was making a bit of trouble for me in the town? I mean, it's absolutely ridiculous! As soon as Trudi and I got married the storm broke anyhow. I mean, well, I knew it would. Why in God's name should I try to kill Isobel because she spilled the beans a few weeks early? Or do you think I'm a homicidal maniac or something?'

'Oh, I agree with you there, sir,' said Dover, reaching across to a small table and opening an exotic-looking cigarette box. ''Strewth!' he muttered. 'Turkish!' He took one all the same. 'Er, got a light? Oh, thank you. Yes, sir, I'm inclined to agree with you. If Isobel Slatcher was just being a bit bitchy because you were marrying another girl, you wouldn't have much of a motive, would you? That's why I didn't regard you as a serious suspect at the beginning of my investigations.' He paused to emphasize his next casual remark. 'However, that was before we found the letter.'

Mr Ofield couldn't help himself. 'What letter?' he asked anxiously.

'The letter from your brother.'

Mr Ofield's habitual sang froid was rapidly deserting him. He looked as though he had been having a particularly unpleasant nightmare and had woken up to find that it was true. His wife was watching him with rather a speculative look in her eye. Marrying Tony Ofield had been rather more of a step up for her in the social and financial scale than her husband, perhaps, realized. Beneath her seductive, extremely feminine exterior she was quite a hard-headed little realist. If Tony had not been an English gentleman, an intellectual, and reasonably well off she wouldn't have married him. She had been wondering for some time if her judgement of the social scene in England had been quite so accurate as she had thought when she had first arrived from Austria. But while she may have been a little uncertain as to the real extent of Tony's nobility, intelligence and wealth, she had certainly not expected that he was going to get mixed up in a murder case. She was extremely annoyed about the whole business.

Her husband however had got beyond mere annoyance. He was frightened. The chief inspector's sinister insinuations were too ridiculous for words, but one heard such disquieting stories about the police these days. He licked his lips again.

'A letter from my brother?' He wished crossly that he could stop this bleating repetition of the inspector's words but, dear God, what else could he say?

'That's right, sir,' said Dover. 'We found it in Isobel Slatcher's belongings. She'd preserved it quite safely. I suppose you reckoned that we wouldn't be able to connect you with it, but it never pays to underestimate Scotland Yard, sir, as no doubt you're beginning to realize.'

'But I haven't got a brother.' Mr Ofield looked as though tears of frustration were not far away.

Dover chuckled grimly. 'No more you have, *now*, sir,' he agreed. 'Not since he was hanged last week.'

'Hanged last week?'

'Oh come, Mr Ofield, let's stop messing about!' Dover was getting bored with all this fencing to and fro. 'Your brother was Cuthbert Boys! The murderer! Bigamous Bertie! Get it? When he was arrested at the beginning of this year he wrote to you from prison asking you for financial help. Cuthbert Boys had a long criminal record and you were obviously ashamed of your connexion with him. Years ago you changed your name and started a fresh life as Ofield. It's quite natural. Lots of people with relations behind bars do the same thing. However, Bertie apparently hadn't lost track of you completely and when he was arrested for multiple murder he wrote to you, his brother, appealing for help. Isobel Slatcher found that letter and she realized the significance of it. The papers were full of Bigamous Bertie's arrest and she was able to put two and two together and get the right answer. She used that letter as a threat. I don't know whether she wanted money, or marriage, or just revenge for the way you'd jilted her, but whichever way it was, you saw her as a real danger and you took appropriate, if violent, steps to remove her from the scene.'

'For God's sake! You don't believe all that rubbish, do you?'

'I believe in facts, sir.'

'All right! Well, here are some facts for you! I haven't got a brother and I've never had a brother. All I know about Bigamous Bertie is what I've read in the papers. I've never had a letter from him in my life, so Isobel Slatcher

184

couldn't have been using one to threaten me with. What the hell is this, a frame-up?'

'I'm sorry you're taking this attitude, Ofield,' said Dover. 'I suppose you think you can still get away with it.' He shook his head reproachfully. 'I had hoped you'd be more co-operative.'

'Now look, Inspector, just let's stop all this playing about. Bigamous Bertie is *not* my brother and I can damned well prove it. My name is Ofield and my family have been living here in Curdley for at least three hundred years! My mother and father are still living in the town. My grandfather was Mayor and one of my uncles was the local Member of Parliament. You've only got to make a few inquiries. We're a well-known Curdley family. How on earth could we have changed our name? Ask anybody about the Ofields. We've been here for generations!'

'Oh!' said Dover, his confidence rapidly ebbing away.

'And there's another thing!' Mr Ofield had now got the bit firmly between his teeth. 'How old is this Bigamous Bertie supposed to be? He was about fifty, wasn't he?'

'Fifty-one,' said MacGregor, who made a point of knowing things like that. He had no doubts at all now that Scotland Yard's master mind had, once again, gone charging off, like an infuriated rhinoceros, down the wrong track. The blithering old fool! Mr Ofield would probably make a complaint, and there'd be reprimands, if not worse, issued all round. Well, this was the last time, it really was! He'd apply for a transfer. He'd demand a transfer. If he got his name linked with any more of Dover's crashing blunders he could say a sweet farewell to all his hopes of promotion, and he didn't relish the idea of staying a measly detective sergeant for the rest of his life.

Meanwhile Mr Ofield had leapt to his feet and started searching through the drawers of a writing bureau. Amongst a collection of prospectuses for the Third Programme and old issues of progressive magazines, he finally unearthed a large leather-bound album. He flicked quickly through it and found the page he wanted. With a triumphant flourish he slapped it down on Dover's knees.

'Now then! Just look at that!'

With his head held high, he went and sat next to his wife on the settee and comfortingly patted her hand. She gave him an absent smile; but her attention was fixed on Dover.

The chief inspector scowled fiercely at the photograph in front of him. It showed a young simpering couple surrounded by bridesmaids and self-conscious men in morning suits, all standing on the steps of St Benedict's Church. The likeness of Tony Ofield to both of them was quite remarkable, and unmistakable.

'My mother and father,' said that young gentleman firmly.

Dover sniffed and looked sullenly at the date which was inscribed in a neat copperplate underneath: June 14th, 1930.

'My mother was twenty when she got married, and my father was twenty-two,' Mr Ofield pointed out, 'I'm sure even you will admit that it is unlikely that they could be the parents of a fifty-one-year-old man! My mother is herself only fifty-two now and my father will be fifty-four in a couple of weeks.'

Dover didn't go down without one last feeble struggle. 'What's your father's Christian name?' he asked.

'John William,' replied Mr Ofield with a knowing sneer. 'And when Isobel was shot he was in New York, on business.'

There was a long silence. Dover turned over the page of the photograph album and was confronted by a charming picture of his host lying stark naked on the inevitable fur rug. He was grinning toothlessly at the camera. Underneath it said: Antony Victor, aged eight months, September 1932.

Dover shut the album with a loud bang. He accepted his defeat as resentfully as usual.

'We shall have to check all this,' he growled.

Mr Ofield waved an indifferent hand. 'Please do,' he said. 'Anybody in Curdley will be able to tell you all about my family. It's a pity,' he added sarcastically, 'that you didn't bother to verify a few simple facts before you came barging in here with your preposterous and outlandish accusations. I have been forced to endure your ridiculous allegations on two occasions but, although I am fully conscious of my duty as a citizen to help the police in any way I can, I do not intend to tolerate a third intrusion. In fact, if I so much as lay eyes on you again, I shall consult my solicitor with a view to taking legal action!'

And that was, really, that. Dover huffed and puffed for another five minutes or so before the Ofields finally managed to get rid of him, but there was no doubt in anybody's mind. Whoever had shot Isobel Slatcher with Freddie Gash's gun, it was not Antony Victor Ofield, F.L.A.

CHAPTER THIRTEEN

WHEN SERGEANT MACGREGOR, in later years, looked back to the Curdley Sleeping Beauty murder case, his dominant memory was of the seemingly endless breakfasts of which he and Dover partook together in the Station Hotel. Rightly or wrongly he remembered them as gloomy, long-drawn-out affairs, during which pathetically ineffectual attempts were made to repair the havoc wreaked on Dover's theories of the night before. This Wednesday morning breakfast was so typical as to be almost a caricature of those that had preceded it.

187

A damp depressing mist hung over the chimneys and slate roofs of Curdley, but it was nothing to the almost visible gloom which hung over Chief Inspector Wilfred Dover. Last night it hadn't been quite so bad. Dover had been so irate at being baulked, once again, of his prey that sheer roaring bad temper had kept him going. The various reports from London and the local police which had come in during the course of the evening were only fuel to an already raging fire. Dover sat with his fat face drooping in sulky petulance while MacGregor sorted things out and gave him a précis. Dover's reaction was a series of contemptuous grunts and snorts which were expressive of nothing except that the chief inspector was thoroughly fed up with everything and everybody connected with the death of Isobel Slatcher, including Charles Edward Mac-Gregor.

The reports, in fact, didn't add up to much, anyhow. They only confirmed the reasonably accurate guesses which had been made in response to MacGregor's earlier, urgent inquiries. The letter had quite definitely been written by Bigamous Bertie shortly after he had been arrested by Superintendent Roderick. There was no indication that his real name had ever been anything else but Cuthbert Boys and, apart from his numerous aliases, assumed for business reasons, he had made no attempt to change his name by deed poll or any other means. He had always been extremely reticent about his family and had never even given a hint that he had any surviving relations. He had no known connexions with Curdley, all his operations having been carried out exclusively in the South of England.

Dover's scowl deepened, and morosely he took his boots off, dropping them heavily one after the other on to the floor of his bedroom. It was now after midnight so there was a reasonable chance that this would disturb the sleep of whoever was on the floor below. Even this didn't cheer

Dover up much. After his ignominious defeat at the carefully manicured hands of Mr Ofield, the two detectives had returned to the Station Hotel three and a half minutes after the bartender had gone home for the night. Dover's curses had been eloquent but he hadn't been able to get a drink. That wine muck, which was Ofield's idea of progressive hospitality, had upset his stomach and after two hasty visits to the lavatory he insisted on giving MacGregor a detailed account of what was probably going on inside him. MacGregor listened squeamishly and wished he dared tell the chief inspector that he had only himself to blame. His inability to refuse a free drink from anybody, even a murder suspect, had now brought its own appropriate retribution.

All this – the reports, the closing of the bar, Dover's boots and his stomach – helped to pass the time, but they didn't bring the case any nearer to a solution. The chief inspector's reaction to the latest setback was typical. He simply washed his hands of the whole affair. He was, he proclaimed, thoroughly fed up with the whole damned business, he'd had a hard day, his stomach was giving him hell, and he was going to bed. He didn't much care if every second man in Curdley was an unapprehended attempted murderer; he'd had more than enough for one day. In fact, the way he was feeling at the moment, he didn't give a tuppenny damn whether the fellow who shot Isobel Slatcher was ever brought to book. Scotland Yard's files were full of unsolved crimes, and as far as Dover was concerned they could add this one to the list and be done with it.

Seven hours later, with a large fat kipper sizzling in front of him, his frame of mind was much the same. His night had not been too restful and several of the guests had already been complaining to the management about the endless flushing of water closets which had gone on throughout the night. And what little sleep he had managed to snatch had brought neither inspiration nor clarification.

In the cold light of a typical damp Curdley morning Dover's mind tetchily flicked away from the harshest fact of all: he was rapidly running out of suspects. The only two men who seemed to have played any part in Isobel Slatcher's admittedly thin romantic life – Rex Purseglove and Antony Victor Ofield – had duly been eliminated. There wasn't anybody else much left. That was the trouble with these blasted respectable women, thought Dover, they didn't have enough enemies to give you a fair chance.

He sighed crossly and poked at his kipper. He wondered what it would do to his stomach. Oh well, kill or cure, in for a penny, in for a pound. He wolfed it down and toppled a quart or so of hot sweet tea on top. MacGregor watched him apprehensively. For a man whose stomach was supposed to be upset, this greedy recklessness seemed a bit drastic. Dover himself was more than a little anxious but, after a couple of minutes of tense waiting, nothing happened. Dover relaxed and MacGregor thought it might be safe enough to open a conversation.

'Mrs Ofield last night was a tasty bit of homework, wasn't she, sir?' he remarked brightly.

'Hm,' said Dover, more interested in excavating a kipper bone which had penetrated the defences of his top set.

'I'm afraid we picked the wrong man there, didn't we, sir?' MacGregor was delicately edging the conversation round to a subject which was usually taboo at this time in the morning – the case in hand.

Dover scowled. He was on the point of retorting that, indeed, MacGregor had backed the wrong horse in the gallows stakes, but it was, he thought, a little too soon to start trying to pull off that face-saving switch.

'Of course,' MacGregor added, anxious to spare Dover's feelings as much as possible, otherwise the old fool would sulk around all day like a bear with a sore ear, 'we obviously couldn't check up all that stuff about his family and them not being old enough to be the parents of Cuthbert Boys *before* we went round to see him. I mean, there wasn't time, was there, sir?'

Dover squinted suspiciously at his sergeant. Was the young pup trying to take the mickey? He contented himself with a non-committal grunt.

'Er, have you any idea yet, sir, of what we're going to do next?'

It was a good question, penetrating and to the point. Didn't somebody say that the true essence of something or other was knowing what questions to ask? Well, whatever it was, Charles Edward MacGregor would have done very well at it.

Dover scratched his head disconsolately. He glumly poured himself another cup of tea and stirred it rhythmically while he thought. What the hell were they going to do next? Start rooting around again in Isobel Slatcher's private life to find if she'd any more boy friends who might have jilted and shot her to get rid of her? Perhaps further investigation would unearth a disgruntled lover whom *she* had jilted? For a second Dover perked up a bit. This was a line they hadn't yet explored. Perhaps . . . no, he simply couldn't imagine Isobel Slatcher arousing that sort of passion in anybody. You just had to face it – she wasn't that kind of girl. Perhaps if they dug around a bit more at the Cuthbert Boys end of things? Surely, with all the resources of the police at their beck and call, they ought to be able to find the brother of the decade's most sensational murderer?

MacGregor was chattering again. 'I think we're on the right lines though, sir, don't you?'

'What lines?' grunted Dover.

'Well, the connexion with Cuthbert Boys, sir. The letter we found in Isobel Slatcher's Bible.'

'Oh yes,' said Dover vaguely.

191

'I'm sure if we can find who that letter was written to, we shall have the man who fired the shots, aren't you, sir?'

'Maybe,' said Dover cautiously.

'Do you think it's any good questioning Violet Slatcher, sir? I mean, Isobel may have mentioned something to her which would give us a clue.'

'Might be,' agreed Dover, 'provided she hasn't gone completely off her rocker.'

'She'd probably be very willing to help us, sir, if she could,' MacGregor pointed out. 'After all, she only killed her own daughter to help get the real murderer punished, didn't she? If she's in any fit state to help us I'm sure she would.'

'It's an idea, MacGregor.' Dover nodded graciously. 'In fact, you can follow it up yourself. I don't know where they've taken her – local loony-bin, probably – but wherever it is you can nip round this morning and interview her. If she isn't chewing the carpet up you might try asking her if Isobel ever mentioned anything about any whited sepulchres in the district. Anybody who seemed respectable enough on the surface but about whom young Isobel could tell a thing or two if she wanted.'

'Do you think the fellow we're after, sir, might be a Catholic? I mean, that was one of Cuthbert's specialities, wasn't it? Posing as a good Catholic himself and making all his contacts through the Church? Perhaps the Boys were a Catholic family so he'd got all the background and so on off pat?'

Dover wrinkled his nose thoughtfully. 'Maybe,' he admitted. 'But in that case, what was she holding her hand for?'

'Holding her hand, sir?'

'Yes! That letter was written, when? The tenth of January, wasn't it? And yet Isobel wasn't put out of action until February the seventeenth, was she? Now, if Cuthbert

Boys's brother is a Roman Catholic, what was Isobel waiting for? You know what she is supposed to have felt about Holy Romans. Surely she'd have denounced him right away, and have enjoyed doing it.'

'We don't know how long the letter had been in her possession, sir.'

Dover chose to take umbrage at the implications of this remark. 'Stop trying to teach your grandmother to suck eggs!' he snapped. 'I know damned well we don't know how long she'd had the blasted letter! But we do know she'd had it long enough for her to threaten her victim with it, and for him to make all the preparations – including hanging on to that gun at the church hall. What was the date of that raid?'

'Twenty-ninth of January, sir,' said MacGregor sullenly.

'Right! Well, we can take a pretty fair guess that not only had Isobel Slatcher got that letter before the twenty-ninth, but that she'd let Cuthbert Boys's brother *know* that she'd got it – otherwise, why should he whip the gun? Now, I'll just repeat my earlier remarks. If the brother is a Roman Catholic, what was Isobel Slatcher waiting for? Why didn't she denounce him straight away? By the time she was shot on the seventeenth of February she still hadn't let the cat out of the bag. Why?'

'Sadism? Enjoying watching her victim squirm, sir?'

'Hm,' said Dover. He hadn't thought of that. 'Well, I suppose that's a remote possibility.'

'Actually, sir,' MacGregor went on, 'I think you're right all the same about the fellow not being a Catholic. We've got to remember that gun, sir, haven't we? Assuming that the Pie Gang were telling the truth, somebody at that Men's Bible Class must have found that gun. And that means he must be C. of E.'

'He must have actually been at that Bible Class, too,' said Dover. 'I'd forgotten about that. We don't have to look all over Curdley for the brother of Cuthbert Boys, we've only got to check the men at that Bible Class.'

Dover could have kicked himself for not having worked this out before, but he was grateful that smartie-boots Mac-Gregor had overlooked the obvious, too.

'All right, MacGregor,' he said, suddenly becoming all precise and efficient, 'you clear off right away and see what you can get out of Violet Slatcher. Then come back here and pick me up. If you haven't got something pretty clear cut from her, we'll follow up this men's Bible Class business. It'll probably mean a lot of work,' he sighed pathetically, 'but we can shed some of it on to the local boys. Mr Bonnington's housekeeper – Mrs What's-her-name – she said the Vicar'd have a list of the members, didn't she? All right, we'll get hold of that and start working through it. We'll check every single bloody one of 'em and see whether they've changed their names. 'Strewth!' he beamed delightedly, 'should be a piece of cake!'

'Perhaps it would be better to start on that straight away, sir, and leave Miss Slatcher till later?'

'No!' Dover was adamant. 'I want to have a bit of a think about the case and I can't do that with you fidgeting around yacking your head off. No, you get off and see Violet. And don't rush it! You'll get better results if you take your time. She'll need patience, you know.'

MacGregor shot off, and Dover ambled away to a quiet corner of the lounge. Although he made himself comfortable with his feet up on a second chair, and although he closed his eyes (the better to concentrate), for once he didn't actually go to sleep. He really did a bit of thinking.

The Isobel Slatcher case had gone on long enough for Dover's money. He didn't like Curdley. He wanted to get back to London and his own home as soon as possible. The quickest way to achieve this modest, and purely selfish, ambition was to solve the problem and get the man who

194

shot Curdley's Sleeping Beauty behind bars, pronto. With this inspiring motivation driving him on, Dover, for the first time really, began to think about his investigation.

He no longer needed to bother about Isobel's actual death in her hospital room. Violet was responsible for that and nobody else was involved. People, like Mr Bonnington, who had been eliminated at first because they had an alibi for the actual killing were now placed firmly back in the picture. All Dover now had to consider were the motives for the shooting outside the vicarage and the movements of everybody known to be in the vicinity at that time.

All right! He scratched his stomach thoughtfully. Who exactly was near the scene of the crime at the vital time? Well, there was Rex Purseglove to start with. And Antony Victor Ofield playing the organ in the church. And Mr Bonnington in his study. And the agnostic Mr Dibb in his fish and chip shop. Anybody else? Oh, there was that senile sponger in the pub on the corner – what was the name? Er, the William and Mary – that was it. And what was his name? Oh damn it! His father was a policeman, or so he said. Twitter? No. Pitter? No. Twitchin, that was it, Harry Twitchin. Then there was that smooth pimp in the café place, the chap who ran Los Toros. Pedro Something, his name was. And, as far as he knew, that was the lot. Of course there might be somebody who was on the scene that he hadn't even heard about, but he'd have another look at this bunch first.

Now, the man who shot Isobel Slatcher must fulfil at least two, what you might call, background conditions: he must have been able to get that gun and he must be Bigamous Bertie's blasted brother. The first condition eliminated some of the fringe characters. It would have to be checked, but Dover felt he was on pretty safe ground if he assumed that the chap at the fish and chip shop, the slimy proprietor of Los Toros and that old soak, Harry

Twitchin, were most unlikely members of the St Benedict's Men's Bible Class. 'Strewth! That narrowed the field down a bit. Who'd he got left? He frowned crossly. Rex Purseglove and Ofield the librarian. Oh God, not those two again! Oh, and there was the Vicar, Mr Bonnington.

A nasty little suspicion began nibbling at the outer perimeter of Dover's mind. He resolutely ignored it and went on deducing, rather frantically. Rex Purseglove, he told himself firmly, hadn't been at the Men's Bible Class, but his father had. Mr Purseglove might have found that gun, kept it and handed it to his son at some later date, so Rex wasn't eliminated on that score alone. Mr Ofield had been at the Class in person. And so had Mr Bonnington.

But what about these three as candidates for the position of Bigamous Bertie's brother? Well, Ofield had eliminated himself. He was just too young. But Rex Purseglove was even younger. Dover blew irately down his nose. Neither Mr nor Mrs Purseglove was old enough to have a fifty-year-old son. They couldn't possibly be the parents of the late Cuthbert Boys. So that left . . . Mr Bonnington, the Vicar.

Oh God! Dover felt a slight chill trickle down his spine. Mr Bonnington, the Vicar. 'Dear Vic.' Suppose it wasn't short for 'Dear Victor' but was just a facetious abbreviation for 'Dear Vicar'? Rubbish, it couldn't be!

Why not? demanded a little voice inside Dover's somewhat apprehensive brain. Bonnington's the right age to be Cuthbert Boys's brother, isn't he? He's not a local man. His family haven't been well known in Curdley since before the Reformation. You don't know anything about his background. And what about that gun? When the Pie Gang attacked, Mr Bonnington hurt his leg, didn't he? Twisted his ankle or something? He couldn't go chasing after the young devils when they ran away. He had to stay behind in the church hall, where he could have found the gun.

Poppycock, Dover told himself, quite out of the question. Is it? the little voice nagged on again. What about the actual shooting? Just stop being pig-headed about it and see how Mr Bonnington fits the bill there.

Unless you're going to assume, at this late stage, that the crime was unpremeditated, the man who fired the shots must have known when Isobel Slatcher was going to leave the vicarage. Now, most of the people concerned knew she would leave at about eight o'clock, so they could have hung around in the darkness of Church Lane waiting for her to come out. A risky business, but a quite possible one. The one person, however, who would know exactly when Isobel left the vicarage was, without a doubt, Mr Bonnington. In addition he could have found Freddie Gash's gun in the church hall, and he was of an age which made him a possibility as Bigamous Bertie's brother. Isobel Slatcher came in regularly to help him with his paper work. She could easily have come across that fatal letter in the Vicar's study. So far nothing was known about Bonnington's background. He could have changed his name long ago, before he was appointed to the living at St Benedict's. And if Bonnington were Isobel Slatcher's victim, it might explain why she didn't make her exposure immediately. Perhaps even she would hesitate to blacken the name of an ordained priest in the Church of England? This delay in taking action still bothered Dover a bit. The obvious explanation was, of course, that Isobel was extorting money from the unfortunate brother of Cuthbert Boys but, somehow, Dover couldn't see the dead girl resorting to common blackmail for financial gain. It didn't seem in keeping with what little he knew of her character.

Well, there it was. Bonnington was certainly a possible candidate for the shooting of Isobel Slatcher as far as certain aspects of the case were concerned. But what about the actual mechanics of the attack? Could he have shot Isobel, and could Dover prove it if he had?

The main point which had proved a stumbling block for the chief inspector almost from the beginning of the case, was how the attacker had got away from the scene of the crime. The two most obvious routes had been under surveillance. Rex Purseglove was standing at the Corporation Road end of Church Lane and Mr Dibb outside his fish and chip shop was on guard at the other end. That left the possibility of somebody climbing the high wall over on to the railway track – a feat Dover considered quite out of the question – or taking temporary refuge in one of the three available buildings: the church, the vicarage or the church hall. All the evidence seemed to show that the church and the church hall were securely locked – and you didn't leave the doors of public buildings open in Curdley. In any case no one could have entered the church without Mr Ofield being aware of it. The more you came to look at it, thought Dover unhappily, the more obvious it became that the intending murderer could have gone most easily into the vicarage. If the man were some third person though, why hadn't Mr Bonnington caught him breaking into his own house? If the man were Mr Bonnington himself, then all became relatively simple.

Dover pulled out a large, greyer-than-grey handkerchief and mopped his brow. He felt there was something rather blasphemous about measuring up a clergyman like this. Dover had quite clear-cut, if erroneous, ideas about what criminals looked like and from what sort of background they came: These preconceptions did not include clerks in Holy Orders.

He sat there in the hotel lounge sweating and grumbling to himself as he reviewed in his mind what had happened outside St Benedict's vicarage at eight o'clock on the night of Saturday, February 17th.

He was still sitting there, gazing stupidly before him, when Sergeant MacGregor came hurrying back to the

198

hotel. The chief inspector's eyes were wide open, so he was obviously awake, and his pasty flabby face was even whiter than usual. MacGregor assumed that his stomach was bothering him again.

Dover stared vacantly at MacGregor, his rosebud of a mouth drooping petulantly downwards and his jowls hanging in ample folds over his collar. His tiny black moustache, worn in the style which Adolf Hitler made so unpopular, twitched slightly in acknowledgement of his sergeant's presence. MacGregor interpreted this as indicating permission to speak.

'I'm sorry, sir,' he said, perching despondently on the arm of a near-by armchair, 'it's absolutely hopeless. The doctors wouldn't even let me see her.'

Dover blinked.

'They don't know if she's ever likely to recover, but apparently she's retreated into a sort of daydream world of her own and she doesn't respond to any questions or anything. It seems she thinks she's a little girl again. It's all rather pathetic, really.'

There was a pause.

Dover's body heaved in a slight sigh. 'It doesn't matter,' he said sadly. 'I know who did it.'

'Really, sir?' MacGregor was apprehensive.

'Came to me all in a flash, it did,' Dover went on miserably. 'Can't think why we didn't see it before. Obvious, really, once you know.'

'Who was it, sir?'

'The Reverend Roland Bonnington, Vicar of St Benedict's.'

'Oh no!' MacGregor's voice rose in a howl of protest. Really, the old fool ought to be put out of his misery! It would be a kindness, honestly it would. He might have been all right in his day, possibly, but it was time now to get him pensioned off.

Dover was not pleased by MacGregor's horrified reaction to his stupendous news. He chose to forget that he had already made two similar announcements during the course of his investigations and neither had proved correct.

'It's all right screaming, "Oh no!"' he snapped. 'I don't like the idea of it any more than you do, but he's our man. There's no doubt about it.'

'Look here, sir,' said MacGregor, trying hard to keep calm, 'don't you think we'd better discuss this thoroughly before we go any further? I mean, we've already accused an Air Force officer and a head librarian of shooting Isobel Slatcher. We don't want to pick on every notable in the town, now do we, sir?'

'Bonnington shot her,' said Dover obstinately.

'He couldn't have done, sir!' MacGregor took his courage in both hands. Somebody had got to do something or Scotland Yard would become the laughing-stock of the place. 'Do you remember Mr Dibb at the fish and chip shop? He saw Mr Bonnington leaving the vicarage *after* the shots were fired. He was quite clear about it. He heard the train go by, he heard the shots and he went outside his shop and then he saw Mr Bonnington leave the vicarage and rush round the corner of his garden to where Isobel was lying.'

'Well?'

'Mr Bonnington must have been *in* the vicarage when the shots were fired. If he'd shot Isobel and then run back into the vicarage, Dibb would have seen him.'

'Only if he'd returned to the house through the front door.'

'But how else could he have got in? We've already agreed he couldn't climb the wall of the vicarage garden – it's just too high and there's all that broken glass stuff on top.'

'He didn't use the front door and he didn't climb the wall,' retorted Dover impatiently. 'He used that side gate in the garden wall. That gate is only two or three yards from where Isobel Slatcher was shot.'

MacGregor sighed heavily. 'We looked at that gate, sir, right at the beginning of the case. It was locked and bolted and every bit of metal on it, including the hinges, was solid with rust. It hadn't been used for years.'

'Oh, I grant you,' agreed Dover generously, 'that it looked in a pretty bad way, but, with patience and plenty of penetrating oil, don't you reckon a determined man could get it open again, if his life depended on it?'

'Well, yes, sir, I suppose you've got a point there. You probably could get it in working order, given enough time. But you'd need to pour pints of oil on to it – the hinges, the bolts and the lock. Surely to goodness we'd have seen some traces of all that when we examined it?'

'You're forgetting, MacGregor,' said Dover, not unwilling to score a minor point off his sergeant, 'that we didn't examine that gate until nearly nine months after the shooting. Let's just suppose that somebody did go to work on it. There was no hurry about it, he could take his time. We know from the way that gun was found and kept that the whole business was premeditated. Our man didn't have to get everything ready overnight. Now then, once he'd shot Isobel, all he's got to do is lock the gate up again, probably wipe off any surplus oil and then simply leave the weather to do the rest. It wouldn't be long before all the metal was as rusty and stuck together as it was before.'

MacGregor thought this over. 'What do you think actually happened, sir?' he asked.

'Too easy, really,' said Dover. 'Got a cigarette, laddie? I think Isobel Slatcher found the letter from Cuthbert Boys in the vicarage. These bossy self-righteous women are usually pretty nosy as well and I imagine she was into everything she could lay her hands on. She takes the letter – having realized its implications. Don't forget she may have seen the

201

envelope as well and that may have given her a clue. Then she tells Mr Bonnington that she's got it and threatens him with it in some way. He decides to get rid of her. Finding that gun was probably an unexpected windfall, but he was bright enough to see how valuable it was going to be to him. Then he gets the gate ready so that he can get it open easily and quietly. When Isobel leaves the vicarage on the Saturday night as usual he nips out through his garden and through that gate. He'd meet her face to face just as she came round the corner. He grabs her and fires both bullets into her head. Then he whips back through the gate again, locks it, rushes back across the garden, through the house, out of his front door – when he's lucky enough to be seen by Dibb – and round to where Isobel is lying, dead, he hopes, on the pavement. From then on he behaves like any normal, responsible citizen, phones for the ambulance and the police and so on.'

'Risky, sir,' mused MacGregor. 'Suppose the local police had examined that gate thoroughly?'

'You can't commit murder without taking some risks,' Dover pointed out, 'and I reckon if Isobel Slatcher had been killed the local boys might have poked about a bit more than they did. But you know what it's like. Why flog yourself to death searching for clues when, in a few days, the victim herself'll be able to give you the name, address and telephone number of the fellow you want? I expect they did look at the gate in a casual sort of way and then accepted Bonnington's statement that it hadn't been opened for years.'

'It was still a bit careless, sir,' said MacGregor reprovingly.

'Well, you know what these provincial CID chaps are like,' agreed Dover with a very patronizing air. 'They do their best, I suppose, but they just haven't got the experience. Besides, suppose they had discovered that the gate would open, that doesn't pin the shooting on to Bonnington, you know. Somebody else could easily have done the oiling, hid in the vicarage garden until Isobel came past, shot her and then gone back in the garden. When the Vicar ran out to see what the hell was going on, Mr X could have slipped into the house and casually walked out of the front door when everybody else was flapping away over the supposed corpse round the corner. The local police had no reason to suspect Bonnington, of all people. I don't know as I would myself, except that he fits the bill as Bigamous Bertie's brother so well – and none of the other suspects do.'

MacGregor tried to find some flaw in Dover's unexpectedly intelligent piece of reasoning, but the chief inspector had a plausible explanation for everything. Much against all his experience and better judgement, MacGregor gradually found himself accepting the idea that Dover might, on this his third attempt, actually be right.

'There's not much in the way of proof so far, sir,' he warned cautiously. 'We're just supposing all the time, aren't we?'

'We should be able to prove that Bonnington is the brother of Bigamous Bertie easily enough. You can get on to the Yard straight away and have 'em put somebody on checking at Somerset House or wherever it is. Now we know what we're looking for it shouldn't be too hard to find – given time: a Boys who changed his name to Bonnington any time in say the last thirty years. Simple routine. Then we can do a real investigation into Bonnington's past, just in case he didn't do the change of name business by deed poll. At some stage we're bound to come to the point where Bonnington disappears and a young Boys is there in his place. Once we can connect the two we're on an easy wicket. We've got the letter and we can prove Isobel Slatcher had it in her possession.'

'We can't prove that she was blackmailing or threatening him with it, though.'

'No, but with the evidence of Rex Purseglove and Mr Dibb we can prove, I reckon, that Bonnington was the only

203

one who could have done the shooting and then got away unnoticed from the scene of the crime. Then the circumstantial evidence about the gun she was shot with isn't too bad. I think we'll get a case good enough for a conviction.'

'It's going to take some time, sir.'

Dover scowled. 'Well, that's as maybe. Frankly I don't intend to stop up here in this godforsaken hole a minute longer than I have to! Anyhow,' he added casually, scraping a bit of dried egg off his waistcoat, 'there's one way we might speed things up a bit.'

MacGregor's heart sank. Surely they weren't going to go through all that again for the third time? Weren't Rex Purseglove and Mr Ofield enough for anybody? 'How do you mean, sir?' he asked faintly.

'Oh, we can go along and have a chat with Mr Bonnington himself,' said Dover, with admirable nonchalance. 'See what he's got to say for himself, eh? Put a bit of pressure on, you know, and he might crack and confess everything. Save us a lot of trouble all round. Bit of the old third degree stuff, without going too far,' he hastened to add.

MacGregor knew it was no good arguing. The chief inspector wanted to get home as soon as possible. The fact that his proposed short cut might well ruin everything by putting Mr Bonnington on his guard was neither here nor there. Bringing the case to a successful conclusion ranked in Dover's mind a bad second to getting away from Curdley on the earliest available train.

MacGregor was sent off to put the more elaborate and lengthy inquiries into motion. If Mr Bonnington were the brother of Cuthbert Boys it shouldn't, given time, be too difficult to prove. While the sergeant got on with the telephoning Dover ordered himself a large cup of coffee and remained comfortably ensconced in the lounge – 'working out his tactics' as he explained later to MacGregor. An hour later he had got no further than deciding to confront Mr

Bonnington with the theory he had built up, claim that it was constructed of provable facts and, if he didn't break down and confess on the spot, thump him in the face until he did. There was, at times, a classic simplicity about the way Dover's mind worked.

CHAPTER FOURTEEN

A S THEY stood outside the front door of St Benedict's vicarage both Dover and MacGregor felt, in spite of certain twinges of apprehension, that the end of the case was in sight. Mr Bonnington was the man all right, though MacGregor would have been happier if they had been calling on him properly armed with a warrant and a substantial backing of real evidence. So, as a matter of fact, would Dover, now that it came to the point, but he recognized with a sigh, you couldn't have it both ways. He was fed up with the whole blasted case and he wanted to be done with it. It might be weeks before they unearthed the evidence he wanted. This way might be risky but at least it would produce quick results – and anyhow it would be more fun. Dover quite enjoyed a bit of heavy-handed bullying every now and again.

The door was opened after some considerable delay by Mrs Smallbone.

'Well?' she snapped.

'We want to see Mr Bonnington,' said Dover putting a corresponding amount of antagonism into his voice.

'You can't. He's having his lunch. You'll have to come back at two o'clock.'

'I'm afraid,' said Dover, moving inexorably forward like a Centurion tank, 'that won't do. We've got to see him now.'

Mrs Smallbone yielded to superior force and let them into the vicarage. 'You can wait in the study,' she announced with a toss of her head. 'I'll tell him you're here.'

'Oh, no need for that,' said Dover smoothly. 'We can talk to him while he's finishing his dinner.' And without giving Mrs Smallbone time to argue he lumbered off in the direction of the kitchen.

Mrs Smallbone was outraged. 'The Reverend's in the dining-room. Just because once a week he has to have a quick snack in the kitchen doesn't mean he lives there, I'll have you know!'

Mr Bonnington, sitting at one end of a huge mahogany table, looked as though he'd had a rattling good lunch. He was reading a book and stuffing biscuits loaded with butter and a crumbly white cheese into his mouth. He looked up when Mrs Smallbone came in.

'Them policemen are here again,' she proclaimed flatly.

Mr Bonnington frowned, but before he had time to make any comment Dover and MacGregor were already in the room.

Dover pulled out a chair at Mr Bonnington's end of the table and sat down, grimly tipping his bowler hat to the back of his head. For a moment nobody said a word and then, with a sniff and another toss of her head, Mrs Smallbone went out, all but slamming the door behind her.

'Well now' – Mr Bonnington produced a bleak smile – 'to what do I owe the honour of yet another, er, unexpected visit?'

Dover ignored him. He spoke over his shoulder to MacGregor. 'Sit yourself down, Sergeant, and get your notebook out.' He turned back to Mr Bonnington. 'I hope you're not going to keep us here too long, sir,' he said.

'I must confess I share your aspirations,' said Mr Bonnington tartly, 'but I fail to see how the length of your inquisition is going to depend in any way on me.'

'Don't you, sir?' asked Dover with a sneer. 'Well, perhaps you will in a moment. Now then, sir, would you mind telling me your full name?'

For a second the Vicar pursed his lips, then he shrugged his shoulders and answered, unperturbedly, 'Roland Bonnington.'

MacGregor carefully inscribed this in his notebook.

'And your age, sir?'

'I'm forty.'

'Have you any brothers or sisters, sir?'

Mr Bonnington's eyes flicked rapidly from Dover to the silent MacGregor and back again. 'No.'

Dover grinned evilly. '*Had* you any brothers or sisters, sir?'

'Now look here, Inspector, I really cannot see the point of your questions. They seem to me to be quite irrelevant to any investigation you are authorized to make.'

'Are you refusing to answer them, sir?' asked Dover. 'They seem to me to be harmless enough. Of course,' he added, keeping his fingers crossed, 'if you feel that you are putting yourself in jeopardy by telling me whether you ever had any brothers or sisters, there's nothing to stop you engaging a solicitor to advise you. Always wisest, I reckon, when you've got something to hide.'

'I have nothing to hide,' retorted Mr Bonnington. 'Kindly don't make insinuations of that kind! If it's so important to you, you may as well know that I did have a brother who is now dead.'

'An elder brother, sir?'

'Yes.'

'Name of Cuthbert Boys?'

Dover dropped his trump card in an off-hand manner but his mean, piggy eyes never left Mr Bonnington's face. He was delighted to see that gentleman go quite white. Silently Dover chalked up the first round to himself.

Mr Bonnington licked his lips. 'How in God's name did you find that out?' he whispered.

'Oh, we have our methods, sir,' said Dover grandly. 'I take it that you were the one who changed your name?'

'Yes,' Mr Bonnington rubbed his hand miserably across his face. 'As soon as I was twenty-one. I had decided to go into the Church and I felt that my connexion with Cuthbert, if it became known, would only prove an embarrassment to me. I had been left a small legacy by an aunt of mine and I let it become known that I was changing my name in accordance with her wishes. My brother – he was nearly ten years my senior – had already acquired a criminal record – petty fraud mostly, I seem to remember – and I flatter myself that I knew his character well enough to know that he would never change. I had to protect myself and my career – and the good name of the Church, of course. There's nothing criminal in that, is there?'

'You severed all connexion with your brother?'

'Indeed I did! He had chosen his way and I, with God's help, had chosen mine. My parents were both dead and we had no other close relations. From time to time I saw Cuthbert's name in the newspapers – usually in the more sensational ones – but this only confirmed me in my determination to have nothing whatsoever to do with him. Every two or three years, however, he used to send me a postcard – one of the "wish-you-were-here" type with a vulgar picture on the front. It was his idea of a joke but it also served to let me know that in spite of changing my name and everything, he still kept track of me. It was a great source of anxiety, especially after my marriage, but,' Mr Bonnington sighed resignedly, 'we all have our crosses to bear.'

'But nobody else was aware of the connexion?'

'No, his postcards were very discreet. Even my late wife didn't know. I am, Inspector, what in a more worldly sphere would perhaps be called an ambitious man.

I wish to serve my Maker to the full stretch of my ability. I have much, with God's help, to give to the Church and to the world. It would have been unthinkable that my not insignificant gifts – gifts from the Lord, of course – should have been allowed to rot in some clerical backwater just because I had a cheap criminal for a brother.'

'Your brother wrote to you for help, I believe, when he was arrested for murdering four of his "wives"?'

Mr Bonnington smiled sadly. 'Ah, I see. You found the letter.'

'Did you answer it?'

'Gracious heavens, no! There was nothing I could do for him, except pray. It was perfectly obvious from the accounts in the newspapers that he was guilty of both bigamy and murder. It was more than ever important that the connexion between us should not be discovered. I don't think I am betraying any confidence if I tell you that I expect some small preferment in the near future. This is the reward for my work and my efforts! I had no intention of letting Cuthbert deprive me of them. I did not answer that letter, but I prayed to God for him.'

'How did Isobel Slatcher get her hands on it?'

'Oh, nosing around as usual. The woman was a quite incorrigible poker into other people's private affairs. I meant to burn the thing but she found it before I had time to.'

'She realized what it meant?'

'Oh yes. She was not unintelligent in some ways.'

'And she tried to blackmail you with it?'

'Blackmail me?'

'Yes, for money, or a wedding ring, perhaps?' Dover glanced slyly at the Vicar.

Mr Bonnington shook his head. 'I wish it had been as straightforward as that.'

'Well, what was she after?'

'God alone knows!' Mr Bonnington's tone was not pious.

'Power? Revenge? A place in the limelight. The woman was a fanatic, of course. Once she got an idea into her head there was no reasoning with her.'

'And what idea did she get into her head where you and your brother's letter were concerned?'

'She was going to expose me!' Mr Bonnington's voice sank a good octave. 'To the Bishop!'

MacGregor's lips twitched, but Dover listened with something approaching sympathy. As a good bourgeois himself he could understand Mr Bonnington's desire to keep himself respectable. Dover had been brought up in a household where what the neighbours might think really mattered. His family had had a disreputable uncle who had brought endless shame and distress to the rest of them. If they could have quietly murdered him . . .

'Didn't you try to talk her out of it?' asked Dover. 'I should have thought what with you being a parson and her such a regular churchgoer . . .'

Mr Bonnington's head shook slowly from side to side. 'I tried everything,' he said. 'I offered her money, very tactfully of course, but that only made her worse.' He gazed reproachfully at the ceiling. 'I even suggested matrimony, but that wasn't good enough for her. You would have thought, wouldn't you, that marriage to a man in my position would have counted for something? Of course, I didn't know the true facts about her birth then, but even so I was making a considerable sacrifice.'

'She turned you down?' asked Dover.

'Flat,' said Mr Bonnington. 'Funnily enough I don't think it was the murders or the bigamy, for that matter, which upset her so much. It was this Roman Catholic side of things that seemed to stick in her throat. I think I could have handled her if it hadn't been for that. For some reason she seemed to think Cuthbert was a Roman Catholic and that we both came from a Catholic family. You know

210

what she was like about Roman Catholics – quite unreasonable, though, of course, her zeal for the Protestant faith on the whole had much to recommend it.'

'When was she going to expose you?'

'The day after she was shot. The Bishop was coming that Sunday for a confirmation. She told me when she was here on the Saturday night that she'd finally made her mind up and nothing could alter her decision. She said she was convinced it was her duty! I thought it was all up then. I turned to the only refuge I had left – prayer. I had just sunk to my knees to place my burden in the Saviour's hands when I heard the shots. Such a divinely prompt answer!'

'Wadderyemean?' snapped Dover, suddenly coming to life. 'When you *heard* the shots? Heard 'em? You damned well fired 'em!'

'I certainly did not!' Mr Bonnington looked quite offended. 'I sincerely believe that I am God's Chosen Instrument, but shooting somebody – no, that's going too far. Besides, I've never fired a gun in my life.'

'You shot her,' repeated Dover obstinately.

'Really, Inspector, if you go on making accusations like that I shall have to consider taking action against you for defamation of character. I am an ordained priest, the Vicar of the leading parish in Curdley. How dare you accuse me of firing a gun at Isobel Slatcher?'

'You're also the brother of a convicted multiple murderer!' snarled Dover, hitting, with no compunction, well below the belt. 'And I'm accusing you of attempting to murder Isobel Slatcher for one damned good reason – because you did!'

'I did not!' bellowed Mr Bonnington in a most unclerical explosion of temper.

'You did!' bawled Dover.

'Liar!'

'Murderer!'

211

At this point MacGregor, very tactfully, dropped his notebook with a resounding slap on the linoleum-covered floor. The two protagonists jumped slightly at the unexpected interruption and lost the thread of their argument.

After a moment's heavy breathing Dover resumed his attack in a slightly more restrained manner.

'Now, look here, Mr Bonnington,' he said, 'you're only making things worse for yourself by taking up this attitude. I know you shot Isobel Slatcher, and I can prove it.'

'Fiddlesticks!' said Mr Bonnington faintly.

'I know how you got the gun,' Dover pointed out. 'You found it, didn't you, in the church hall the night the Pie Gang raided it? It was,' he sneered, 'what you no doubt would call a heaven-sent opportunity, especially when you found that there were two bullets left in it. I suppose you never thought we'd be able to trace that gun, did you?'

'I did not find any gun!' The Vicar spoke through clenched teeth, though he was beginning to feel a little uneasy. Memories of how American detectives behaved on TV came flooding disturbingly into his mind. 'I tell you again – I don't even know how to fire a gun. To the best of my knowledge I have never held a weapon of that nature in my hands in my entire life.'

Dover ignored him. 'You've told us yourself how Isobel Slatcher was going to ruin your career by telling the Bishop you were a convicted murderer's brother. You realized that the only way you could save yourself was by shutting her mouth' – dramatic pause – 'for ever! You made your preparations. You found the gun and kept it. Then you went to work on that gate in your garden wall – the one that leads directly into Church Lane. You made it so that it would open. Oh, I know you probably think it's all rusted up again by now, but I don't doubt we shall be able to find traces of oil in the lock.

212

'I don't know what you're talking about,' moaned Mr Bonnington.

'Then on that Saturday night you made a last appeal to Isobel Slatcher here, in this room!'

'It was in the study, sir,' hissed MacGregor helpfully.

Dover ignored him too and swept magnificently on. 'You offered her money, marriage! You begged for mercy! She wouldn't listen!' He was getting really worked up now. 'You knew there was only one way out. You had to kill her that very night, before the Bishop could hear the scandalous news. Isobel Slatcher left the vicarage to go home. You seized the gun, you rushed out through the garden, opened the gate and stepped out into the darkness of Church Lane. When Isobel Slatcher came round the corner, you shot her twice in the head. You dashed back into the garden, pausing only to lock the gate behind you. You ran into the house and hurried out of your front door as if you'd heard the shots and were looking, like any decent dutiful citizen, to see what had happened. You thought she was dead, didn't you? It must have been quite a shock when they told you she was still alive. You must have been quite worried for a bit, until you knew for certain that she would never regain consciousness. That left you with just one little problem, didn't it?'

'I don't understand what you're talking about!' Mr Bonnington held up his hands as if in prayer. 'Dear Lord, this is like a nightmare! I must be going mad!'

'Not you,' snorted Dover. 'You've kept your head very well, all things considered. Must run in the family,' he added unkindly. 'However, I'll bet when you were pretending to examine Isobel after she'd been shot, you didn't forget to have a look in her handbag, did you?'

What little colour was left in Mr Bonnington's face drained away. 'How did you know that?' he gasped, running a trembling hand down his cheek.

213

'You wanted that letter back, didn't you? You killed Isobel, or tried to, but that incriminating letter was still kicking around, wasn't it?'

'All right, all right!' screamed Mr Bonnington. 'I did look to see if the letter was in her handbag! Dear God in heaven, wouldn't you have done the same?'

'And that's why you kept hanging round Violet Slatcher, isn't it?' roared Dover with a sudden inspiration. 'That's why, after she was arrested, you were so damned keen to stay behind and lock the house up. You wanted to have a look for that letter.'

Mr Bonnington appeared hurt by this suggestion. 'My main aim was to bring Christian consolation to poor Miss Slatcher in her hour of need. I am her spiritual pastor, after all.'

'But you wanted to get that letter back.'

'Of course I did! It was mine, wasn't it? Isobel Slatcher stole it from me. And what if I did want to stay behind when the house was empty?' he added testily. 'It was the first real opportunity I'd had in all those months. Trust Violet to let anyone have a quiet look round! You'd have thought she'd had the crown jewels stowed away somewhere – suspicious old devil!' He rose, not without dignity to his feet. 'But I repeat, I did not shoot Isobel!'

Dover glared at him. Blast the man – didn't he know confession was good for the soul? 'But Isobel Slatcher knew you were Cuthbert Boys's brother and she was threatening to expose you – you don't deny that, do you?'

'No. I have no wish to speak ill of the dead but what you say is perfectly true. We shall probably never know what black motives prompted her to such a dreadful deed, but if she had not been, er, removed from the scene, she would, I have no doubt, have ruined my life.'

'And you removed her,' prompted Dover.

'I repeat, I did not. It was an act of God.'

214

'You found that gun,' insisted Dover, 'you opened up your garden gate and you shot her.'

'No!' thundered Mr Bonnington.

Dover's scowl grew blacker. 'All right,' he threatened, 'if that's the way you want it! I shall have to ask you to come down to the station with me.'

Mr Bonnington passed a pink tongue over his dry lips. 'Are you arresting me?' he asked in a choked voice.

Dover leered maliciously. 'Not yet,' he said. 'I'm just taking you in for questioning. It'll be quieter down there.'

The Vicar slumped heavily in his chair. 'You're quite serious about this?' he asked, running his finger round his dog collar. 'It isn't some kind of a practical joke? No, I suppose not. Well, in that case, Inspector, I think there is something which, under the circumstances, it is clearly my duty to tell you.'

'Well, make it quick!' bawled Dover. 'I haven't got all day!'

Mr Bonnington bowed his head and placed one hand over his eyes. Having presumably received the Lord's blessing on his intentions he looked up and smiled forgivingly at the chief inspector. Before he could make any utterance, however, the dining-room door was flung open with a crash which nearly made Dover jump out of his skin. He whipped round furiously to find Mrs Smallbone standing, arms akimbo, in the doorway.

She spoke to Mr Bonnington. 'Save your breath,' she said. 'I'll tell 'em myself.' Her gaze swung contemptuously to Dover. 'Call yourself a detective?' she scoffed. 'You don't really believe this weak-kneed specimen would ever actually *do* anything, apart from mumbling a few prayers, do you? Just look at him! Does he look capable of shooting Isobel Slatcher?'

Mrs Smallbone was so dominating that Dover's eyes

215

automatically turned back to have another look at Mr Bonnington. He was now a picture of sheepish embarrassment.

Dover pulled himself together. Damn it, it was his blasted case, wasn't it? 'Well, if he didn't shoot her,' he demanded furiously, 'who did?'

'I did,' said Mrs Smallbone calmly. 'And if this snivelling coward could have been trusted to keep his mouth shut, you'd never have found out!'

Dover could have wept – or strangled Mrs Smallbone with his bare hands. How dare the bossy old hag come storming in here where she wasn't wanted and confess to the attempted murder of Isobel Slatcher!

'I suppose you were listening at the door?' he blustered.

'Naturally. What else do you expect me to do? A woman's entitled, I hope, to look after her own interests and he' – she nodded her head tartly at Mr Bonnington – 'he happens to be mine!'

'Oh,' said Dover, rather inadequately.

'I suppose he didn't tell you that we are engaged to be married? No, I thought not. Well, we are and have been' – she glared scathingly at Mr Bonnington who avoided her eye – 'these many months. That's one little secret that Isobel Slatcher with all her poking and prying around didn't find out. His lordship here didn't want anybody to know until he got the promotion some other idiot had hinted he was in line for. Thought if he announced he was going to marry his housekeeper it might harm his chances. He didn't want to marry me, mind you, but by Christmas last year things had gone a bit too far.'

Dover's mouth dropped in unflattering astonishment. 'Do you mean you and he were . . .?'

'We were,' agreed Mrs Smallbone grimly. 'Even parsons are human, you know.'

'And you're saying,' said Dover, still not sure he'd heard

aright, 'you're saying it wasn't him who tried to kill Isobel Slatcher, but you?'

'That's right. I'm confessing. Not that I'm sorry for it – she deserved everything that was coming to her, nasty, interfering little bitch! I heard everything that was going on in here. Another couple of seconds and he'd have blabbed the whole story to you. Anything to save his own skin, the yellow-bellied rat!'

'Here!' said Dover, brightening up a bit. 'D'you mean he's known all along that you tried to kill Isobel?' The words 'accessory before and after the fact' were almost legible in Dover's piggy little eyes. At least he'd be able to get Bonnington on something.

'Not him!' sneered Mrs Smallbone. 'There's none so deaf as those that won't hear! He's all for a quiet life, he is. Doesn't like a lot of fuss and bother. It upsets him. Soon as Isobel told him she'd found that letter and that she was going to tell the Bishop about him – and all his congregation here too – he comes rushing to me. I knew if anybody was going to save the situation it'd have to be me.'

'She did it for love, Inspector.' Mr Bonnington leaned forward. 'Surely that will count in her favour?'

'Love?' Mrs Smallbone laughed rather unpleasantly. 'Don't you kid yourself! I've lived in Curdley all my life and I've not had an easy time of it, I can tell you. I've never had a chance and I've had to watch others, no better than I am, getting themselves fixed up nice and comfortable like. I'm entitled to a bit of luck after all these years. And I'd have made a good Vicar's wife – don't make any mistake about that. Then Isobel Slatcher had to find that letter. Well, I wasn't going to see all my hopes go down the drain without putting up a fight for 'em. Isobel thought she was going to ruin him. She didn't realize she was going to ruin me as well.' She looked down her nose at Dover. 'She might have been a bit more careful if she had.'

'How did you get the gun?' asked Dover faintly.

'I found it in the church hall when I went in to help clear up after the battle. Been kicked behind one of the lockers.'

'But you don't know how to fire a gun,' protested Mr Bonnington.

'I got a book out of the library and learnt!' snapped Mrs Smallbone.

'And the garden gate?' asked Dover.

'I got that open too.' Mrs Smallbone laughed wryly. 'Fancy you thinking he could manage a job like that. He wouldn't know how to work an oil can if you gave him from now until Doomsday!'

'And you didn't go home that night as usual?'

'Of course not! I said good night to him and he thought I'd gone – if he ever thinks about anything. I waited in the kitchen in the dark. When I heard Isobel leave I ran out through the garden and opened the gate. It didn't make a sound. When she came round the corner I grabbed her and fired the gun into her head. Then I went back inside the vicarage and hid in the kitchen again. I waited until about midnight when everybody'd gone and it was all quiet. Then I took a tin of petrol out and cleaned all the oil off the gate. I soaked all the hinges and things in water, and then I went home. I told the police I'd left at seven o'clock, same as usual, and nobody bothered any more about it. Every now and again I'd go out and give that gate another soaking. You won't find a spot of oil anywhere on it now.' She proffered this bit of information proudly.

'And you're seriously asking me to believe that Mr Bonnington didn't know?'

Mrs Smallbone shrugged her shoulders. 'We never discussed the matter,' she said primly. 'I'd told him to leave Isobel to me and not to worry about it – and that's exactly what he did do. He's a great one for pushing his burdens off on to someone else's shoulders – delegation of responsibility, I think he calls it. Anyway, he pretended not to know who shot Isobel and I certainly wasn't going to enlighten him. Least said, soonest mended, that's my motto.'

Mr Bonnington was naturally anxious to confirm his housekeeper's statement. 'My dear Inspector, of course I had no idea that Mrs Smallbone had done anything so dreadful. I just thought she was going to talk to Isobel and persuade her to see reason. And I knew nothing about the gun. How was I to know that she'd found a gun, of all things, in the church hall? I mean, that sort of thing just doesn't happen, does it?'

Dover sighed heavily and avoided MacGregor's eye. ''Strewth, if he had much more of this he'd go barmy himself! He dragged himself to his feet. 'I think you'd better come down to the station,' he said.

Mr Bonnington relaxed in his chair, his hands clasped piously together.

'Both of you!' snapped Dover.

'So that's how it was, sir,' said Dover, waving a casual hand in the direction of the Chief Constable.

Colonel Muckle's eyes sparkled with excitement. 'Brilliant,' he cooed. 'Just brilliant! My, it's a real education to watch you fellows at work.'

Dover smirked modestly and held out his whisky glass for a refill.

'And you knew all along that Mrs Smallbone was the guilty party, eh?'

MacGregor was not present at this rather high-level get-together so Dover was free to discuss the case without an accompaniment of disbelieving gasps from his sergeant.

'That's right,' he admitted with a wise little smile. 'I spotted her right from the start. A sort of detective's instinct I suppose you'd call it. But, of course, as you know, sir, it's one thing to know who the villain is – and quite another to prove it.'

'My word, yes!' said Colonel Muckle. 'How right you are!'

'So,' continued Dover, lying peacefully back in his chair like a trooper, 'I had to conduct my investigation in an indirect way.'

'Ah,' said Colonel Muckle, as though that cleared up a number of points which had been puzzling him.

'And, of course, I had to keep my suspicions strictly to myself. I daren't confide in anyone – in case they inadvertently gave the game away. Couldn't risk breathing a word, even to my own sergeant.' Dover smiled briefly. That'd spike young MacGregor's guns!

'Ah,' said Colonel Muckle again, indicating that it had.

'I let it become known,' Dover went on, getting rather pompous, 'that I thought one person had been responsible for both crimes, the original shooting last February and then the final murder in the hospital. That was just to put the guilty parties off their guard – lull them into a false sense of security, you know. Meanwhile, I pursued my investigations under cover, as you might say.'

'I thought at first you were going to arrest young Rex Purseglove.'

'That,' retorted Dover smugly, 'is what you were meant to think. Actually I was after a very important bit of evidence from him but I didn't want to have that gossiped about all round the town. What he did, in short, was to stop up the Corporation Road end of Church Lane. When I found the man in the fish and chip shop who could stop the other end up, I knew I was on the right lines. Incidentally, I can't think how your men missed questioning Mr Dibb. His evidence that nobody passed his shop after the shooting was absolutely vital, you know.'

'My chaps aren't very experienced, I'm afraid,' apologized the Chief Constable. 'That's why I called the Yard in.'

220

'Very wise,' said Dover. 'Well then, I decided to show my hand a bit by arresting Violet Slatcher. She was such an obvious suspect for the actual murder of Isobel that I thought it would look queer if I didn't get her under lock and key.' He wondered if the Chief Constable was naïve enough to swallow this. He was.

'A sort of mercy killing?' asked Colonel Muckle, who had been playing a bit too much golf lately to keep fully abreast with what was going on in his own force.

'Not really,' said Dover. 'Violet was devoted to Isobel – she was, after all, her own daughter. She'd made a mess of her own life, or at least thought she had, and she'd pinned all her hopes and ambitions on Isobel. Above all, she wanted to see her respectably married. But when Isobel was shot like she was, I think Violet went a bit off the old rocker. As time went on she knew there was nothing more that she or anybody else could do for the girl, except see she was avenged. She wanted the chap who had, in effect, murdered Isobel brought to book and hanged, and when she thought nobody was doing anything to catch him and people were beginning to forget about what had happened she decided to help things on a bit. She checked up on the law. If Isobel died, it'd be capital murder and a job for the hangman, but Isobel had to die within a year and a day. Violet made sure that she did.'

'Bit grim,' said Colonel Muckle.

'Yes, but it worked. The whole case took on a new lease of life and you sent for me. It was just what Violet wanted. She thought Rex Purseglove had shot Isobel and she did her best to make us think so too. She wanted Isobel's death to look as though it was the delayed result of her original injuries, but in case we weren't taken in by that, she fixed it up that young Purseglove was the Number One suspect. Luckily,' observed Dover with an irritatingly complacent smile, 'I saw through her little game fairly early on.'

'Fascinating,' said Colonel Muckle.

'Just routine,' said Dover.

'And you knew all the time that Mrs Smallbone was the real culprit?'

'Well, let's just say I strongly suspected it,' lied Dover modestly. 'Couldn't have been anybody else, really.'

'Not Mr Bonnington, himself? After all, he was the one with the motive, wasn't he?'

'Yes.' Dover pursed his lips judicially. 'I suppose that's what an amateur might have thought, but I flatter myself I'm a bit of a student of human nature. I couldn't see Mr Bonnington attempting cold-blooded murder. Just wasn't in keeping with his character.'

'But you accused him of the shooting, didn't you?'

'Oh yes, but only to make Mrs Smallbone talk. I knew she'd done it all right, but we hadn't any proof and didn't look like getting any either. I was pretty certain Mr Bonnington knew what had been going on, and by threatening him with the crime I thought he might well try and save his own skin by telling us the truth. As you know, he was on the point of doing just that when Mrs Smallbone herself burst in and saved him the trouble. She made a full confession. Very satisfactory.'

'And he and Mrs Smallbone had actually been – well – er, lovers?' asked the Chief Constable, not averse to having a little gossip over some juicy Protestant peccadilloes.

'Apparently so,' sniffed Dover, 'though I reckon Mr Bonnington might say with some justification, "The woman tempted me." Isobel Slatcher wasn't the only one in Curdley who wanted to take a walk up the aisle. Mrs Smallbone was determined to marry Bonnington and be the first lady of the parish. She managed to get him to seduce her, and I reckon she'd nearly got him to agree to lead her to the altar when this letter came from Cuthbert Boys and Isobel threatened to blow the whole show sky high. Bonnington

222

just wrung his hands and turned to prayer, but Mrs Small-bone got cracking. She never actually told Bonnington that she'd shot the girl, but he must have had a pretty good idea that she was behind it. When Isobel didn't die, the pair of 'em were afraid of arousing suspicion if they got married and, much to Bonnington's relief, they just carried on same as usual, waiting until all the fuss and bother died down.'

'But they reckoned without you, eh, Chief Inspector?' The Chief Constable beamed at Dover.

Dover beamed and basked a little longer in this, to him, unusual atmosphere of admiration and approbation. When he finally left to catch his train, Colonel Muckle jovially insisted on accompanying him to the waiting car.

Outside the police headquarters three little girls were grimly intent on playing some elaborate game with an old tennis ball to the accompaniment of a shrilly chanted song:

> 'I'm Bigamous Bertie,
> I rise at seven thirty
> And off to the altar I go.
> I'm marrying my seventh,
> Or is it eleventh?
> I'm Bigamous Bertie the beau!'

Dover scowled and ignored them as he shook hands with Colonel Muckle, a ceremony which was recorded by a gentleman of the local Press.

And that was that. History, in the form of the chief inspector's own report, tells us that the murder of Isobel Slatcher was solved by Chief Inspector Wilfred Dover in less than a week.

As for the gun which Dover had promised to return to the Pie Gang, they never did get it back. Freddie Gash used to wax very bitter about it. 'Coppers!' he would complain poignantly. 'You can't believe a ruddy word they says!'